Sandra James

STAR-SPANGLED SUMMER

Star-Spangled Summer

✦ ✦ ✦ ✦ ✦ ✦ ✦ ✦ ✦ ✦ ✦ ✦ ✦ ✦ ✦ ✦ ✦ ✦ ✦ ✦

BY JANET LAMBERT

Illustrated by Sandra James

✦ ✦ ✦ ✦ ✦ ✦ ✦ ✦ ✦ ✦ ✦ ✦ ✦ ✦ ✦ ✦ ✦ ✦ ✦

E. P. DUTTON & COMPANY, INC.

New York ✦ ✦ ✦ ✦ ✦ ✦ ✦ ✦ ✦ ✦ 1941

First printing ....January 1941
Second printing ....January 1941
Third printing ......November 1941
Fourth printing .....November 1941
Fifth printing ....August 1943

TO

MOTHER

"Of myself I am nothing"

LIST OF CHAPTERS

STAR-SPANGLED SUMMER

CHAPTER ONE

CARROL MEETS THE PARRISHES

"WE'RE ALMOST there, now," Penny said, after a quick glance from the train window.

"Do you think we should call the porter to take our bags?" Carrol began gathering up her purse and gloves and leaned toward the little mirror between the windows as she put on her hat.

"Oh no, he'll get us. We've loads of time."

Carrol stopped adjusting the blond curls framed by a wide-brimmed sailor and turned blue eyes on Penny. "Do you really think I won't be a bother to your mother?" she asked anxiously. "A month *is* an awfully long time."

"Don't be silly." Penny looked up from the odds and ends she was cramming into an overfilled purse. "Didn't she practically beg your grandmother in a special delivery letter and two telephone calls? Why, just think, if you hadn't come with me I'd still be at Aunt Julia's waiting for Uncle Jim to bring me home in the car. Mums doesn't believe that I could travel all the way from Chicago to Kansas by myself. Why, she's grateful!"

As Penny paused for breath, Carrol smiled happily. "It's exciting, isn't it?" she asked, an eager little quiver in her voice. "I never thought I'd be visiting on an army post."

"I know. It's lucky for both of us that I went to visit Aunt Julia."

"And that Grandmother made me go and call on you. Do you think your family is as excited about our coming as we are?"

"Excited! They're in a dither. You've never seen excitement until you've seen my family. The least little thing gets everybody all stirred up. Every time we move from one post to another Daddy says he'd like to take sleeping powders until we get packed up and where we're going and unpacked again. Mummy says the excitement is half the fun and I really believe Daddy thinks so, too. Would you like to hear what they are doing right now?"

Carrol leaned back in her seat. "I'd love to," she said, preparing herself for a lengthy narrative which, coming from Penny, was bound to be complete and very descriptive.

"Well," Penny leaned an elbow on the window-ledge and thought for a moment. "Right now," she said, "Mummy is probably leaning out of one of the back, up-stairs windows. The orderly—he's a colored soldier from the regiment, named Williams, who shines boots and does the cleaning and waits on the table—the orderly has forgotten to clean out the car. He always does. And Mummy is waving her comb at him and telling him, for heaven's sake, to hurry because it's filled with bathing suits and a horse blanket and some groceries she forgot to take out. He says, 'Yas'm,' and drops the rug he's shaking and trots around the house.

"Then Mummy spies David over on the post tennis courts. So she shrieks at him that it's time to meet the train, and isn't he going to take off that horrible sweatshirt? and that if he doesn't care how he looks for his own sister he should at least want to appear respectable before a lovely guest, meaning you. David mumbles under his breath but he starts loping over, because if there is anything a senior in high school likes it's to show off before a pretty girl."

Penny rolled her eyes at Carrol. "You don't need to look so embarrassed and guilty," she teased. "You are pretty. I wish I were. Oh well," she went on in a matter-of-fact tone before Carrol could assure her, and justly, that she was attractive in a gold-and-brown gypsy sort of way, "Mummy is flying down the stairs now, to the kitchen. She has to be sure that Trudy baked the chocolate chiffon pie she knows I like. And Trudy is saying, 'Law, Miz' Parrish, it's only two o'clock. 'Tain't time yet. You jes' keep calm. Miss Penny'll have her pie.' Trudy has been all over the world with us so she takes liberties.

"Feeling safe there, Mummy dashes through the house, making last minute changes in the bowls of flowers and being sure there aren't any skates and riding crops to fall over. She has Tippy locked in the screened porch, hoping she'll keep clean. Tippy probably started out in a white dress but she'll be a sight by the time we see her. Mummy will scoop her up and then she'll disentangle Bobby from about six other little boys who are jumping on the hose and squirting water on each other. She'll dump Tippy in the car and shove Bobby in after her, then she'll have to go back to hunt David. After she has blown the horn and threatened to leave, he'll come out. Then they'll argue about who is going to drive. When they get that all settled and David is driving, and they're all in the car with the doors safely locked, they'll discover that Bobby has his police puppy."

"Will they bring him, too?"

"Oh, sure. They'll have to because they'll be so late they won't have time to go by the riding hall to pick up Daddy if they don't. They'll have more excitement there because Daddy won't be ready. After they finally get him in and the children have stopped begging to see their pony, he'll have about four places he has to go. He'll say, 'Do you mind stopping here for just a minute, Marge? I won't be long.' They'll stop, and he will be long. So, they'll slam on the brakes at the station just as the train pulls in. You wait and see."

Carrol was entranced with the picture. "I hope I can keep them all straight," she said. "Bobby and Tippy and David. Is David good looking?"

"The girls think he is." Penny squinted up her eyes and considered David appraisingly. "I guess I do, too," she decided. "He's tall and blond and thin, and has the bluest eyes with long, dark eyelashes that make me positively furious every time I look at them. His hair curls up when it's damp and he's always trying to make it lie down. He looks just like Dad, and I think Dad's handsome, so I guess David is too. He plays football and rides and swims—boy, how he can swim! He just graduated from high school last week and he's going to West Point next month."

"Does he like girls?"

"Not much. They're all crazy about him but he doesn't seem to care. We used to have lots of fun together when we were little, but he doesn't want to drag me around with him now. I suppose, when you're eighteen and ready for the Point, a fourteen-year-old sister does seem kind of young. He may be nicer to you because you're fifteen. I wouldn't count on it, though." She made the last statement in a flat tone that gave Carrol a complete picture of David as far as girls were concerned. Then she looked out of the window and her voice crackled with excitement as she exclaimed: "Oh, good, we're coming in!"

The porter appeared to take their bags and they straightened their hats and gathered up their small belongings. He hovered about, making vain and ineffectual jabs at them with his whisk broom, but they were pressed against the window as Penny pointed out the dearly loved landmarks.

"See, there's the officers' club and the golf course," she was saying. "And here are the quartermaster buildings and some corrals where the horses are turned out in the daytime. And those buildings are stables and those are barracks. The soldiers live there."

Carrol peered through the glass, eager to miss nothing, her eyes straining to follow Penny's acrobatic finger. "Oh, look!" she suddenly cried. "Look, up there on the hill. I see a flag!"

"Umhum, that's the parade ground." Penny gave the

tall flag pole with its flying banner a mere glance. For her, rain or shine, it was always there. Its base provided a meeting place and a playground for her crowd; its colors, bright above the treetops, meant protection and that all was well. Now it was waving, "welcome home," and she pulled Carrol away from the window. "Come on. We're here."

They started down the aisle just as the porter returned for them. He nodded and grinned. "Fort Arden, ladies," he said. "But I reckon you all knows that."

"Indeed we do." Penny gave a joyous hop as the train slowed to a gentle stop.

The porter set down his little box of a step, and as they stood above him Penny nudged Carrol and pointed. "Look," she said.

Beside the station a car slammed to a stop. Brakes screeched, doors flew open and an avalanche of excited people hurtled out onto the graveled path. A small blue figure and a shrieking white one took a flying lead and Penny, as she stepped from the train, was staggered by the clutching embraces of a wild man of eight and a copy-cat of three. By the time she had got herself untangled from them, her mother and father, between them, had knocked her hat off. Their hugs were hurried, but thorough, before they turned to the tall, quiet girl who was watching the little scene with interest. Penny mumbled some sort of introduction and threw Carrol to the wolves as she mopped her hot face.

"My goodness," she grumbled, "you'd think I'd been gone two years instead of only two weeks."

"But we've missed you so, pet." Her mother kissed her again. "It's been awful."

David, who had remained in the background until the first explosions had subsided, sauntered up. He seemed to be the only calm member of the reception committee as he offered a casual: "Hi, Sis." He gave Penny a brotherly pat on the shoulder, and made short work of his introduction to Carrol by shaking hands with her quickly and turning to help his father with the bags.

Carrol, in the brief touching of their hands when David's blue eyes looked straight at her, thought Penny had been right. He was handsome, and though he was totally unaware of it, he was probably the best-looking boy she had ever seen. She glanced from him to his father who was the fulfillment of all David could someday be; the same eyes, but the man's made kindly and keen by life; the same mouth, but the older one firmer, and jollier in its welcoming smile.

From them, she glanced at Mrs. Parrish who was vainly endeavoring to start the two little children back toward the car. "Why, she looks almost like Penny's sister," she thought. "Her hair's so brown and her dimples pop in and out. She must be fun." She catalogued the entire family, even to the noisy Bobby and the dumpling of a Tippy, in the few seconds while Major Parrish was tipping the porter, and found them delightful.

The porter picked up his little step, grinned delighted thanks and climbed aboard. The train tooted cheerfully and away it went; the interested passengers, turning reluctantly from the group on the platform, resumed their reading.

"Come on, everybody, let's get in the car." Penny's mother put an arm around each girl and drew them along with her. "I don't know when I've been so happy," she confided. "I do hope Carrol is going to like it here."

"Oh, I am," Carrol said earnestly and received a smile so loving that whatever shyness she had felt disappeared like magic. Marjorie Parrish's smile was delightful. It flashed out at the slightest provocation and refused to be erased even when, as now, she was trying to be stern with Bobby and Tippy who were clambering through the car door like two little burrs attached to Carrol's dress.

After the usual Parrish commotion everyone was at last stowed away.

"Well, are we ready?" Major Parrish asked as he and David came around the car after closing the luggage compartment. "Nobody left behind? Nothing lost? Be sure now, before I start." He looked at his wife and laughed. "It will be a miracle," he said, "if we don't have to come back for a coat or a camera or one of the children."

"Everything is actually in." Mrs. Parrish gave him an answering grin. "I even noticed Penny's luggage; she has every piece she started with, plus a large box which has simply been driving me mad." She twisted about in her seat, indulgently pushing the puppy's face away, so that she could look at Penny. "Did Aunt Julia send me something?"

Penny shook her head and said sternly: "You're not to ask." But her eyes twinkled as she said it, and fearful that she would say more she looked out of the window, searching for something of special interest to point out to Carrol.

"That's the headquarters building," she said as they wound up the long hill. "There, on the left. It's a sort of courthouse."

Carrol leaned forward to look at a large stone building set among tall trees, and suddenly found that she had five guides on her personally conducted tour. Her head was busy bobbing in all directions as she tried to follow each pointing finger.

"These are barracks," one would say. "That's the post office, 'way over there." Or: "You can just see the children's swimming pool through the trees."

She turned and twisted and looked, and at last her own eager eyes found the thing she had been searching for. "There it is!" she cried, leaning forward to peer between Mrs. Parrish and David. "There at the top of the hill. The flag."

"That's the parade ground," said Major Parrish bringing the car to a stop.

The flagpole was set near the curb and stretching away from it, green and close-cropped, was a large flat field. A cinder path led through the middle to buildings on the far side, and in one corner a few soldiers were drilling.

Carrol looked at the scene without speaking. Her eyes traveled to the top of the high pole and remained there for some time. "It is just as I've dreamed it would be," she said at last. "I hope I can see them take the flag down some evening."

"Oh, you can," Penny assured her as the car started on

again. "It's called 'retreat' and we often come up to watch it."

They turned into a long, shaded street lined with old stone houses. Each was set in a square, green lawn and all had screened porches across the front and were surrounded by shrubbery nodding under a wealth of white blossoms. At the end, one house stood alone, like a sentinel, and divided the street into a Y.

"These are officers' quarters," explained Mrs. Parrish, "and the one by itself is the general's."

Carrol looked at the two long rows extending before her. "But how can you tell which is yours?" she asked in wide-eyed amazement. "They're all exactly alike. I know I'll get in the wrong one if I ever come home alone in the dark."

"I don't doubt it." Major Parrish laughed as he stopped the car. "Penny's grandmother did once. She walked into what she thought was our house and called: 'Why, Marge, where did we get this awful-looking footstool?' You can imagine how she felt when the woman who lived there answered her."

Everyone laughed and David volunteered: "You can tell our house by the sign that's painted below the top step. Every officer has his name on his quarters."

Bobby and Tippy, eager to be out, began tugging at the doors. The general exodus was swift, and before she knew it Carrol found herself standing on the walk with Penny hopping excitedly about the luggage compartment.

"Hurry, Daddy," Penny was urging. "Just give me the big package."

"Take it easy. You'll have me so curious I can't find

the key hole," Major Parrish laughed as he opened the yawning cavern. He set the box on the grass and Penny snatched it up, bumping it along with her as she led Carrol up the walk.

"Everybody come on the porch," she called as she dumped her burden inside the screened door.

Bobby and Tippy and her mother needed no second invitation. They hovered over her as she struggled with the knot and Bobby produced a dull and broken knife from the end of an enormous chain. They hacked at the cord and, between them, managed to saw it in two. Major Parrish came and stood looking down with inquisitive interest.

"Where's David?" Penny asked as she laid back the rustling paper.

"He's gone to tell Williams to take in the bags." Her mother bent over to push Bobby's exploring fingers away. "What have we here, anyway?"

"I want you to know," Penny said, looking at each one, "that I brought you all presents. And I bought them with my own money."

As they seemed properly impressed, her mother and father even overcome, she admitted honestly: "Except the biggest thing. That's from Carrol."

"It isn't any bigger than yours, Pen," Carrol blushed, "and you bought some of it."

"Oh, yes, that's right, I did. Well, here." Penny began lifting out the carefully wrapped packages. "This is yours, Tippy. Bobby, this has your name on it."

The children took their boxes and Tippy screamed with delight as a flaxen-haired doll, pink and beruffled, stared up at her with a blue unwinking gaze. Bobby, savoring the unexpected windfall to its utmost, finally produced a cowboy outfit that surpassed even his wildest dreams.

"Oh, boy!" he shouted. "Just what I needed!" He gave Penny a hasty kiss and, checkered shirt and chaps waving, disappeared inside.

Penny laid David's gift to one side. "It's just a tie," she explained as she burrowed deeper into the box. She lifted out a heavy, square package and handed it to her father. "That's the part Carrol bought." She gave a lighter one to her mother. "And that's from me."

Sitting back on her heels she watched in eager anticipation as her father untied the string. Carrol's eyes were on him, too, and on Mrs. Parrish's bent head.

"Marge!" he exclaimed. "Look. It's those volumes of Shakespeare we have been dying for." He caressed the blue leather of the beautifully bound books tenderly as his wife cried:

"And I have the loveliest book-ends for them! Oh, you dear, dear children." She waded through the paper and hugged the self-conscious girl standing shyly by the screen door and made a swoop for the exuberant, sitting one. "How can I ever thank you?"

Major Parrish, cross-legged on the floor, his long legs in polished boots tucked under him, was already turning the pages. "Thanks, girls," he said, looking up and grinning. "I'd get up to hug you both but I've got to have one quick look before I go back to work."

Mrs. Parrish dropped down beside him. She lifted off

his service cap by its leather visor and laid it on the floor. "Let me look, too," she said.

As the girls went inside, her chin was resting on the shoulder of his olive drab uniform and they were utterly deaf to the chattering of Tippy or the repeated pleas from Bobby that someone would "pu-lease" come and help him with his buckles.

The girls found him in the upstairs hall, which was as far as he could bear to retire for his change of costume, and Carrol sat down on the top step to adjust his tin spurs while Penny tied a violent red handkerchief around his neck. When they had him buttoned, buckled and equipped with his belt and cap pistol, he clapped his ten-gallon hat on his head, emitted a piercing "yip-pee" and clattered into his mother's room where he could admire himself in a long mirror.

Arm in arm, the two girls went on to Penny's room.

CHAPTER TWO

CARROL MEETS THE CROWD

"MOTHER!" Penny shrieked from upstairs. "You did my room over. I can't believe it's mine!"

"Do you like it, darling?" Mrs. Parrish was running up the stairs, as eager and excited as Penny.

"Like it? I adore it! And twin beds. Did we get rich or something?"

"No, we aren't any richer, but I thought it was about time we did something to it. How do you like the drapes?"

"I love them. Look, Carrol, aren't they the most heavenly shade of pink? And a chaise longue," she went on before Carrol could answer, "a real one, just like you and Daddy have." She threw herself onto the chaise longue, scattering its lacy pillows to the floor, then jumped up and caught her mother around the neck. "It's all much too fine for me," she exulted as she covered her mother's

24

face with kisses. "I'll be in terror of those organdy bed-spreads every minute."

"For the first two days you will. After that . . ." Her mother's predictions were never finished for Penny swung her about over the gay rose rug until their skirts swirled out and Penny's brown curls were flying in the breeze.

Carrol watched them in fascination. There never had been such excitement at her grandmother's over the redecoration of a room. In fact, there was no room in Grandmother's whole house so gay as this one. Carrol's own bedroom was staid, with fourposter and draped net curtains; and the other rooms held furniture which had been in the Houghton family for generations. Everything was old and charming, and her grandmother moved about among her treasures, as old and charming as they were. She loved Carrol devotedly, and saw to it that she had the same comfort and care that would have been hers had her mother lived. But there was no gayety there. Carrol's father, too, paid his duty visit each summer and waited with cold, aloof patience for the day when he could return to New York. He was proud of her, over-indulgent and kind, but never would she have shouted to him over the banisters as Penny was doing now:

"Hey, Dad, come up here this minute! Santa Claus has been here."

There was a clatter on the stairs and Major Parrish, trailed by Tippy, the resplendent Bobby, and the puppy, burst in.

"It's beautiful, Dad. Thanks a million." Penny kissed her father, then swooped up Tippy, doll and all, and in the midst of tickling her under the chin, exclaimed: "I think it's silly for Carrol to sleep 'way off in the guest-room. Couldn't she stay in here with me?"

"I thought you would want her to," her mother answered. "If you will notice, her bags are in here and half the closet is left vacant, and half the drawers. That is, if Carrol doesn't mind being crowded."

"Oh, I'd love it, Mrs. Parrish," Carrol assured her. "It would be so much more fun."

"Then it's settled. Come on, everyone. Trudy will want to get at these bags. She has iced tea for us on the porch."

She shooed the younger children out, and linking her arm through Major Parrish's moved out into the hall.

"My goodness, you haven't seen Trudy, yet." Penny caught Carrol's hand and hurried her to the back stairs. "She's practically the most important member of the family."

They ran down the stairs and burst into a big kitchen. Penny rushed to a wiry little colored woman who was bending over the stove, peering into its oven. She straightened her up and hugged her.

"Trudy, you horrible thing, you didn't come out to see me."

"Law, Miss Penny, it's that chiffom pie. I just . . ."

"You think too much about our tummies. This is Carrol Houghton, Trudy. She's going to spend a whole month with us."

"How de do, Miss Carrol. It sho' will be nice to have you." Trudy beamed on Carrol, asked her if she had had a pleasant journey and was turning back to her oven when Penny uttered an exclamation of dismay.

"Good gracious, Trudy," she cried. "I forgot your present. It's out on the porch."

"No 'tain't, Miss Penny," Trudy stopped her as she was dashing for the door. "Your mamma brought it out an' I jus' had to take a little peek. Yo' shouldn'ta spent so much on me, honey."

"I didn't spend much, Trudy. And you do need a nice purse to carry to church. Do you like it?"

Penny watched Trudy hopefully, sure of extravagant

thanks, but to Trudy's alert nostrils came the faint odor of browning pie-crust and she jerked open the oven door. "I loves it," she mumbled hurriedly, "but you two scat now, I got my pie to tend to."

As the two girls went through the swinging door into the butler's pantry, Carrol said: "She's sweet. With such a big family, you'd think she might be cross at having one more to wait on."

"Oh, not Trudy. She loves us as much as we love her. She thinks the sun rises and sets in Mummy."

"I do, too." Carrol smiled shyly at Penny as they crossed the dining room and came into a large, square hall which was used as a living room. It was bright with flowered chintz; books lined all one wall, a radio and a comfortable chair stood near the broad first landing of the stairway, and all about were interesting souvenirs of a life of travel. Beyond it was a more formal drawing-room. "I wish I had a mother just like her," Carrol said.

Penny's arm slid quickly around her shoulder. "You can have part of mine," she whispered. "Mummy will adore having another daughter."

When they came through the vestibule onto a big shaded porch Mrs. Parrish was sitting alone among the bright cushions of a glider. Her lips were puckered and she was frowning at a needle she was poking in and out of some blue yarn. "I will never learn to crochet," she said resignedly as she stuffed her work into a bag that hung on the arm of the swing and reached for her glass of iced tea.

"You've been trying ever since I can remember," Penny declared, taking a tray from a low table and holding it out to Carrol. "Maybe you're just not the type for it, Mums."

Carrol, carrying her tea and her little plate, came and stood before Mrs. Parrish. "I can crochet," she said shyly. "My grandmother taught me. Perhaps I can help you."

Mrs. Parrish looked up at the eager face before her. She saw a beautiful girl, tall and slender. Blue eyes looked soberly out between long, dark lashes, and a contradictory dimple at the corner of the mouth and the merest hint of a tilt to the patrician nose gave life to a face which, without them, would have been cold and too carefully sculptured. As it was, in one quick glance, she thought: "The child isn't happy. She's too serious for fifteen; and she isn't gay enough. She needs a summer like this."

She looked at her own daughter sprawled in a wicker chair. Penny's brown locks, in an attempted page boy effect, sprayed out around her face. Her brown eyes danced and her mouth, normally very sweet, was stretched to its limit around a slice of cake. Life was wonderful to Penny. Mrs. Parrish hoped it always would be.

So she smiled up at Carrol and said: "Thank you, dear, but this is going to be a very busy summer. I hope you won't have many odd moments for crocheting. I hope I won't, myself."

"Where's Dad?" asked Penny as she brushed the cake crumbs from her face.

"Today is the Cavalry parade. He almost forgot it in the pleasure of looking at our books, so he had to dash over to the barracks."

"Any of the girls phone?" Penny pulled Carrol down

onto the arm of her chair and touched her hair lightly. "Isn't her hair lovely, Mums?"

"Beautiful. Yes, the girls have been telephoning by the dozens. They're making plans for tonight and said they would meet you up at the parade ground. You'll have to take the bikes. Daddy has the car."

"The bikes?" Carrol looked inquiringly down at Penny. Did they expect her to ride?

"She means the bicycles. Mummy is very slangy. I'll have to ride David's and Carrol can have mine."

"Oh, no," declared Mrs. Parrish emphatically. "Can't you hear David on the subject? 'What, Penny use my bike? Ruined, that's what it will be. Can't a fellow have anything of his own sacred from the rest of the family?' Oh, no." She shook her head. "This is to be a peaceful summer. There's a bike out in back for Carrol."

"Really? Where did you get it?"

"From the Martin girl, who will be away."

Through the conversation Carrol had been listening with a dubious expression. "I'm not sure I can still ride a bike," she began. "You see, in a city we don't have a chance . . . Listen, what was that?" Her head lifted as she strained to catch the clear notes of a bugle that sounded in the distance.

"Heavens, it's retreat! They'll sound 'to the colors' in a minute. Hurry!"

Penny spilled Carrol off the chair arm and dragged her, half laughing, half protesting, down the steps and around the corner of the house. At the back steps she let go of her hand and ducked under the high back porch. Such a rattling and banging followed, that as Carrol stepped hastily in after her the whole semi-darkness seemed filled with bicycles. Under, surrounded by and topped with them sat Penny.

"For the love of Mike, what happened?" Carrol pulled at the top bicycle, which seemed to be the key piece of the puzzle, and Penny crawled out, laughing.

"I just learned a lesson. You can't take the bottom of anything out and expect the top to stand up." She flung her hair back out of her eyes and surveyed the wreckage. "Just roll that idiotic tricycle of Tippy's off someplace," she said, "and I can get at the rest of them."

Carrol gave a fat, three-wheeled affair a push and sent a small sidewalk bike after it, as Penny trundled out a glittering red two-wheeler, covered with bells, horns and baskets, and evidently intended for a full-sized brownie.

"How about this one?" she asked, dumping it on the grass.

"Goodness, is that for me?" Carrol looked at it in dismay. "Why, I could stand up and walk with it."

Penny laughed and ducked inside again. "That's Bobby's new one. Here," she called, "give me a hand with David's racer. He'll die if we chip the paint." She passed out the racer and as Carrol set it carefully upright on its standard she could hear Penny muttering.

"Ours *would* be on the very back." A blue bicycle rolled out and was followed by Penny, hot but triumphant with the last of the pile. "This is yours," she said, shoving it to Carrol. "It's a honey, isn't it?"

Carrol took hold of the handlebars of the "honey" and thought that "monster" would be more expressive.

She looked at it prayerfully and then at Penny who was urging haste.

"Come on," Penny ordered. "I'll start you off."

Carrol had never felt less sure of herself in her life than when she thrust one leg through the frame of the bicycle. But she was fairly hopeful of Penny's holding her from the rear, so she gripped the handlebars, placed her feet on the pedals and carefully eased herself into the saddle. No sooner was she seated than Penny gave her a mighty push. The front wheel shot to the right, then jerked back to the left: and as she wobbled off it was wagging like the tail of an overjoyed puppy.

She managed to circle the back yard, ducking under a clothes line and bisecting a flower bed, before she braved the nasturtium-bordered walk which led around the house. Keeping to its narrow brick bumpiness required the greatest concentration, so that the grin she flashed at Mrs. Parrish, standing on the side steps, was of necessity fleeting.

"I'm doing it," her voice came back. "It's fun!"

"Bless her heart," Marjorie Parrish thought, "she needs this. I never saw a girl who needed it more."

Penny zoomed past her mother with a confident wave of her hand and a "cheerio, see you at dinner," then bumping off the curb, she pedaled along furiously until she caught up with Carrol.

"You're doing fine," she encouraged. "Keep up the good work, we're almost there."

"I think I'll make it." Carrol's cheeks were pink and her curls were damp on her forehead, but the tracks her wheels left behind on the pavement were straight and her hot hands were not so tense on the handlebars.

The band was playing when they came to the corner and a complete regiment of men and horses was lined up across the parade ground. Carrol ventured a look and almost spilled.

"I think I'd better get off now," she said, promptly taking a flying leap. "I'd rather meet your friends right side up than on my back. Besides, I'd like to see what's going on."

Penny laughed and hopped off too, and they trundled their bicycles among the people and the cars that were parked along the street. Penny's eyes, darting this way and that, discovered a group of girls and boys under a small tree and she motioned Carrol to follow her.

"Hi," she screamed, ringing her bell and waving her arm. "Hi, there!"

Bicycles crashed to the ground and the band found itself playing an accompaniment to yells of welcome and the triumphal re-entry of Penny into her crowd. Their waving tennis rackets, gay print dresses, slacks and bright shirts made such an attractive picture that many people glanced from the long lines of pawing horses and smiled.

"This is Carrol Houghton," Penny introduced her, beaming. "And, Carrol, this is the crowd." Laboriously, as they gathered around, she began the individual introductions. "This is Mary Prescott," she said, "and that is Bob Prescott, there in the yellow sweater. And this is Louise Frazier, and Jane Carter, Dick Ford, and Michael Drayton."

Carrol smiled shyly at each one and received a varied collection of smiles in return. The boys were frankly delighted with her and their grins said so. Dick Ford was clowningly effusive and made a great show of elbowing Penny aside as he said, "Just run along, child, I'll look after Carrol." Mary's candid grey eyes smiled with her mouth, and Jane held out a welcoming hand. Only Louise, dark of hair and stormy-eyed, gave her lips a little twitch and looked away.

"She doesn't like me," Carrol thought. "She doesn't even know me, and she doesn't like me." A little of the sparkle died out of her face, but the others were dragging her forward.

A cannon boomed. There was a second of breathless silence, then the band began to play "The Star-Spangled Banner." Like carved figures the spectators stood rigidly at attention. Hands dropped to sides, hats were removed and the officers among the crowd stood in a stiff salute. On the parade ground, hundreds of horses became statues. Sabers flashed. And all eyes were lifted to the stars and stripes, brilliant against the early evening sky.

Slowly the flag came down. Carrol felt tears stinging her eyes as she watched. The whole world slipped away and she was conscious only of the great billowing folds sliding slowly down into waiting upstretched arms.

"What? Oh." She came back with a start as Penny nudged her. Penny was pointing to the horses, which had come to life again and were prancing and tossing their heads as they turned in orderly lines of four. A stirring march leaped from the band and the regiment swung along with it. Down the field they came, the band leading the way, and the officers leading their troops. Red and white guidons fluttered at intervals; there was the clanking of bits and stirrups, and the rattle of little machine guns bringing up the rear.

When the last man had passed, Carrol sighed and turned reluctantly back to the others. They were already diving for their bicycles and a heated argument was going on about the evening's activities.

"I say we coax the general to let us have the pool open," Dick was urging.

"And I say we haven't a chance of getting it." Michael was positive in his answer. "We had it last night."

"Well, you ought to know." Snub-nosed Dick's broad grin flashed as he leaned toward Carrol and whispered, loud enough for the others to hear: "His old man is recreation officer—and the stingiest man on the post. Why he hates to change the water in the pool so much he has it all dipped out and poured back again so we'll think it's clean."

Everyone laughed and Michael pretended to glower at him. "You're wrong there," he answered witheringly. "No one can use the water after you come out of it, with your red hair three shades lighter than when you went in."

"That's right, blame me." Dick turned again to Carrol. "They pick on me all the time," he said, trying to look forlorn.

"Well, why do you put all that gooey stuff on your hair?" Jane was frankly inquisitive.

"Because, if you must know, I don't like red hair. Now, if I could be the dark movie hero type like Mike or even sandy-haired like Bob . . . But red curls! Gosh, no one cares what I suffer."

Penny walked over and gave him a push. "Suffer, my eye," she said. "You're delighted that you're the center of attention."

"Yes, and he's making us miss our dinner." Mary, the only one on foot, shouldered her tennis racket and turned away. "Come on, Bob. You know how mad Mrs. Prescott gets when her children are late."

"But we haven't decided anything," Jane called after her.

"We can talk on the way home."

They walked down the middle of the street, trundling their bicycles. Plans were offered and discarded, and only Carrol and Louise were silent. Carrol, feeling strange, had no suggestions to make; but Louise was entirely disinterested and held herself aloof. Only when the huddle was formed again at the Prescotts' front walk did she make a remark.

"We may as well go to the movies as usual," she said in a bored tone. "Afterward, something may turn up."

"Okay." Mary was anxious to be in the house and she pulled Bob along with her. "See you at seven, then. Same seats," she called. " 'Bye, Carrol."

"Goodbye." Carrol walked along between Penny and Dick, listening to their chatter, and thinking what a strange world she had dropped into. Just a few hours on a train, and her orderly existence was changed into a happy-go-lucky whirlwind where anything might happen —and probably would. She, who rarely saw a horse suddenly had seen hundreds of them. And flags and cannons and bands, and bicycles. She chuckled to herself as she and Penny bumped their wheels onto the curb at their own walk and waited eagerly to hear if any more plans would be made. It was Louise's voice that surprised her, saying casually.

"How about persuading David to come tonight? Since Carrol is here it makes nine in the crowd."

"What difference does that make?" Penny asked, wide-eyed. "We don't have to be even."

"No, but it's nicer. David would make one more boy, so ask him to come anyway."

Louise walked on and the boys grinned and winked. They waved and mounted their bicycles, as they lived over on what was known as "the upper post," and Michael called back:

"We'll stop by for you. I may get the car."

"How did you like them?" Penny asked, stopping in the middle of the walk and waiting eagerly for Carrol's answer.

"I thought they were darling." Carrol leaned on her handlebars as she thought about the different ones. "Which is older, Mary or Bob?"

"Bob, by about a year. He's nuts about Jane and doesn't mind saying so. Jane's cute, isn't she?"

"Precious. She has such a perky face. I suppose it's because of her little pointed chin and the way her eyes slant up. She looks like a good sport."

"She is. She's a good rider, too. Mary's the only one who doesn't ride. She says she just doesn't like it."

"Mary's a darling. I imagine she would be a wonderful friend if you needed her."

"You're exactly right. She's one of the most loyal girls I have ever known. And speaking of loyalty . . ." Penny stopped and looked side-wise at Carrol. Then she asked the question Carrol had been dreading. "What do you think of Louise?"

"She's beautiful." Carrol's answer was prompt and sincere.

"I supposed you'd say so, everybody does. All that cloudy black hair and smoldering sort of eyes with eyelashes about two feet long. But what did you think of her? Now, truthfully."

"Well . . ." Carrol looked straight at Penny. "I don't know what to say. She . . ."

"She's a spoiled brat." Penny finished the sentence to her own liking. "I saw how she acted this afternoon. She's all right when just girls are around, but she's got the idea that she's the most beautiful creature that ever lived. Her parents aren't much help to her because Mums says they ruin every party by boring everybody all evening, raving about her. She thinks the boys should hover over her and simply swoon with joy when she looks at them. You heard her tell me to bring David to the movies. She thinks David should be her private property—and she can't bear it because you are going to live right in the house with him."

Carrol shook her head and asked: "Does David like her?"

"No! David doesn't like any girls."

"Well then, perhaps I can convince her that I am really a very nice person, and she may get fond of me."

Penny laughed and they went on, leaving their bicycles

propped against a large maple tree that drooped its branches over the porch.

David was pillowed comfortably in the swing when they came in. He looked up from his book, said "hello" and returned to his reading.

"I have a message for you," Penny said, going over and looking down at him. "Louise said to bring you to the movies tonight."

She got no response so she gave the swing a jiggle. "Hey, can't you hear me?" she asked.

"I hear you."

"Well, then answer."

"Can't go."

Penny turned away with a shrug. "You see," her shoulders expressed eloquently, "there's nothing to be done with him."

The girls were just stepping into the vestibule when the air was shattered by shrieks and howls. Bobby, for once unattended by the faithful Tippy, was streaking across the lawn.

"What's the matter, boy?" David was out of the swing and down the steps in a flash.

"It's Woofy," Bobby sobbed. "He's lost. Woofy's lost."

"Oh, we'll find him," David consoled as the screen door banged behind his mother. Carrol and Penny followed her, and Trudy's head appeared at an upstairs window.

"Are you hurt, Bobby?" Trudy called. Then without waiting for an answer she offered an upsetting piece of information. "His milk's still asittin' in its saucer."

This started Bobby's screams afresh and Tippy suddenly added to the din by coming around the house, beating on the walk with a toy shovel and yelling at the top her lungs.

"Well, do something!" Mrs. Parrish cried to David. "We can't just stand here. The military police and the fire engines and the ambulance will all be here in a minute, if this keeps up."

"I can't do anything until I find out where they saw Woofy last. Listen Bobby . . ."

But his mother was too excited to wait for details. "Just go in all directions," she urged, waving her arms vaguely. "Take your bikes and ride around. I do hope he hasn't been run over. Oh, poor Woofy!"

"You're worse than Bobby," David grumbled. But he grinned at her as he stood up. "If you will just try to keep calm and hold onto the brats we'll . . . Well, for Pete's sake!"

There was a rattling under the shrubbery and Woofy, pink mouth open in a mighty yawn, came wandering out. He looked sleepy and bored and none too pleased when Bobby pounced on him.

"There, you see!" Penny turned to Carrol. "The dog takes a nap and we all act as though we'd gone crazy. I never saw such people."

Carrol was laughing as she had never laughed at Grandmother's. She was laughing because these were such dear, funny people; because Mrs. Parrish was just as excited over Woofy's return as she would have been had he been found miles from home; because David looked so rumpled and good-natured as he pretended to spank

Bobby; and because, beneath her seeming indignation, Penny secretly adored her family's ways.

They began to go their separate ways again. David took up the hose to sprinkle and Mrs. Parrish walked over to the next porch to explain the mishap. Penny and Carrol wandered into the house to freshen up for dinner, and peace, for a few moments at least, descended on the Parrishes.

CHAPTER THREE

A RIDING LESSON

"Penny. What's that?" Carrol leaned out and shook the occupant of the other twin bed.

"What? Huh? What's what?" Penny rolled over and blinked sleepily into the early morning light.

"That bugle. Listen."

"O-o-oh, that's reveille. For the soldiers to get up, you know. It says, 'you can't get 'em up, you can't get 'em up, you can't get 'em up in the morning.' But we don't have to get up. It's too early." Penny snuggled down, a little pink cocoon in her blanket, but Carrol lay listening.

"I've been here three whole days," she thought. "Three beautiful, wonderful days have flown by like magic. I've never heard just that bugle call before or heard the birds sing so sweetly. It seems a shame to lie here and miss any of it."

She slipped noiselessly out of bed and padded to the window. The world was drenched in early morning sunshine and robins were hopping about, while a blue jay sat in a lilac bush and scolded.

"You silly thing," she whispered. "It is much too lovely a day to be so cross.

Tiptoeing to the closet she got out a pair of blue slacks and a white cotton sweater, then, gathering up her underclothes, she stole around Penny's bed and into the bathroom. She splashed quietly and dressed as quickly as she could, anxious to be out in the sunshine. When she sneaked down the back stairs and through the kitchen, she could hear Trudy stirring about in her room in the basement. She unlatched the screen door and stepped out.

For a time she sat on the back steps watching the birds and sniffing the fragrance of the syringa. Then Woofy poked his cold nose into her hand and she wandered around into the front yard to throw sticks for him. She was sitting in the grass exploring an ant hill when the porch door opened and David came out.

"What are you doing up so early?" he asked in surprise.

Carrol looked up and smiled. "It's too lovely to stay inside," she answered. "I had to come out. Are you going to ride?"

"Umhum. I'll be back for breakfast." David started down the walk, then he turned around. "Want to come?" he asked casually.

"No, thanks. I'm not dressed to ride and, besides, I don't ride very well."

David looked at her as though he were seeing a stranger from Mars. Not to ride! It was unbelievable. He half turned away, then looked back again. She was a guest; the family would sleep for hours—and that left her his responsibility to entertain. So he came over to her and held out his hand to help her up.

"Well, come on. I'll show you the horses."

Carrol looked up at the outstretched hand, making no move to take it. "Please don't bother," she said. "I'm really enjoying it right here."

"Okay." David let his hand drop. He looked at her as she stood Woofy on his hind legs and tried to make him sit up. Suddenly he didn't think it would be a bother at all. In fact . . . He held out his hand again trying to suppress the eagerness in his voice as he said: "Come on! You've been on a cavalry post three days and you haven't been close to a horse. I want to show you mine."

"Do you, really?"

"Sure I do."

"All right." Carrol dropped Woofy in a heap and David pulled her to her feet.

"I'll tell you what we might do," he suggested as they walked across the grass. "You go in and put on some of Penny's riding stuff, then we can jog around a little."

"I have jodhpurs."

"Swell. You go put 'em on and I'll bring the car around while you're gone."

Carrol ran into the house and tiptoed up the stairs again. She felt excited about riding and decided that David might be human, after all. For three days he had completely ignored her. What he did with his time she had no idea. Now and then she saw him stretched out in the swing with a book on chemistry or history, but he always disappeared when she and Penny came to occupy the porch. He was no older than most of the boys who hung about and she had heard him on the telephone making plans with them when he was sure no girls would be about.

"He's busy studying for West Point and practicing for the horse show," Penny had explained the second day when David appeared for lunch as the others were leaving the table. "Dad bought a new horse last year and David's training him. He wants to jump him in the show."

"I thought perhaps he doesn't like having me here."

"Oh, no-o-o! I told you he doesn't like girls. But they don't bother him any. He doesn't even see you. I'll ask Mums if she can make him behave."

"Oh, please don't!" Carrol had cried in panic. "I don't want him to go around with us. It's much nicer without him and . . . I hope you won't be angry—but I think he's terribly conceited."

Penny had laughed uproariously. "He isn't," she had answered. "Not a bit. He likes to show off, about his riding and playing better tennis than anyone else, but he really isn't conceited."

"Perhaps he isn't," Carrol decided this morning, humming softly as she put on the new jodhpurs. "I'll give him the benefit of the doubt, anyway. Maybe I can discover what makes him tick."

David was waiting for her in the car. He swung the door open and started the motor as she climbed in. Again he seemed to have retreated within himself and

Carrol was at a loss for conversation. So they rode in silence.

"He's about as talkative as the great stone sphynx," she thought. "It's going to be a jolly morning."

Once, so suddenly that she jumped, he waved a hand across her and murmured: "That's the riding hall."

Carrol admired the riding hall, commenting on its vast size as long as she felt she could decently string adjectives together, then they rode silently on. When at last they reached the stables, David stopped the car and got out. Not knowing what she was supposed to do, Carrol sat. Halfway up the cement runway David turned and beckoned to her.

"Hey, come on," he shouted.

For a moment she was furious. Then common sense returned to her. "He doesn't realize," she thought, "that this is all strange to me. I suppose the army kids come down here, pile out and go and get their horses. He can't believe that I really don't know what to do."

So she got out of the car and walked toward him. This time he waited for her. He even pointed out the long line of stables, explaining them.

"Those are for the horses in the troops," he said. "The next one to this is the polo stable, and this one is for officers who own their own horses. The one on the other side belongs to the horse show team."

"Are those the horses that jump in the Olympics?"

"Yeah."

"I saw them jump once. I was in New York and my father took me to Madison Square Garden." Carrol's eyes shone. "It was wonderful."

"There are a lot of famous old horses in there. Would you like to see them?"

"I'd love to."

David seemed pleased. He even walked beside her as they went into the vast dimness of the stable. Soldiers were busy grooming and watering the horses as Carrol and David wandered up and down the long aisles, peering between the slats of the box stalls.

"And this is famous old Cherokee!" Carrol's face was filled with awe as she chinned herself on the top of the stall in order to see the big bay. "Wouldn't it be wonderful to ride him?"

"Someday I will." David leaned against the stall and he and Cherokee looked thoughtfully at each other. "Someday I'll be on the horse show team."

"Oh, David, really? When?"

"Not for a long time after I'm out of West Point, silly." He helped her down and they wandered on.

"Good heavens, he helped me down," she told herself. "He *actually* helped me down."

When they finally came into the stable where David's horse was kept, he said: "Wait here a minute."

He disappeared into a box-stall and Carrol could hear him murmuring, "Hello, baby. How's my boy this morning?"

When she had given up all hope of ever seeing him again he came out leading a beautiful chestnut thoroughbred. Carrol reached up to stroke the soft muzzle and the horse nipped gently at her hands with his lips.

"He's perfectly lovely, David," she said. "And he's young, isn't he?"

"What makes you think so?"

"Well, I suppose," Carrol laid her cheek against the velvety nose, "because you called him baby—and because he has long hair."

David whooped. The startled animal threw back his head and reared. Carrol fled into the empty stall. When he had quieted the horse, David called: "You can come out now."

Then he added, as Carrol inched around the door; "You mustn't say 'hair.' That's his mane and lots of horses wear it long. But you're right; he is young."

Carrol blushed and for the first time in their brief acquaintance David was tactful. He handed her the halter and said: "Here, you lead Lucky up to the door."

"Is that his—his name?" she stammered.

"It's Lucky Souvenir, but I call him Lucky. You lead him and I'll go and find a horse for you."

Carrol led Lucky and prayed that he wouldn't step on her. She found some tufts of grass by the door, and they were having a delightful time together when David came back. He was followed by a soldier with a rangy animal that seemed unhappy about the whole thing. He closed his eyes and stood on three legs while the soldier tightened the saddle girth.

"I don't think he likes me much," Carrol volunteered as he refused a sprig of grass she offered him.

"He doesn't like anything much, but sleep."

David was busy saddling Lucky, so the soldier boosted her up and shortened her stirrups. "What's his name?" she asked him.

"Robin, Miss."

Robin blinked one eye and sagged in the middle. Anything less like a robin Carrol had never seen. She was giving him a pat to win his affections when David mounted and, without warning, moved forward. For reasons known only to him, Robin roused himself and shot through the stable door as though he had just remembered a fire call. Carrol jerked backwards, lost her stirrups and grabbed the saddle. David reached out and caught her bridle as she passed. They stopped in a huddle and he glared at her.

"What are you trying to do?" he scolded. "Hold on to your reins. You can't just let him go any place he likes."

"Well, how did I know you were going to start?" Carrol was indignant and, for her, unusually explosive. "There ought to be such things as traffic signals, even on a horse. I'm not a mind reader."

She gathered up her reins and David was surprised to see that she knew how to hold them. In silence, they walked down the road. Suddenly, in a voice that blasted her ear drums, David shouted:

"Fifteen feet—then prepare for a left turn!"

Carrol gave him a withering look. "I'm not deaf," she said.

"You wanted signals. I'm giving them to you."

"Well, please don't."

She looked ahead at the path they were to take. It lay before her, broad and straight, so she gave her horse a vexed dig with her heels. He ambled into a trot and she rose and fell with him, rose and fell, in her best riding academy manner. She hoped David was impressed. Surprisingly, he was.

He watched her straight little back going up and down and wondered how long she could keep it up. But Robin tired before Carrol. He tired suddenly and completely.

"Kick him," David urged, as he rode up beside her. "Keep him going."

"You know, you're really not bad," he complimented when Robin was on his way again and they were walking along side by side. "You're darn near as good as Penny. I'll give you a better horse next time."

"Really? Do you think I do all right?"

"You do fine. Can you jump?"

"I've never tried." (He *would* ask me something like that, she thought. Just when he's beginning to unbend a little.) So she added bravely: "I'd like to, though." She was more astonished at her words than David and wanted to snatch them back, but he gallantly offered her a reprieve.

"We'll go down on the Island and I'll take a few jumps on Lucky," he decided. "I wouldn't want you to try it on Robin. He's so dumb he'd probably fall down with you."

They wandered under a railroad trestle and into a green maze of forest paths. The little tract of woodland was called the Island because it was cradled in a bend of the river and could only be reached by the one bridle path. Lucky broke into an easy canter, and by beating, kicking and clucking, Carrol kept Robin loping along behind.

At last David signaled her to halt. He turned Lucky off the path and sailed easily over a pile of logs. This way and that they turned, over logs and mounds of brush,

with Lucky's mane flying in the breeze and David leaning forward, a part of him.

"It was wonderful!" Carrol praised when they came
back. "Do you suppose I could learn to do it?"

She forgot he was the insufferable David as she asked,
and he forgot she was just another girl to worry with as
he answered:

"Sure. I'll teach you."

They started their horses again and eventually made
the whole outer circle of the Island. Sometimes they
trotted and sometimes they walked, bending their heads
to avoid green overhanging branches. Once David suggested that they let their horses graze, and they pulled
into a glade where the grass grew thick and lush. Lucky
stood looking around him, listening to the quiet forest
sounds; but Robin bent his head and went greedily to
work as though each mouthful might be his last.

"Isn't he a pig?" Carrol laughed. "Still, I suppose it's
like being turned loose in a candy store."

"And speaking of candy stores—I'm hungry." David
looked at his wrist watch. "Good grief," he said, "it's
nearly nine o'clock."

"Oh, it can't be!"

"It is." David held up his arm and Carrol looked at
the watch in amazement. "We've missed our breakfast,
but I'll take you over to the Post Exchange," he consoled.
"We can get a malted milk there."

"A malted milk sounds perfectly divine, but what is
the Post Exchange?"

It was David's turn to look amazed. "Hasn't Penny
taken you there?"

Carrol shook her head. "Not yet."

"I can't believe it. I thought her crowd live there." David went on to explain. "It's a sort of general store that has everything from groceries and meat to cosmetics and clothes. There's a barber shop and a restaurant and a soda fountain . . ."

"Oh, you mean the P. Ex.," Carrol interrupted. "We've been in the soda fountain after the movies. I'd just never heard it called the Post Exchange."

David laughed. "I didn't think Penny would neglect that part of your education," he said. "She likes ice cream too much."

"Don't you ever go there?" Carrol pulled Robin away from a patch of grass he was trying to steal from under Lucky's very nose, and looked at David curiously.

"Sometimes, not often." David turned sidewise in his saddle, one leg thrown over the pommel. "You see, Carrol," he explained seriously, "I'm studying pretty hard. I'm going to the Point straight from high school and most of the fellows have had a year prepping for it. I've got a lot of reading to do and I go over to one of the second lieutenants and he helps me. I have to enter the first of July."

"Michael and Dick are going, too, aren't they?"

"Yes, but Mike's been studying in Washington all winter and Dick went to a coaching school in Missouri. They've got an edge on me."

"I see, David. And I think it's awfully fine of you to do it. But you really should play some."

"I do. I swim every day and I ride, but . . ." he hesitated a moment, then: "It's the girls," he blurted out. "If you play with them at all they just won't let you alone."

"I know, there's always something going on."

"Yeah, and," his face looked troubled, "I don't mean Mary and Jane, they're swell, but . . ."

"Louise?"

"Louise, and a bunch of others like her on the post. They don't have anything to do but make a play for the boys. Oh, I don't think it's because I'm so hot, don't get that idea of me; I'm just another scalp to add to the collection."

"It shouldn't be that way, David," Carrol said seriously, thinking how right Penny had been about his conceit. "But a lot of it is because girls don't have any ambition. They aren't planning a future as boys are, and aren't trying to amount to something someday."

"Are you?"

"Yes, I am. Oh, of course I don't have anything definite like you, knowing you want an army career. But I'd like to major in languages and then do something after I finish college."

David looked at her curiously. "You're a funny girl," he said.

"Why?"

"Because I can sit here and talk to you as I would to Dick or Bob, or Mike. I didn't care much for you at first. I guess you knew that, didn't you?"

Carrol smiled. "I guess I did. But why didn't you like me?"

"It wasn't that I didn't like you," he answered. "I just didn't trust you. You were so pretty I thought you'd turn out to be another Louise."

Carrol threw back her head and laughed. "Do all girls who are fairly good-looking have to be designing?" she asked. "If they do, I might buy some horn-rimmed glasses."

"Oh, don't do that." David vetoed her suggestion with such a warm, flattering look that, for the first time, Carrol could understand the charm he had for her sex. "Your eyes are too pretty to hide."

They both laughed self-consciously, and he said suddenly: "Do you know what made me like you?"

"No. For goodness' sake, what?" Carrol was frankly curious.

"The way you got so mad at the stables. I was horrid to you, and if you had been Louise's type you'd have pouted and looked hurt and had to be coaxed back into a good humor. But you just went trotting off. You looked cute."

"And do you know what finally made me like you?" Carrol asked. "Oh, I didn't like you, either," she said quickly. "I thought you were the rudest boy I had ever known. *And* the most conceited." At his incredulous stare she was inclined to laugh, but she went on. "I didn't want to come with you this morning, but I thought I'd see what you were really like. I thought I'd found out. And I hadn't changed my opinion, either. Then you were so nice about not letting me jump on Robin, and getting me a better horse, and teaching me to ride. I liked you," she finished simply.

"Then we're friends?"

"Friends. No foolishness. Just—friends. Like Penny and I are."

"Shake."

They reached gravely across to each other and shook hands.

"Now that we have that settled," David said, "I'll buy you the biggest malted milk that P. Ex. has to offer."

They dragged up their horses' unwilling heads and turned toward home. Robin, knowing that his stable was in the offing, began to lift his feet and became almost jaunty. He clop-clopped along beside Lucky, and, as his red tiled roof shone through the trees, even volunteered an unassisted sprint. Like the mad dash of Paul Revere he charged up the runway, and was impatient as Carrol swung out of the saddle. She reached up to pat him but he was hurrying off and she brushed only the tip of his tail.

"Now what?" she asked as David gave his bridle to a groom and slapped Lucky into a departing trot.

"Now we go eat." David caught her hand and together they ran to the car.

When they came into the soda fountain, engrossed in a discussion of football, a shrill voice brought them to with a start.

"Well, I wish you'd look!" Penny was exclaiming. "Where have you two *been*?" She jumped up from the table she shared with Jane and Louise and beckoned to them.

"Where would you think, from our clothes?" David stood glaring at her, then he followed Carrol over. "Have you paid for your drinks?" he asked looking down at the cluttered table. At her nod he pulled out a chair for Carrol. "All right, then we'll sit with you."

He lounged in complete silence, which bothered Penny not at all, for she was explosively repeating to Carrol: "I never was so surprised in my life. I got up and you were gone. You were simply *gone!* I couldn't imagine *where.*"

"My dear little nit-wit." Louise lifted her shoulders and smiled sweetly at Penny. "I can't imagine *why* you wouldn't know *where.*" She set her glass carefully in the center of the table, her lower lip caught between her teeth, eyes guardedly lowered. "Haven't you heard the saying—about the early bird getting the worm?"

CHAPTER FOUR

PLANS ARE MADE

THE NEXT MORNING, not all the bugle calls in the world could have moved Carrol at an early hour. She hobbled about the house and moaned every time she sat down and groaned every time she was forced to get up. Breakfast on a straight-backed diningroom chair was a painful event not to be dawdled over, and the long trip from the table to the front porch seemed as endless as a walking tour across the continent. She had just stretched out in the swing, comfortable at last, with pillows wedged under sore muscles, when Penny's cheerful voice called from inside:

"Hey, Carrol, where are you? It's time to go riding."

"Oh, dear," she wailed, as Penny bounced out, shirted and jodhpured and waving a riding crop. "I can't ride today: I just can't!"

"Sure you can. You have to. It's the only way to get the stiffness out."

Penny bent over her and began pulling out the comforting pillows. In a business-like fashion she got Carrol on her feet, and with remarks meant to be encouraging got her started on her return trip through the miles and miles of halls and stairways.

Carrol protested, but she went. She changed into her riding clothes and the sweetest voice she had ever heard was that of Penny's mother calling: "I'm going marketing and if you girls are ready, I'll drive you to the stables in the car."

"Oh, joy," she thought, "I'm spared the bicycle."

The ride over was fairly painless and to her surprise after the first few jounces in the saddle, the stiffness disappeared. She had a sweet little horse named Ragamuffin, that made it clear from the start he had come out to enjoy his morning exercise. He cantered along like a rocking-horse and trotted in a sure-footed manner, proving to her that he knew his business. When he walked he looked around as though enjoying the sights, and Carrol loved him.

"You're a precious," she told him as she dismounted at the stables. "I hope I see you often."

"You can always have him," Penny said, as they started through the ravine, taking a short cut home. "Captain Carlyle, who owns him, is in the hospital, and he'll be glad to have someone exercise him."

They swung along, chatting and laughing at each other's nonsense, and before they realized it were at home. As they came onto the porch Mrs. Parrish met them at the door.

"Mary and Jane have been calling about every ten minutes," she said to Penny. "They want to plan a scavenger hunt for tonight."

"Grand! What did you tell them?"

"Heavens, I didn't know what to tell them. I just said it was all right with me and that they can use our house, or anything they want. You had better go in and call them."

Penny and Carrol went inside and Mrs. Parrish began her usual tour of the block to see if she could round up Bobby or Tippy, or both. When she returned, overcome to find them in their own back yard, five girls had taken over the front porch.

"Oh, Mums," Penny called, "please come here a minute."

She opened the screen and came in. "Hello, Mary," she greeted them. "Hello, Jane, Louise. Please don't get up for me." She dropped down on the swing beside Carrol and patted her knee. "Feel better, honey?"

"Much, thank you. I'm not stiff at all now."

"That's good. Penny," she turned to her daughter, "I'm dying of thirst. Please ask Trudy to bring the pitcher of lemonade that's in the refrigerator. Then I'll listen to anything you have to say."

Penny skipped inside and was out again in a few seconds, talking as she came. "Don't you think a scavenger hunt would be fun, Mummy? Or would you like a treasure hunt better?"

Mrs. Parrish considered it. "Why, I don't know," she said. "What do you think, Jane?"

"Well, it's a problem of cars, Mrs. Parrish," Jane answered. "A treasure hunt isn't much good unless you cover a lot of ground, and I don't think our parents will let us take the cars."

"I know mine won't." Mary spoke up in a matter-of-fact tone. "Dad says Bob is too careless, and since he smashed up a fender he's confined to the post."

"Well then, I believe I'd plan on a scavenger hunt and use the bicycles. I like scavenger hunts better, myself." Mrs. Parrish made a place on the low table before her and was busily planning as Trudy arrived with the tray.

"I don't know what arrangements you have made," she said as she poured the lemonade, "but you'll need prizes and you'll have to have a meeting place. How many do you want to invite?"

"We thought we would ask everyone on the post our age," Louise said consulting the list she held. "That would make about twenty."

"You know, Mums," Penny cut in, "we don't see the other crowd on the post very often, but they always ask us to their big parties. I think we ought to have 'em, but . . ." She shook her head and looked disconsolate. "I don't know what we could use for prizes—we're all so broke."

Mrs. Parrish sipped her lemonade thoughtfully. "Let me think," she said. "Oh, I know! I bought a green tie with horses' heads on it, for David. Someone gave him one for a graduation gift and I have never returned it to the store. That would do for the boys. Then for the girls . . . I have a lovely isinglass box filled with sachets. Would that be all right?"

"Perfect!" The chorus of approval was unanimous and Penny upset her glass of lemonade in her enthusiasm.

"Shall we meet here?" she asked, rubbing the sticky sweetness from the chair arm and holding out her glass to be refilled.

"Why don't you? And you can bring your loot back here to be checked. Now, about the food. If you will just tell Trudy . . ."

"Oh, Mrs. Parrish," interrupted Mary. "You're doing too much as it is. We'll each bring a package of sandwiches or something. When we call the girls we'll tell them what to bring."

This started a discussion as to what they would serve, and Mrs Parrish seized the opportunity to make her escape. "You won't need me any longer," she said, as she stood up. "And I promised to help Trudy before lunch. So if you'll excuse me, I'll run along."

She started to go inside, laughing away their thanks, but Penny stopped her. "Oh, Mums," Penny called, "the list! Will you make out the list?"

"The list?" Mrs. Parrish turned back. "What list?"

"Why, the list of things to hunt for. We can't make it out because we want to hunt, too. We mustn't know anything that is on it."

"Of course you mustn't. All right, I'd love to make it." She went on, but called back over her shoulder, "I know one perfectly grand thing—but it's going to be hard to find."

The girls looked questioningly at each other and Jane asked: "Now, what do you suppose it could be?"

"I don't know," Penny answered, "but you can bet she'll make up a honey. Do you think we should go in couples, or just any old way?"

This started them off again.

"I think couples would be best," Jane said. "After all, it isn't much fun to go riding around in the dark by yourself."

The shrieks at this remark brought Woofy's sleepy face out from under the swing where he had been hiding. "Listen to her," Mary teased as she went over and pulled him out. "She doesn't want to ride around by herself. Whom do you suppose she wants to ride with, girls?"

"Bob," answered the chorus.

Penny tucked her foot under her and grinned. "If she and Bob go out together they can kiss the prize good-bye"

"Penny Parrish, you're a beast. I do not want to go with Bob!" Jane was blushing and stammering in her confusion. "I'd—I'd every bit as soon go with—little Jimmy Peterson as anybody. Just because I said . . ."

"We know what you said, darling." Mary sobered and tousled Jane's hair as she passed her. "We know you like my brother, and we know it's mutual." She sat down with Woofy, a boneless ball in her lap, and added: "It's all right for Jane and Bob to pair off—but gosh, it's going to leave some of us with awful punks."

"I know it." Louise made a wry face. "We can't ask the boys for dates."

"Why can't we, I'd like to know?" Penny sat up and looked at her. "We know 'em, don't we?"

"Of course, Penny," Louise answered her in a voice meant to be crushing, "we *know* the boys, but we don't ask them to date us. *I* don't anyway."

"Oh, you do, too." Penny, unawed, refused to be squashed. "We're always calling each other up to do something, and I don't see any difference in this."

"But, Penny, a *date* . . ." Louise, resorting to the supercilious tone one might take with a child of three, was interrupted by Jane's brisk voice.

"That isn't the point, Louise. I see what Mary means. We don't mind asking the boys, but most of the attractive ones are in our crowd. It isn't fair for us to take them and give these other girls we're inviting all the goons like that little Peterson boy, who's practically a baby even if he is a sophomore."

"Well," Louise tossed her head. "I'm not asking any boy—and I'm not going with any left-overs, either. If I don't get a good date, I'll stay at home."

"Why don't you make it fair for everybody," Carrol

suggested, "and draw lots?" Up to now she had been an interested listener, and this was her entrance into the conversation. "You could write the names on pieces of paper and draw, or you could cut cards in half and match them up."

"Oh, grand! Let's!" Penny, ever-enthusiastic, was only halted from an immediate operation on the kings and queens of her mother's best bridge cards by Carrol's detaining hand.

"Wait and see what the others think of it," she cautioned.

"I think it's the thing to do," Mary said. "Then there won't be any hard feelings. Of course," her eyes twinkled as she looked at Jane, "I don't suppose you and Bob will care for it much."

"Don't be silly." Jane tried to look cross, but her frown was completely denied by the upward quirk of her lips.

"I suppose I'll draw someone utterly impossible," Louise said sulkily. "Oh, well . . ." She shrugged her shoulders and looked at Penny. "Is David coming?" she asked.

"No!" Penny answered shortly. "You know he never comes. He isn't on the list and we have an even number without him. Shall I cut up the cards now?"

She dismissed David lightly, and receiving no opposition to her suggestion, appropriated a deck from the table drawer. After selecting eight face cards, she found a pair of scissors and snipped them neatly in two.

"Thanks, Mrs. Parrish," she said, dumping the remainder of the deck into the waste-paper basket. "It's all for dear old Arden." She shuffled the bits of pasteboard and laid them in a cigarette box. "Now what?" she asked.

"Well, the food." Louise, restored, for no known reason, to good humor, checked her list again. "We never have decided about the food."

"How about sandwiches?" Mary asked. "They're easy, and when Louise phones the girls she can tell them each a different kind."

"All right. And you might have them bring a quart of milk too. We can have Trudy make us some cocoa," Penny added shamelessly. "I'm always hungry."

"Aren't we all?" Louise looked up from her writing. "How about splitting this list with me, Jane? You can telephone half and I can telephone half. It saves so much time."

"Okay." Jane took the paper Louise tore off. "How come I'm getting all the girls?" she asked as she glanced at it.

"They just happened to be on top." Louise had the grace to look embarrassed. She saw the amusement on the other faces and held out the second list instantly. "You can have this one," she offered.

"I like this one better." Jane folded the slip of paper and stuck it in her pocket as Major Parrish came home to his lunch.

"What's the pow-wow about?" he asked, reaching for Penny's empty glass and some lemonade.

"It's a scavenger hunt, Dad," Penny explained.

"It's going to be fun, Major Parrish," Carrol added. "Mrs. Parrish is making the list of things we're to find."

"She is? Then I'd better go in and give her some

suggestions. I know one *peach*." He went inside and the girls got up to leave.

After lunch, which was a noisy affair punctuated by whispered conferences between Major and Mrs. Parrish, Penny gave Trudy instructions about cups and plates. Then she and Carrol wandered upstairs. They were lounging about until time to go swimming when David's head peeked around the door.

"Hey," he asked, "what's this about a scavenger hunt?"

Penny looked up from the outrageous color she was painting a finger nail. "If you'd ever come home to eat, you'd know. Look, Carrol." She waved her hand about, admiring it. "Mummy'll make me take it off, but doesn't it look elegant?"

"I asked about the scavenger hunt." David came inside and leaned against the door. "Come on, tell me."

Penny winked at Carrol. "You aren't thinking of coming, are you?" she asked saucily.

"*I asked about the scavenger hunt.*" David put a threatening foot forward.

Penny gave a shriek, and in fear of battle clapped the stopper on the nail polish. "We're having a scavenger hunt," she explained hastily.

"I *know* you're having a scavenger hunt. I asked about it. When is it, where is it, who's coming?"

"Everybody's coming. It's tonight, and it's going to be all over the post—and we're to eat here. How did you hear about it?"

"Mother and Dad have their heads together downstairs and they're whispering and giggling like nobody's business. What time is it to be?"

"Oh, David," Penny sat up in distress, "you aren't thinking of coming, are you? We didn't count you in—you never come—and now you'll get the list all uneven."

"Well," David grinned, "you can even it up again." Far from feeling hurt at not being wanted, he was delighted to be teasing Penny. "I think I'll come."

"But you *can't!*" Penny wailed.

"I'd like to know why I can't. Aren't you having it at my house? and hasn't Mother announced she's giving my necktie away for a prize? I certainly ought to have a chance to get my own necktie back. Don't you think so, Carrol?"

Carrol could hardly keep a straight face as she looked from one to the other. Penny's dismay was so comic and David's glee at teasing her so apparent. The more Penny protested, the more determined David became.

"It won't matter," Carrol said, when the battle was becoming heated. "We can dig up another face card to match one we have and some lucky girl can have two dates. I think it is very polite of David to be so interested." She gave Penny a long look and added, "You know, Louise suggested having him."

"Oh, she did, did she?" David glowered at them both, and for a moment looked undecided. The list might have remained even and peace been restored, if Penny hadn't blurted out:

"Then that settles it! David won't come!"

"Oh, won't I!" David chose between suffering Louise and being bluffed out of what he felt to be his rights.

"Sure, I'll come. Thanks a lot." He disappeared and could be heard laughing as he slammed his door.

"Now what do you suppose made him do that?" Penny moaned. "He never butted in before, and lots of times we've simply begged him to help us out." She looked at Carrol. "I bet he's coming because you're here!"

"Oh, Penny, he isn't." Carrol was very positive in her answer. "David took me for a ride, and was nice—but I haven't seen him since even to talk to. He's only coming to tease you."

"No, he isn't. I know David. And will Louise be wild!" Penny threw herself back among the pillows and laughed. "Watch out for Louise," she warned. "She looks like such a sweet little thing butter wouldn't melt in her mouth, but has she claws! I ought to know—she's always digging them into me."

"I wouldn't do anything to make Louise mad," Carrol said seriously. "Goodness, you make me feel as though I'm some kind of a vamp or something. I don't want David."

"Of course you don't. I don't see why any girl should; he's too stuffy." Penny spoke with all the intimate knowledge of a sister. "But Louise wants him. She wants every good-looking boy that comes along. She purrs at Jane, but she'd like to murder her because Bob never minds saying he likes Jane best." She thumped the pillows viciously. "I don't see," she declared, "why boys have to spoil everything."

"They don't," Carrol told her wisely. "Not if you forget girls like Louise and have a natural sort of good time.

I know David is just being nice, and he's probably lonesome. My goodness, Penny, he's only eighteen. He can't sit around the house like an old man."

"Probably not. But he never came before."

"Well, he's coming this time." Carrol put the bottles back into her manicuring kit. "And I'm not going to be self-conscious and foolish. It's silly at our age. I'm not going to let the thought of Louise make me act like a dope, either."

She began to hum as she got out her bathing suit and Penny flew to her and hugged her. "Oh, darling," she cried, "you've got more *sense!*"

CHAPTER FIVE

THE SCAVENGER HUNT

THE HOUSE was in an uproar. Bobby and Tippy were helping Williams, the orderly, clear the table while Trudy arranged glasses and plates on the buffet. The two-fingered clacking of a typewriter echoed from upstairs as Mrs. Parrish struggled with the last minute copying of her list. On the stroke of seven girls began arriving with their contributions to the feast, and Penny was rushing about and wailing:

"I'm furious. Simply furious. Bobby has given my whole quart of milk to Woofy! We won't have enough, now, I know we won't."

"Oh, we'll have plenty," Carrol consoled her. "The whole kitchen table is covered with bottles of milk and we've enough sandwiches for an army."

At precisely seven thirty the booming volume of boys' voices swelled the din. Bicycles crashed against the porch and Major Parrish looked up from the list he was dictating to his wife.

"I hope your petunias live through it," he commented dryly.

"I hope so, too, but I can't bother about it now. How do you spell tombstone?"

He told her and she jerked the sheets out of the typewriter. They sorted out the carbon copies and she rushed downstairs with them. "Hot off the press," she called as she waved them.

"Wait a minute, Mums." Penny darted to the stairway. "Don't give them out yet, we haven't drawn for partners. Do you and Dad know everyone?"

"I think we do."

The Parrishes smiled around the crowded hall and made an attempt to shake the few hands that could reach them. All the girls and boys from the post were familiar to them, and two tall boys who had come out from town came over to introduce themselves.

"I'm Stanley Mathews," one said, holding out his hand. "And this is Dwight Conley."

"How do you do." Mrs. Parrish greeted them and Major Parrish said: "I believe we know your father, Doctor Conley."

"Yes, I believe you do."

They chatted for a few minutes while Penny darted in and out. At last she mounted a footstool and began counting, audibly and vainly, the moving heads.

"Oh, please keep still," she begged. "I think you're all here, but I keep getting a different number every time."

"You might check us off," a voice called. "Me, I'm Dick Ford."

"I know you!" Penny laughed as she searched the different groups. "Bob, Chuck Carstairs, Ed . . . Where's Ed Lyman?"

"I'm down here." The voice came from the floor and a long arm waved like a semaphore. "It seemed to be the only place left to sit down."

"All right, don't move then." Penny's eyes passed on. "Florence Rush?"

"Present," a tall girl answered, and added: "I'm hanging onto Martha. This is no place for anyone who only measures four-feet-eight."

Everyone began to tease Martha except Penny, who was scowling at her list. "I can't find the Abbotts," she said at last. "Has anyone seen Peg and Tubby? I know they were here."

"We're still here." Two girls rushed in from the diningroom. The first one, breathless and excited, pointed to her younger and much fatter sister and said crossly: "Of course Tub forgot the sandwiches. We had to run all the way home for them."

"Now, Tub," Dick drawled, "I bet you just went out in the kitchen to do a little sampling and Peg had to go and drag you back."

"I did not!" Tubby wiped her hot face on her sleeve and explained, "Why, I even made the sandwiches all by myself and I didn't so much as eat one. To hear Peg talk you'd think she did all the work."

Peg made a face at her which she returned with a grin. Penny climbed down from her stool and took the cards from their nest in the cigarette box. She arranged them in each hand, fan-wise and face down, as she announced:

"We're going to draw for partners. The boys will take from my left hand and the girls from my right."

She had just begun her tour of the room when David, immaculate in a white suit, appeared. Penny saw him and gasped. The boys yelled, "Hi, David, going with us?" and the girls looked up from their choosing in surprise.

"Why, David," Louise cooed, rushing over to him, "are you coming, too?"

"Thought I would." David waylaid Penny and reached for a card, but she jerked her hand back and looked at him with troubled eyes.

"I forgot to put a card in for you, David," she said. "What can we do about it?"

"He can come with us," several of the girls offered, while the boys looked glum.

Carrol crossed the room to Penny. "There's an extra card in there," she explained. "I put it in before dinner. It's half of the joker but I wrote 'king of diamonds' on it and the two who get the king of diamonds can take David with them."

"Oh," Louise smiled sweetly at Carrol. "So you knew David was coming?"

"We all knew it," Penny answered hotly. "But I was so busy I forgot to fix his card. Thanks a lot, Carrol." She went on passing out the cards but she stuck them out stiffly when she came to Louise."

There was laughing and confusion as they matched their bits of pasteboards. Penny drew the little Peterson boy, owlish behind horn-rimmed glasses, and undesirable as the others thought him to be, was quite satisfied. He stood at the top of his class and Penny thought he should be smart about finding things. Jane and Bob were beaming because they had drawn each other.

" 'Tain't fair, 'tain't," Dick taunted. "It's a put up job."

Mary had drawn Dwight Conley, and Carrol had Michael. Louise could be heard above the din assuring the other boy from town that there was no one in the world whom she would rather have for a partner. David was going with Tubby and Dick; and Tubby was overcome with her own importance.

"I think we're ready," Penny said at last as she looked at the couples grouped about. Some were sharing chairs, the springs of the divan were wailing, and Mary and Chuck Carstairs were sitting on the hearth of the empty fireplace.

Mrs. Parrish came down from the stairway-landing with her papers, and Major Parrish, who had been an interested spectator, stood on the bottom step and held up his hand. "Before you look at your lists," he said above the rustling of the paper, "I think you should set a time limit. Say you study them for five minutes. That will make it exactly eight o'clock. Then, at ten sharp, we start checking you in here. That will give you two hours —and the most complete list wins. How about it?"

Everyone hurriedly agreed and the reading began. The silence, punctuated by giggles and whispered comments, was shattered by a shriek from Mary. "I wish you'd listen to this one," she exulted as all the bent heads lifted. "Down at the bottom of the page it says 'a second lieutenant's bar. Oh, boy!'"

"Now I don't think that's fair." Dick threw his paper down in pretended disgust. "Major Parrish," he drawled, "I'm asking you as man to man, do you think it's right for us boys to stand out in the dark while our girls go in and chin with those good-looking young officers? After all, they have *uniforms* on. We haven't even got to West Point, yet!"

"You can go in with us," Jane laughed.

"Not me!"

"Nor me." "Nor me." The boys set up a chorus of protest while the girls enjoyed their discomfiture. Through it all Carrol looked blank, and Penny scrambled from her place to go over and whisper to her.

"A second lieutenant's bar," she mumbled hurriedly, "means one of those little gold bars the lieutenants wear on the shoulders of their uniforms—like Dad's major leaves, you know. Be sure and go to Lieutenant Hayes, because he's the youngest one, and the best-looking. He's a bachelor and lives with his mother in Jenkins Hall. Now remember," she hissed, " 'cause Mike won't *tell* you where to go."

Carrol nodded and Penny sped back to her place.

"Time's up," Major Parrish called. "Get set, every-body. One, two, three . . . Go!"

There was a scramble for bicycles. Bobby and Tippy cheered lustily from an upstairs window and, as the clat-ter died away Mrs. Parrish sank with a sigh into the dark and peaceful haven of the swing. "That is *definitely* the end of my petunias," she mourned.

Carrol, riding along beside Michael, became more eager and more excited as their baskets filled. "Where shall we go now?" she asked, as they stopped under a street light to study their list.

Their heads were bent over the paper, and with a stubby pencil Michael was checking off the items, when an arresting "yoohoo" came out of the darkness. Penny, followed by the cherubic Jimmy, tore around the corner and coasted to a stop.

"How are you doing?" she asked, one hand on her handlebars and one clutching a bulky pillowcase slung over her shoulder. "Any luck?"

"We have nearly everything." Michael looked up from his scratching and asked doubtfully: "Did you get up nerve enough to ask the general for his signature?"

"It was easy." Jimmy wiggled his glasses farther up on his nose and said earnestly and with pride: "I was pretty scared of him because I broke his window once with a baseball, so Penny and I kinda inched up on his porch. I felt like the dickens asking him—but I made up my mind to do it." He swelled out his chest and looked as boastful as his five-feet-five would allow. "I had a piece of paper all ready and my fountain pen, and I was just going to ring the bell when Penny spied a whole box of papers by the door. Oh, boy, was I relieved when we saw they had his scrawl on 'em."

They shrieked at his round-eyed seriousness, and overjoyed at the unusual impression he was making, he waggled his head and mopped his brow in dramatic agony. "Oh, boy," he anti-climaxed, "it was somepin'."

He was casting about in his mind for further tid-bits of information when Carrol and Michael mounted their bicycles and were off like rockets.

"Thanks," they called back, and Carrol heard Penny say:

"Come on, dope, let's get going."

Carrol and Michael coasted down the hill and slammed on the brakes at the general's curb. Michael sprinted up the walk and returned in a record-breaking lope, triumphantly waving the cherished paper. Their collection swelled—and their pencil left its mark again.

"Now where?" Carrol looked at Michael, knowing that the next item on their list read, "one second lieutenant's bar."

Michael knew it, too, but decided to be perverse. "I guess we have them all," he said.

"No, we haven't. I know of at least one more." Carrol looked at him and laughed.

"What?" Michael's answering stare was all bewildered innocence. "I can't think of any."

"The second lieutenant's bar—surely you haven't forgotten that."

"Oh, *that.*" Michael shook his head. "I don't know any second lieutenants; they're too high-ranking for me. Do you?"

"I know one."

"Who is he?"

"Lieutenant Hayes."

"Oh, heck," Michael groaned, "you would know him. Do you know where he lives, too?"

"In Jenkins Hall."

Michael threw a leg over his bicycle and pushed away from a little maple tree that shuddered as though being rudely waked from a pleasant dream. "Come on then," he groaned. "We might as well get this over."

He pedaled off and Carrol laughed as she followed him. She had no idea where Jenkins Hall might be, so she pretended to be slow on the hill, leaving him to lead the way. Had Michael known it, he had her at his mercy and they could have checked in their list minus one of its most sought-for items.

"Here you are, pal," he said as they parked their wheels before a long two-storied apartment house where most of the younger and lower-ranking officers had small suites. "Go to it."

"Oh, Mike." Carrol looked up at the lighted windows and lost her courage. "Please come with me," she begged.

"No sir, not me." Michael sat down on the stone steps and shook his head. "If you want the bar you'll have to go and get it. I'll just take a little nap." He settled himself comfortably, then grinned up at her. "It's the first apartment on the second floor. Go on, and good luck."

Carrol looked at him beseechingly, but as he remained stubbornly inert, she squared her shoulders and went timidly up the stairs. She hardly knew what she expected to find. There had been so much discussion about it that, should it turn out to be a trivial incident it had been made to seem a great adventure. A second lieutenant, as far as she could see, was merely a young man a few years older than the boys, who had finished his college education and was established in his career.

"There's nothing to it," she told herself, as she gave a weak rap on a battered and uninspiring door. "I've talked to men his age before—and he's probably not so much, anyway. I'll just dash in and dash out and . . ."

She was so engrossed in her thoughts that the voice which called, "come in," was merely an obligato to the thumping of her heart. The repetition, a shout, startled her so that her hand turned the door knob, and she found herself in a cluttered room staring at a young man sitting at a drawing board. His back was to her and she had a swift glimpse of soiled white slacks, and a green shirt that was not impressive. Then he turned around.

"Whew!" she thought, "he's the handsomest man I ever saw." She would have explained about the gold bar but she saw that he held one in his hand. He poked it toward her with a brief glance, turned back to his board and went on with his pen-scratching.

"Come on, take it," he grumbled. "It's the last one I've got—and what I'll wear tomorrow, I don't know."

As she walked across the floor he turned in his chair again and looked at her. A puzzled frown came into his eyes and he laid down his pen. "I don't know you, do I?" he asked.

"No." Carrol felt her calm returning and she smiled. "I'm Carrol Houghton, and I'm visiting Major and Mrs. Parrish."

"Well; how do you do, Miss Houghton!" He ran his hands through his rumpled hair and made an attempt at straightening a tie which wasn't there, as he stood up. "Won't you . . . er . . . sit down some place?" He swept a roll of drawing paper from a chair and kicked a pile of magazines to one side. Stepping over a small statue of a horse, he made a sweeping gesture toward the chair, but Carrol shook her head.

"Thank you, I really can't stay. If I could just have the pin . . ."

He took no notice of her refusal. "I probably look a little informal," he went on, "but my mother went out and I thought I'd do some work. I seem to have made pretty much of a mess . . ." He looked vaguely around the room then back at her. "Why haven't I seen you at any of the dances?" he asked. "Don't you dance?"

His blue eyes were disconcerting in their eager stare but Carrol managed a laugh. "Oh yes, of course I dance," she answered. "But I'm much too young for your parties. Now, if I may have the pin . . ."

"Really? That's too bad." He looked downcast for a moment, then his face brightened. "Would you care to see the horse I'm drawing?" he invited. "It's for a magazine."

Carrol gave the pen-and-ink horse a quick glance. Its front end was rising nobly over a fence and there was the promise that in a few more hours its rear would follow.

"It's very good," she praised. "But, please, don't let me disturb your work. If I may just have the pin!"

"Oh yes. The pin. Now what did I do with it?" He began looking through his pockets with an expression so naive that, in spite of her irritation, Carrol smiled.

"You know what you did with it," she was surprised to hear herself say. "Come on, please give it to me. I have to go."

"Well, all right." He handed her the coveted bit of gold but his expression was stern and he scowled at her. "Now, you bring it back," he ordered. "Tomorrow."

"Oh, we will." Carrol, safely clutching the little bar,

was willing to promise. "I'll ask David to stop by with it in the morning."

"I don't mean David. He studies with me nearly every night. I meant you." The blue eyes twinkled. "How about me coming over to the Parrishes for it?"

"Oh no. That won't be necessary at all. We'll have it here very early—really we will."

Carrol began backing away and, as she slid through the partly open door, he followed her and said: "Why don't you keep it? For a souvenir of Fort Arden, I mean."

"I couldn't do that, but thank you." She groped behind her for the newel-post, and as her hand touched its comforting smoothness, turned and bolted.

She scurried down the stairs, and from the safety of the landing dared a quick look upward. His laughing face was peering down at her and he was leaning far out over the banisters. "Boo!" he said. She hurried on down, and could hear him laughing as he slammed his door.

"The man's crazy," she told Michael as he rose up out of the greenery by the steps. "Plain crazy."

"He's not crazy." Michael snorted. "Not Hayes. He's just nutty."

Carrol mounted her bicycle and laughed. "I don't believe you like him," she called back.

"I like him all right, but he's only been out of West Point a few months and he hasn't grown up."

They pedaled on and, now and then, met other hunters. As time grew shorter the frantic search became more frenzied. Bicycles screeched around corners, lights blazed in most of the houses as the occupants trotted from cellar to attic and back again. "I did have a picture just like you want," they would say. Or, "My grandmother had a . . . Now, let me think."

Suddenly it was ten o'clock.

There was a mad dash for 11 B Seymour Avenue. Bang, went the bicycles in the yard. The screen door beat a rat-a-tat-tat in its slamming. Pillow cases, pockets, sacks and laundry bags were emptied in little piles about the house. Cries of "check us, we're ready," followed Major and Mrs. Parrish in a chorus.

The Parrishes, equipped with pad and pencil and a copy of the list, selected the divan as the best vantage point and waded through the displays and the squatting owners to their seats.

"A black diamond," Major Parrish called when everything was quiet. Lumps of coal were waved and he nodded as he checked them. "Two hairs from the tail of a white horse."

"I hope they aren't all from the same horse," Mrs. Parrish said feelingly, as long white hairs streamed out. But it seemed they were. Old Plutocrat was in the nearest stable and he had had a painful evening.

"Oh dear, I wouldn't have gone there if I had known," Penny lamented. "There are lots of other white horses." She twisted the hairs about her finger and looked at them sadly. Poor old Plutocrat." Only her father's voice brought her back with a start.

"A used laundry list." Three had to admit failure.

"A 1939 license plate." Two more dropped out.

"We're still in," Carrol whispered to Michael. "I don't see how we can lose unless someone had a better pink handkerchief than the one I dunked in the red ink."

"A second lieutenant's bar." Gold bars showered around the checkers, for no girl had missed that one. Voices began to buzz and there was so much chattering and giggling that Major Parrish cupped his hands into a megaphone and shouted:

"A movie stub."

Bits of cardboard were fished out, examined critically, and three ruled out. "These are whole tickets," he said. "Your list, if you will notice, says *stubs*. And this one looks as though someone might have seen a football game." The two whole tickets were demanded back by their owners, as representing an investment of fifteen cents, and the checking went on.

"The general's signature."

"Oh dear," Mrs. Parrish covered her face with her hands. "I won't dare face the man tomorrow," she said. "I hope he wasn't furious."

"Oh, he wasn't!" Billy Peterson squirmed to the edge of his chair. His tale, which had brought so much applause from an audience of three, seemed just the drama for this crowded theatre and he launched into it. "I was pretty scared because I broke his window once with a baseball, so . . ."

"Little man, you've had a busy day. Sit back and rest." Penny pushed him back into his seat and as he looked up in hurt surprise, Dick added: "I know it was hard getting the old boy in a good humor for the rest of us. Thanks, old man." So he smiled again and searched importantly among his treasures.

"A piece of paper from a certain tombstone in the cemetery."

They all had the pieces of paper and they all had gruesome stories to relate of their finding.

"I declare, Mrs. Parrish, I never was so scared," Tubby said. "And Dick was, too. He fiddled around at the gate so long I was halfway across before he caught up with me."

"I was not scared!" Dick shouted above the teasing. "The sign says to lock the gate and you didn't go two feet alone. You just stood and squealed, 'oh, Dick, Dick, I see a ghost.'"

His imitation was so funny that they laughed, even to Tubby, who blushed. "Well, it was spooky," she defended herself. And they all agreed that it was.

"A June bug." June bugs began to come out.

"O-o-h, don't let them loose," wailed Mrs. Parrish. "Throw them out! The whole house is going to be owned by June bugs."

The bugs were dumped back into the night and Major Parrish hurried through his list. "A picture of a President." Presidents waved from Washington to Roosevelt.

"And a pink handkerchief." The last was greeted by silence.

"Go on, Carrol. Dig it out," Michael urged her.

Carrol flourished a pink square in the air. "I don't know if it will do," she said. "We dyed it in red ink and water."

"Well, it certainly is pink." Major Parrish took the handkerchief, inspected it and nodded. "The winners!" he called. "And very clever ones, too."

Everyone crowded around. "Why didn't we think of doing that," Jane groaned. "I thought Mother had a pink chiffon handkerchief some place, but we couldn't find it. We wasted about half an hour."

"We did, too." Dick said. "Everybody dug out evening handkerchiefs for us, but nobody had a pink one."

"I have." Mrs. Parrish said as she handed the winners their gayly wrapped packages. "Didn't you remember it, Penny?"

"Heck, no. I never thought of coming back home for anything."

"Well, it pays to be smart, my child." Michael was waving his tie in the air. "Or, if you can't be smart, pick yourself a partner who is." He removed his own blue-and-white necktie and replaced it with the horse bedecked scarf. "Boy, will I look swell on the hunt Sunday," he crowed.

Carrol thanked Mrs. Parrish for the sachets, and sprang up to help the girls with supper.

"Well, our work is done," Major Parrish said, propelling his wife toward the stairs. "Goodnight. Save us some house."

"Goodnight," they called. "Thanks for helping us."

There was a general exodus to the kitchen. "Listen," Penny said in despair, as she tried to fight her way to the refrigerator. "You boys will simply have to get out. There isn't room to move."

The boys departed noisily, and when the girls were ready in the diningroom they were on the floor, too much absorbed with a bag of Bobby's marbles to be enticed away.

"All right," Jane said, "we'll eat without you."

That brought them. Stacked sandwiches, leaning like the Tower of Pisa, crumbled into ruins, and only a few crumbs and spots of spilled chocolate gave evidence that there had been food. Conversation buzzed. And as though loath to let the day go, the clock's hands clung together at twelve before the last bicycle trundled across the lawn.

"It was swell, wasn't it?" David asked as he went about turning off the lights. "I've been thinking that we ought to have a moonlight picnic."

"Really, David?" Halfway up the stairs Penny leaned over the rail. "When?"

"I'll let you know when I get it all worked out. We'll go on horseback and I'll have to see about the grooms. Don't say anything about it to the rest of the crowd."

"All right, but make it soon." Penny stifled a yawn and her enthusiasm. For, with a sisterly knowledge of David, she thought she had about as much chance of going on a moonlight picnic as she would on a trip to Mars. David had enjoyed tonight, but tomorrow he would be back at his chemistry and practicing his tennis. "He'll never think of it again," she told herself, "so why get all hot and bothered about it." She would have been surprised could she have heard him as he waylaid Carrol in the diningroom door.

"There should be a full moon pretty soon," David was saying, "and I think you had better ride with me. You might need some help."

"All right. I'd love to." If a smile tugged at Carrol's

lips, she controlled it. The dimple near her mouth flashed only once as she added: "I expect you'll have to show me a lot."

"Funny, funny David," she thought as she slipped into Penny's room. "He does so hate to ask a girl for a date."

CHAPTER SIX

A STORMY AFTERNOON

CARROL came into the kitchen from the back porch, a pile of bathing suits over her arm. Trudy turned from the sink and the mountain of spinach she was washing to smile at her.

"It's a good thing you brought them suits in, Miss Carrol," she said. "I don't think you-all is goin' to get yo' swim this afternoon, 'cause it sho' is fixin' to rain."

"I don't believe we will, either." Carrol walked to the window and looked out at the threatening sky. "It looks pretty black, doesn't it?"

"Sho' does. I reckon a little nap won't hurt yo' none, yo' was all up so late las' night. You was mighty smart to win the prize, Miss Carrol. Miz Parrish done tol' me how yo' dyed a han'kch'f. I never would have thought of that."

Carrol laughed. "It was such fun!" She turned and sat down in the broad window-sill, studying her white shoes

extended before her. "I don't know when I've had such
a good time, Trudy," she said. "I don't know when I've
ever had such a good time. This is the happiest place.
Everybody on the whole post seems happy."

"Well now, Miss Carrol," Trudy inspected a torn leaf
carefully as she answered, "some folks here is happy and
some ain't, jes' like any place. You is only seein' the
happy folks. This is a happy house."

"That's just what it is." Carrol's face lighted up. "A
happy house. It's wonderful to be able to say to yourself,
'I live in a happy house,' isn't it, Trudy? What do you
think makes it a happy house?"

Trudy shut off the cold water and turned around, her
eyes narrowing. "Miss Carrol," she said, wiping her
hands on her apron, "you is mighty young to be seein'
what lots of folks don' know about the Parrishes. They
all makes it happy. But I reckon if yo' gets right down
to it, Major Parrish, and mostly Miz Parrish, started
things right an' keeps 'em goin' that way. Nothin' ain't
ever too much trouble if somebody can get some fun out
of it, an' they can get fun outa mos' nothin' at all. Lots
of folks would be worryin' 'cause they didn't have a new
car or a new dress or somethin', but the Parrishes ain'
like that. You seen how tickled Miss Penny was about
her new room? Well, she'd a'been jus' as proud to have
you sleep in her old one. An' Miz Parrish, she figured
an' figured on that room, an' she had jus' as good a time
goin' to the dance in her old dress as she would in a fine
new one. Nex' thing you know, Miz Parrish'll have a
new dress an' Major Parrish'll grin at her, an' she'll never
let on she knows he done without somethin' he wants

so's he could give it to her. That's jus' the way they is,
Miss Carrol, an' I been with 'em fifteen years."

"You love them a lot, don't you, Trudy?"

"They's my family. But law," Trudy lifted her pan of
spinach to the table, "I been talkin' to you like you was
a grown-up lady. You run along now an' get your rest."

"I *am* a grown-up lady." Carrol laughed as she swung
herself to her feet and tucked the bathing suits under her
arm. "But you forgot one person beside the Parrishes
who makes this a happy house."

"I reckon you means me," Trudy chuckled modestly.
"Well, maybe you're right, maybe you're right. I guess
I makes their stomachs happy, anyway."

"You make more than their stomachs happy." Carrol
gave Trudy's bent shoulders a pat as she passed her.
"You're grand, Trudy."

As she went through the pantry into the dining room,
Trudy's pleased chuckles were drowned out by Bobby's
shrill voice. "Postman. Postman," he shouted as he stood
on the bottom step of the stairway, a stack of letters in his
hand.

"Anything for me?" Penny's head appeared above the
rail, followed by her mother's.

"Or for me?"

"Yep. Come and get it."

"Oh, bring it up, Bobby."

"Nope. The postman's tired." He sat down on the
step and mopped his brow as he leaned against the newel
post.

"After walking all the way in from the front porch!"
Penny scolded. But she slid down the banister never-

theless and gave a leap from the landing. Her mother sat down on the top step. "Throw me mine," she begged.

"Okay." Bobby pitched a letter up to her as he jerked out of Penny's reach.

The letter fell short and she retrieved it. "Pooh, a bill," she groaned. "Haven't you anything else?"

"Yep." Again Bobby moved away from Penny's clutching hands. "Be patient, can't you, Pen? Here." He looked hard at a post card before he gave it to her. "Miss Penny Parrish," he read laboriously. "It's from Gram. She says she's having a good time at the World's Fair and sends you her love. I guess that's what she says, she writes so awful I can't read it." He handed the card to Penny and tossed another letter up to his mother. "It's from Gram, too."

Carrol sat down in a chair to await her turn and, with a shy grin, he sorted through his pile and gave her a long thin envelope. He hurled several more at his mother, brought another one to Carrol and then announced, "The rest are for Dad. I didn't get any. Shucks!"

As though daily letters played an important part in his life, he plunked the remaining envelopes on a table and stalked out.

Penny turned her card over and looked at its picture. "Oh, it's the perisphere. See, Mums!"

She ran up the steps again, and Carrol took her letters out to the porch where she might read them quietly. She weighed the thin crinkly envelope, embossed and businesslike, against the stiff square grey, precise as a lesson in penmanship. With a sigh, she dropped the grey into her lap and slit the flap of the other. A check fluttered out and she let it lie unnoticed as she read the few typed lines:

"Dear Carrol:

Hope you are enjoying your vacation. Am leaving for San Francisco tonight, so enclose check. Wire me if you need more money. Address, St. Francis Hotel until June 25th.

Yours,
Dad."

She folded the letter slowly, then took up the check and looked at it. Five hundred dollars. Thoughtfully she laid it inside the letter, and slipped them both back into the envelope before she broke the second seal. This letter was longer and it was written, like the address, in a firm even hand. She read:

"My dear little Grandaughter:

I trust that you are enjoying your stay with Major and Mrs. Parrish and that you are not inconveniencing them greatly. You must be very careful to be neat and orderly, as I imagine they do not have many servants. I have written Mrs. Parrish today to thank her for her kindness. I hope you will remember to send her flowers upon suitable occasions, and . . ." (*Carrol looked up from the letter to the masses of bridal-wreath bending under white blossoms, to the roses, fragrantly pink, to a corner of the back garden riotous with nasturtiums and pansies. "Poor Grandmother, in her city," she thought. Then, reluctantly, she began to read again.*) ". . . upon suitable occasions, and that you will take Penny and her friends to luncheon, and that you will always bring home a box of candy when you go shopping." ("*Grandmother!*" *Carrol shook the letter and sighed.* "*You mean well, but you haven't any idea about anything. If I have any sense of smell, Penny is making fudge right now—and as for luncheons and shopping, no one lunches out or shops. I'll do something—but why don't you let me figure out for myself what it will be?*")

(*Once more she struggled on, and this time was determined to see it through to the end.*) "Everything is very serene and quiet here. Several of my friends are going East and have urged me to accompany them, but I shall await your return and then we will go to the beach as usual. I was unable to take my drive yesterday afternoon as Charles felt the car needed some minor repairs. They have been attended to and Minna has come to say that Charles is waiting with the car. So I shall close that I may post my letter.

I do miss you very much, my dear, and wish that I could have you on the seat beside me instead of Miss Turner who is very dull, even if she is a gentlewoman. You have ever been a joy to me and I do want you to know that I am always,
Your loving
Grandmother."

Carrol put the two letters together and sat tapping them against her knee. She felt depressed. She had been so happy before she read the letters. Nothing was changed, nothing was wrong; Grandmother was well,

Daddy had sent a check. Both had written, and yet . . . What was it? She looked around the porch as though searching for an answer. Five hundred dollars. That would mean chromium and glass and bright awnings to Dad. He'd chuck it to a decorator and say, "Here, fix me up a terrace for my penthouse; you know what I want." It wouldn't mean a grass rug and bright pillows and deep wicker chairs, so big he could sit down and pull you onto his lap. It wouldn't mean that to Grandmother, either. It would only be chauffeur's wages and gifts to charities; though Grandmother had let herself be inconvenienced and her whole way of living changed, so that a motherless little girl might come into her house. Grandmother's house. . . . Carrol sat up straight. That was the trouble, the whole trouble. Grandmother's house, and Daddy's penthouse, weren't happy houses!

"They just aren't happy houses," she thought wistfully. "And I don't want to go back to them."

A sudden clap of thunder cut her unhappy meditations short and she shot through the door in time to hear Mrs. Parrish call from upstairs: "Are all the lights out down there, too?"

"I'll see." Carrol flipped the switch of a lamp, but no cheerful gleam answered her. "Yes, they're out here, too."

"It's as dark up here as Aunt Miranda's old black hat." Mrs. Parrish could be heard fumbling down the hall-way. "It's going to be an awful storm and I wish I knew where those children are. Penny?" Her voice echoed down the back stairs.

"I'll go and hunt, Mrs. Parrish." Carrol was in the

kitchen now and she came out into the back hall. "Penny says the fudge won't harden and she's practically beating it to death."

"Practically beating my arm off, you mean," Penny mumbled between set jaws. "You take a turn and I'll go and hunt the kids."

Carrol went over and gave the fudge a critical stir. "We'll have to cook it again," she decided. "It's nothing but soup. Come on, we'll both go and hunt."

There was another deafening crash and a flash of lightning tore past the window. It was followed by a faint shriek from under the floor.

"That's Trudy." Penny sped to the basement door. "Hey, Trudy, are you hit?" she called.

"No'm, but I sho' am scared," came weakly back.

"Well, you come on up here. Go upstairs to Mother; she's scared too."

"I am not." The voice from above was indignant. Then, realizing Penny's drift, it added from the darkness: "Yes I am, too. Come on, Trudy."

There was a scrambling on the basement stairs and Trudy's white apron scuttled through the hallway and disappeared above. Penny and Carrol took their raincoats from a closet under the front stairs, tied scarves over their hair and each found a small coat for the children.

"They're probably down at the Prescotts and as dry as can be," Penny said as they let themselves out into the wind. "Doesn't it smell good?"

"Um. Heavenly."

They hurried along the street pelted by enormous

drops which were beginning to fall. The leaves were twirling around on their flimsy stems and shrubbery was bending and swaying amid a snowfall of white petals. Penny tipped her face back into the wind and rain and skipped with delight.

"I love it," she exulted.

As they turned into the Prescott's walk they could hear shrieks of mirth from inside. Bobby and Tippy and the two little Prescott's, Jack and Jimmy, were wrestling in the middle of the livingroom, while Mary, her book tipped to catch the dim light, was placidly reading by a window.

"What's going on in here?" Penny asked as she and Carrol looked in the door.

"Oh, hello." Mary laid down her book and Tippy rushed over to clutch Penny around the knees.

"We don't want to go home," she begged. "We're having a good time and I'm just going to get scalped."

Penny laughed and gave her her raincoat. "Slide into it," she ordered. "Scalped or unscalped, Mother's having a fit."

The game broke up with wails from Bobby, and the children were shooed out onto the porch. "Come on down awhile," Penny said to Mary. "We're making fudge and we can pop some corn."

"All right. Wait till I call to Mother. She was taking a nap, but she ought to be awake by now. If she isn't, she's either deaf or dead." Mary called up the stairs and, receiving a favorable answer, snatched her raincoat and joined the girls who were waiting on the porch. They corraled the children and braved their way down the steps. The rain was coming down in sheets now and they made a dash for the sidewalk and the nearest tree.

"Wow," Penny said as they reached its shelter. "We'll be soaked."

A car cruising down the street began a great blowing of the horn. Heads and arms waved from its windows. "Taxi! Taxi!" Michael shouted from the curb.

Someone opened the door and there were cries of, "Hop in. Quick. You're soaking us," as the girls piled the children on top of the back seat occupants.

"What are you doing out in all this?" Carrol asked as she squeezed onto Jane's lap.

"Dick and I were just riding around," Michael answered, "and we saw Jane and Louise hot-footing it across the parade ground from the Post Exchange, so we waited for them."

"And were we glad to get in!" Jane added. "They didn't have to beg us."

When they reached the Parrish front walk they were greeted by a cloudburst. They ran up the windows against it and sat in cheerful steaminess until it began to slacken a little. At the first lull they hustled the children out and made a dash for the porch.

"Last one in is a tailless monkey," Dick shouted as he sprinted up the steps and grabbed for the door. The whole screened structure shuddered as everyone hurtled through, fearful of being a tailless monkey. But it remained upright, and only Tippy collapsed, as flat on her stomach, she provided a barrier for the others to stumble over. She was picked up and petted, her howls stifled with kisses, until Bobby led her proudly upstairs to have adhesive tape plastered over her wounds. The rest shed their raincoats in a heap across a chair and Dick sat down at the telephone to begin a search for David and Bob.

"You might try the stables," Penny suggested as she started out to the kitchen. "Or they may have gone to the movies."

The crowd followed her and in a few minutes Dick came out. "They're in the movies," he announced. "The old sergeant called David to the phone and they said they'd come when the picture's over." He went straight to the refrigerator and, squatting down, began poking about among Trudy's jars and bowls.

"Dick Ford, you keep out of there." Penny made a dash for him and bowled him over. "Hasn't Trudy told you about fifty times to stop eating the Parrishes out of house and home? Doesn't your own family ever feed you?"

Dick laughed and sat on the floor crunching a stalk of celery. "The Parrishes are stingy people," he said to Carrol, waving the celery. "When you get too thin from not having enough to eat you can come over to my house. This refrigerator is always empty." The last leafed tip disappeared. "Look and see if it isn't." He started to open the door again and Penny swooped at him.

"Don't you touch it! Do you want me to call Trudy?" She opened her mouth as though to shout and he clasped his hands in prayer.

"Please don't call Trudy," he begged. "Oh, please, please!"

"All right, then behave yourself."

Penny went back to her stove and Dick got up from the shiny linoleum. "Dirty floor," he said, dusting imaginary spots from the seat of his trousers.

The fudge, once more above the fire, began to bubble cheerfully and Penny got out the popcorn, a large iron skillet and a lid. She set them on the stove and Michael rattled the skillet back and forth above the blaze.

"Shake it faster," Penny ordered. "Faster! Faster!"

Michael shook faster. His right hand rattled the skillet so wildly that his left was unable to keep up with the lid. White grains popped out. Like waiting vultures they snatched them up and the kitchen rang with shouts of merriment. In the midst of the fun, Bob and David came in. With a few jibes at Michael as a cook, they joined in the chase, imploring him to lift the lid a little higher since there were more people in the game.

"Someone can butter me a plate," Penny suggested presently. "And someone can melt butter for the corn, and the rest of you can go out on the porch. It isn't raining now."

"I'll butter the corn." Carrol opened the refrigerator door, warding off Dick, as, with an eye on Penny he made what he considered were hungry, snarling noises as he lunged at it.

At last, with a cheerful grin, he said: "No soap," and followed Louise and Jane.

"Sure I can't help?" Mary asked.

"Sure."

She wandered away and David took Bob and Michael down into the basement to his workshop to show them a bookcase his father was making.

"You'll come back, won't you?" Penny called.

"Be right back."

The two girls left alone in the kitchen hurried with their buttering and beating. Jane and Louise, coming out onto the porch, saw a wrecked and devastated scene. The wind had twisted one of the smaller grass rugs into a cornucopia; a bowl of flowers was overturned, and magazines and papers lay on the floor.

"I'll fix the flowers and you pick up the papers," Jane suggested. She righted the bowl and was arranging tall roses when an exclamation from Louise made her turn around. Louise was staring at a small piece of paper in her hand.

"I wish you'd look," she gasped, holding it out.

Jane took it. "Why, it's a check," she said, staring. "Carrol Houghton, five hundred dollars. Where'd you get it?"

"There on the floor, with those letters. She certainly is careless with it."

"Five hundred bucks. Gosh. You'd better put it back." Jane gave the check to Louise as Mary and Dick came out.

"Look," Louise said, going over to them and holding out the check. "A check made out to Carrol for five hundred dollars. It's from her father."

"Five hun . . . Let's see it." Dick stared down at the bit of paper while Mary peered over his shoulder. Good grief!"

"No wonder she can be so snooty." Louise sat down and angrily jerked her skirt away from a damp pillow. "She thinks she's got so much money . . ."

"Carrol isn't snooty." Jane came over to the swing and sat down, too. "Carrol is just as sweet and—and unassuming as anyone else. Why, I didn't think she had any more money than the rest of us."

"Well, I did. Her clothes look like they cost a fortune and she's always talking about her father's penthouse."

"She is not," Dick cut in. "You asked her where her father lived and she just answered. Besides, I've got an uncle who lives in one. *He's* not rich."

"Well, I say she's snooty. She's got a lot of money and that's why the Parrishes all bow down to her. Penny acts perfectly ga-ga, and David follows her around looking as though he'd like to have a tail so he could wag it for her."

Mary winked at Jane, but she said seriously: "The Parrishes don't give a darn about money and you know it. As for Penny *and* David, you're just being jealous."

Louise looked at her witheringly. "Now you've gone Carrol-minded. Dear Carrol, sweet Carrol. I suppose you're thinking of how much she can do for you. And all the rest of you. You make me tired!" She flounced out of the swing as David and Bob and Michael came out.

"What's all the fuss about?" David asked, looking from her angry face to the others.

"It isn't anything, we were just talking." Jane looked warningly at Louise, but Louise interupted her.

"It is too. We were talking about your rich guest who leaves five-hundred-dollar checks around so that people will be sure to see them."

"Rich guest? Five-hundred-dollar checks? Sounds like a mystery novel," David grinned.

"It is—and don't pretend you don't know it." Louise tossed her head.

"Oh, shut up Louise." Jane looked at the three inquiring faces. "It wasn't anything at all. Louise and I came out to straighten up the porch and Louise picked up a check that had fallen out of one of Carrol's letters. It was for five hundred dollars, and from the way Louise is acting you'd think it was for a million. It's none of our business, anyway, and I don't see why we're talking about it. Put it back in the letter and let's forget it."

"Five hundred . . . ? Let's see it," Michael and Bob breathed together, just as Dick before them, while David stood scowling at Louise, a slow flush mounting to his face. He walked over to her and held out his hand.

"Give me the letter and the check," he said.

Louise thrust the letter at him and sat down in the swing again, leaning back haughtily. She smiled about the circle and remarked tauntingly: "Doesn't our hero look dramatic as he defends Lady Bountiful! Maybe she'll buy him something nice."

"Louise! I never saw you act *quite* like this." Mary looked at her with troubled eyes. "You're making a regular fool of yourself, and about nothing. How do you know Carrol's so rich, or what the money's for?"

"Yeah, maybe it's to lift the mortgage on the old homeplace, or somepin'." Dick stretched his long legs before him as he straddled a chair.

"Oh no, it's not," Louise flung him an exasperated glare. "And you're not being a bit funny. A piece of the letter stuck out and I saw that, too. It said 'if you need more, wire me.' Imagine! Wire me."

They stared at her in silence, too amazed to speak. That she would pry into another person's letter! That she could be so angry and so vindictive because one girl had more money than the others! It was unbelievable. Her voice, undaunted by their incredulous faces, rasped on.

"Half the time she sits around and doesn't say anything, just looking at us as tho we were something out of a zoo. I think, even if she is your guest, David, that she's the snippiest, most snobbish girl. . . ."

She stopped suddenly. Heads turned, following her eyes. Carrol, carrying an enormous Japanese bowl filled with popcorn, was standing in the door. Penny was behind her with the platter of fudge. Penny's eyes were stormy, and Carrol's were brilliantly blue as she came across the porch with her popcorn. She stooped to set it on the low table before the swing so that her curls screened her face. No one saw her wink back the tears. When she turned around she was smiling. She motioned to the bowl and with a, "help yourselves, everybody," walked over to take a piece of fudge from Penny who was still standing in petrified silence.

"Go on and put your plate down," she whispered. "Just act as though nothing had happened and we hadn't heard. Go on."

Penny went over to the table like a sleep-walker in a trance. She clapped the plate down and cutting off a piece, mumbled with a gulp: "I think I'll take some up to Mother." She could be heard sobbing as she stumbled up the stairs.

Carrol sat down on a low stool. "I can't make a scene," she thought. "I'll have to sit here and pretend . . ." She forced herself to eat the fudge she had cut off and to smile up at David who was saying:

"Here are some letters you dropped, Carrol."

"Thanks." She held out her hand for the letters, slipped the check inside, and said as casually as she could: "I must have dropped them when the thunder startled me. I'd better go in and put them away."

She was hardly inside, her bright head pressed against the mantel, tears spilling down, when David was beside her. He turned her around, hands on her shaking shoulders and his clear blue eyes looking down at her. "It's that little beast, Louise," he said. "She saw your check and she's jealous of you. They're all mad at her."

"Are they? Was it *just* Louise? I thought . . ." The light began to come back into Carrol's face.

"Heavens, yes! The others have been ripping into her, and the more they praised you the madder she got. She's jealous, Carrol, because you're prettier than she is—and now she's found out you have a lot of money. But you mustn't let it worry you."

"I won't." Carrol laughed shakily. "Not if you and the others weren't talking about me. You see, Daddy does give me a lot of money. But that's because he doesn't want to bother with me, and it makes him feel better about it if he writes a check. I don't cash most of them and he doesn't even know the difference."

"You poor kid."

Carrol dabbed at her eyes and smiled, nodding her head. "It really is being poor when you're rich, isn't it?" she said. "Now we'll forget all about it and I'll go and get Penny. You go out to the others."

David returned to the porch and Carrol routed Penny out of her mother's room where she was huddled in a big chair, dissolved in tears.

"You see, Mrs. Parrish," Carrol said after they had talked and Penny had gone to wash her face, "Louise doesn't realize how much she has, with a father and mother who adore her. She's got spoiled, and she thinks the whole world should bow down to her. I've seen girls like that before."

"Well, I haven't." Penny came back in time to hear the last few words. "She's the limit. But I don't mind as long as the others weren't dumb-bunnies, too. I thought they had more sense."

"Of course they have." Her mother put an arm around each girl. "Now, you two run down and behave as though nothing had happened. After all, Louise is the one who should be unhappy. I think she has behaved abominably, and I am sure she'll be terribly ashamed. Carrol is very sensible and, fortunately, the others are too, so I don't believe there will be any embarrassment from an overheard remark. Just pretend you didn't hear and the rest will follow your example. Now run along."

Both girls were laughing when they came out onto the porch. Penny dived for the popcorn, Carrol took another piece of fudge, and each entered into the conversation nearest her. At six o'clock, when bowl and platter were empty, and the telephone was transmitting irate messages from parents, the crowd wandered out to Michael's car. Louise had the grace to look embarrassed as she was saying goodbye, but Carrol's eyes were serene as she said, "See you all tonight."

"I—I may not go to the movies with you," Louise stammered. "Mother and Daddy might want me to stay at home with them."

"Oh, come on," Carrol invited. "They won't care."

A question had been asked, an answer given. Assured that no unpleasantness was to result, Louise followed the others out to the car, light of heart and unabashed.

"Why did you do that?" Penny asked, slamming the screen door. "She ought to be left out of things for awhile, then she wouldn't be so smart."

"She doesn't feel so happy, anyway," David put in. "Did you see the way the boys treated her? She didn't like it a bit."

"No, but she'll make you all forget it, just see if she doesn't."

"Not me, she won't." David stretched himself out in the swing and clasped his hands over his stomach. "But I wish I hadn't eaten so much popcorn," he mourned.

CHAPTER SEVEN

THE HORSE SHOW

"WE'RE TURNING on the lights in the horse show ring for awhile tonight," Major Parrish said at dinner. "Would you kids like to come down?"

"We'd love it!" Penny was glowing as she turned to Carrol to explain. "We've talked and talked about the horse show and you've seen Dad running around like a madman, and tonight you can see what it's all about."

"Is anyone going to practice, Dad?" David asked hopefully.

"All the officers, and anyone who wants to get his horse accustomed to the lights. That is, they will if the ground isn't too wet. I've got to go over now and see."

"The rain should have made it just about right." David pushed his plate away and looked at his father eagerly. "How about me joining in with Lucky?"

"All right, but don't get in the way of the officers."

"Okay, I won't." He jumped up from the table and dashed out to the telephone.

"David, your dinner!" his mother called after him.

"Can't bother now. I've got to call the stables."

Mrs. Parrish shook her head. "I do wish, Dave," she chided, "that you hadn't told him until after he had eaten."

"He's full of popcorn, anyway," Penny said, looking at her plate with distaste. "We all are. How about me riding around, too, Dad?"

"No, not you," her father answered as he pulled a crumpled paper from his pocket. "I've got a swell job for you and Carrol and your mother. Here." He tossed the paper to Mrs. Parrish. "That's a list of the trophies, and Sergeant McWade is to bring them over from the office. I wish you'd unpack them for me and tie a card on each one, with the class in which it's to be used, so I can grab them up quickly as we need them. I know it's a messy job but . . ."

"It's a grand job," Mrs. Parrish interrupted. "I love beautiful silver. Did you get some good prizes this year?"

"I think they're the best we've ever had. There is a silver tray that's a honey, and vases and cigarette boxes— and a silver horse. I'd like to win that, myself."

"I hope you do, then." Mrs. Parrish smiled at him but he shook his head.

"I haven't a chance. Next year I'm going to let someone else run the thing and I'll just ride. I can't ride and run the horse show, too." He pushed back his chair. "I've got to get over to the ring."

"But there's dessert."

"Can't wait for it. Tell Williams to put it in the refrigerator. I'll eat it when I come home."

"I'd like to save mine, too," Carrol said. I'm so full of fudge . . ."

"Let's all have ours later," Penny chimed in. But the two youngest set up such a howl that Mrs. Parrish hurriedly assured them they would not be left out.

Williams chuckled as he changed the plates. It was nothing strange to him to see the entire family vanish in the middle of a meal. He brought Bobby and Tippy each a dish of ice cream and hovered over them while they ate it. When they had scraped up the last spoonful he took off their napkins and enticed them kitchenward.

"You better help me an' Trudy feed Woofy," he coaxed. "He's kinda persnickety about the way he's fed." And when he had lured them safely out he motioned to Trudy. "We oughta keep 'em awhile," he suggested. "They's goin' to be awful busy in there."

So they kept them, and the children missed seeing the cartons which were being stacked on the porch. As the excelsior and tissue paper began to pile into a mountain, Mrs. Parrish realized how much she was being spared by their absence.

"Look!" she or Carrol or Penny would exclaim as each piece of silver was lifted from its nest. It was admired and set, with its carefully checked card, on the closed, grand piano. Eventually, the entire piano top was covered, and the three went into the drawingroom for a more leisurely inspection.

"I don't know which one I'd rather have," Carrol said thoughtfully. "They're all so beautiful."

"Boy, I know." There was no doubt in Penny's answer. "I'd like the horse."

She lifted the little statue tenderly. It was the figure of a beautiful thoroughbred, saddled and bridled, the head turned and the ears up, as though watching for its rider. It was mounted on an onyx base; and the whole statue stood about a foot high.

"Look at those delicate silver reins," Mrs. Parrish pointed out. "And the tiny stirrups. It is sweet; but for myself, I'd rather have this cigarette box. My coffee table is simply crying for it." She set the box on the low table and stood off to admire it.

"Well, Dad wouldn't. Every time we go to town he hangs around a jewelry store looking at the horses."

"Mightn't he win it?" Carrol asked.

"Nope. He hasn't time to ride."

"Perhaps David could."

"I don't think so. And anyway, it's probably in an officer's class. Let me see the cards."

Penny peered at the card which was tied around the horse's neck. "Open Jumping," she read. "Oh boy! David might win it, at that, because open jumping means that anybody can ride in the class."

"Wouldn't it be wonderful, Pen?"

"Dad would simply expire, he would be so thrilled."

Mrs. Parrish returned the cigarette box to its place. "I wouldn't get too excited about it," she cautioned. "There will be too many officers and a lot of fine horses in the class. David is just a boy, and he's riding a colt. The jumps are going to be pretty high."

"I know it." Penny looked disconsolate. "Dad doesn't even think David should try Lucky in that class. But I'm glad he's going to. He might win. Lucky's good. Everybody says so; and he won in the riding hall this winter. Oh, dear, I wish Dad were riding him."

"Is your father so much better?"

"Oh, Dad's a whizz. When he and Lucky take a jump they seem to be made all in one piece. Dad would really have a chance."

"*Couldn't* he do it?"

"No, he says he's too busy. Come on, let's go over and see what's going on."

The show ring was behind the houses that lined the other side of the street. In a ravine, the bottom leveled and covered with turf, it made a natural amphitheater. A low hill encircled three sides of it and into the hill bleachers had been built. Above the bleachers, on one side, were two tiers of concrete boxes. Each box held six chairs, and each was enclosed by a rail of silver-painted pipe. These were for the officers and their families and for exhibitors from other posts who were coming to ride in the show. One box, larger than the others and in the exact center, was for the general, and over it was stretched a bright, striped canopy. Across the ring was the judges' platform. It held comfortable chairs and was fitted with a loud-speaker, through which to call the classes and to announce the winners. The fourth side opened into a level tree-shaded space that was roped off as a paddock. There the riders could wait with their horses and could exercise them until their turn was called.

Penny and Carrol crossed the street and came between the houses to the top of the hill, above the first row of boxes. Men were busy stringing bright banners between tall poles that held brackets of floodlights; and the flags made a gay circlet around the show ring, their colors flying in the soft evening dusk. Someone was testing the loud-speaker and it said "hello, hello, hello" as though greeting them. Scattered about with clever ingenuity but seeming carelessness, were the hurdles. Some were made of candy-striped poles and others were painted to resemble brick walls and stone fences. Soldiers were setting little bushes in green tubs at either end of each jump, and across the ring lights reflected in a miniature pond that was merely a trough, sunk into the ground and filled with water. Before it stood a high rail over which the horses must soar if they were to reach firm footing.

"Will David have to jump over all those mountainous things, and over that water, too?" Carrol asked Penny as they stood looking down on the scene.

Penny nodded dismally, and added: "It's goodbye silver horse."

"Well, I should think so."

They wandered down the steps and sat in one of the boxes as the lights came on. "It looks like fairyland, doesn't it?" Carrol said.

"Umhum. I love it out here at night. It's so cool and nice. It gets pretty hot during the day, but we don't have to come over except for the classes we want to see."

"Will your class do any jumping?"

"Mercy, no. It's for the kids on the post and we just ride around. It's called the Good Hands Class, and the trophy is given by the A.S.P.C.A."

"What's that?"

"The American Society for Prevention of Cruelty to Animals. We're supposed to have our hands light on the reins so we don't hurt the horse's mouth, and to ride well and to know all the aids for backing and cantering on the right lead, and so on."

"Does David ride in that, too?"

"Oh no. He rides in another kid's class. But they jump and are really good. Bob and Dick are in it, and Jane and Louise. I wish I could jump well enough."

"Are these classes at night?"

"No. David's is in the afternoon and mine is in the morning. We'll get a programme when we go home and look them up."

While they were talking, officers had begun to gather and dim groups of horsemen could be seen coming through the trees into the paddock. A number of women were sitting in other boxes, some in riding clothes waiting for their horses. Penny waved to her mother who had joined one of the groups.

The darkness came softly down until the outside of the arena was only a faint grey blur caught in the glow from the blazing floodlights. The turf in the show-ring was the brilliant green of artificial grass, jumps stood out in startling clearness, flags were gaudy against the black of the sky. All the hurrying figures disappeared, grooms took their stations beside each jump, and the ring filled with horses and riders. Rails came crashing down as they practiced taking the hurdles and water was splashing in the little pool as many a luckless horse missed the grass-rimmed edge.

"There's David!" Penny cried. "See, there, straight across from us. He's going to take the ditch."

"Oh, I see him." Carrol leaned forward as David and Lucky approached the jump that Lucky must clear in a flying leap if he were to land with dry feet on the other side. They were galloping in a long, easy stride; Lucky's ears were up and he was looking at the barrier as though gauging its height. Suddenly, instead of rising into the air, Lucky planted both front feet—and stopped. His nose was over the bar and he was looking down into the water with dismay.

"Oh, dear," Carrol slumped back into her chair but Penny was still watching.

"It's all right," Penny said. "He's never seen one before. David will give him a good look at it now."

David and Lucky remained some seconds immobile. David was patting the horse and talking to him. Then they turned back, circled, and headed for the jump again.

Again Lucky's ears came forward, and again he stopped. They repeated the performance several times and were at last forced to move away as other horses came thundering by.

"That's that," Penny said in disgust. "He says he won't take it."

"Can't David try again?"

"Oh, he'll keep on trying every time he gets a chance. Lucky wants to do it; you saw how he almost did it the last time, but he doesn't know quite how."

The girls were so interested in David's battle with Lucky Souvenir that, so far as they were concerned, there were no other horses in the ring. They watched every jump the pair took and breathed sighs of relief when every difficult barrier was safely hurdled. At last the ring was cleared, the horses returned to the paddock, and the riders came in one by one to take the entire course, each jump in its order. Most of them did well, but a great many poles were knocked down and water often splashed into the air.

"Here comes David." Penny clutched Carrol and pointed. "And there's Dad going over to tell him what to do. Maybe he can help."

Major Parrish was motioning toward the water jump and David was nodding. Lucky was looking at the flags and the lights as though far more interested in his venture out into the night than in winning a coveted replica of himself.

Then they were off. Lucky settled down to the serious business of meeting each obstacle as it appeared before him. He galloped, jumped, turned, jumped again; up and down and around the field. Easily David headed him toward the fatal water. His hooves thundered over the grass, his eyes were looking, looking; his ears came up . . .

"He's going to do it," Penny breathed. "He's going . . ."

Then abruptly Lucky sat down. He sat down in the middle of all the poles. Poles flew up into the air; poles flopped into the water. The decorative little trees bounced over—but David stayed on.

Penny leaned back and giggled. "I can't help laughing," she exploded. "I'm just sick about it, but they looked like a cartoon. Lucky sitting there with all four feet stuck out in front of him and David hanging around his neck. They can try twice more."

When the poles had been put back in place David tried again. The third time, his last chance, Lucky decided to cooperate. He made a valiant effort, knocked the bars in all directions, landed in the middle of the water, but got across.

"He did it!" The girls beat on each other with joy as Lucky trotted off.

"I wish he had more time to try," Penny said. He might get better at it. The other horses won't knock it down."

"Can't he do it any more?"

"Unhunh. He won't see it again until tomorrow night. Come on, let's go over to the movies and find the gang."

They stumbled out into the darkness, their eyes blinded from the glare of the ring. Favorite seats in the War Department Theatre, occupied when possible by

the crowd, were empty. No one in the ticket booth had
seen them, no one in the soda fountain.

"We've missed them at the stadium, somehow,"
Penny decided. "Let's go home and get a good night's
sleep so that we'll be rested for the show tomorrow."

"It suits me perfectly." Carrol stifled a yawn. "I'm
almost asleep, now."

The house was silent when they came in. They un-
dressed quickly and Carrol called to Penny who was
splashing in the bathroom:

"Pen, if David can't win the horse, would your father
like to have one, anyway?"

Penny came in, her face rosy and scrubbed. "I suppose he would, he's so crazy about them," she answered
as she slid in between the sheets. "But I don't think it
would be quite like winning one. That little silver plaque
on the base that says, 'won by so and so' seems to mean
such a lot. But let's not worry about it." She gave a little
grunt as she burrowed about comfortably in her pillow.

Carrol turned on her side and smiled into the darkness. "Grandmother," she thought, "I think we have one
parting gift lined up."

The next morning the girls were wakened by rever-
berating yells from David's room. "Who took my spurs?"
he was shouting. "They're gone! My spurs are gone!"

Sunlight poured into the room and heavy shoes were
clumping along the back hall.

"Hold on, Mr. David," bellowed Williams' voice in
cheerful answer. "I got 'em. Wouldn't do for you to ride
with all the gen'lemen in dirty spurs. I done cleaned
your boots, too. You find 'em?"

"I've got 'em on."

Penny bounced out of bed. "Jeeminy, it must be late!" She poked her head out the door. "How about my jodhpur boots, Williams?"

"Comin' up. Comin' right up." Williams back-tracked down the hall and sorted among his collection at the head of the stairs. "Here you are, Miss Penny, as black and shiny as new." He dropped the shoes at her door and Penny inched them in.

"Good old Williams," she said as she scrambled into her riding clothes.

Carrol sprang out of bed, too, and in a surprisingly short time both girls had dressed, swallowed a fair amount of breakfast, and were on their way to the stadium.

"Don't you have to go for your horse?" Carrol panted as she ran.

"No. Major Gray is letting me ride his horse, and he'll have him here for me when it's time."

They tore down the steps and sank, breathless, into the box which Penny pointed out as theirs. Horses were being brought in for the second class of the morning, which was a walk, trot and canter class for ladies. The girls sat, one eye on the women riding in a circle and one on the young Prescotts who were scrambling down the slope.

"Hi," Mary shouted, when within hailing distance. "Where were you last night?"

"Right here." Penny removed her riding hat from a chair and Mary dropped down onto it. "Where were you?"

"Over on the other side of the bleachers for awhile. We were on our way to the movies and saw the lights, so we stopped. We were all so dead we didn't stay long."

"David had himself a time, didn't he?" Bob's voice came from behind them. He swung one leg over the iron rail and sat down on it. "Think he'll have better luck tonight?"

"I don't know." Penny shook her head. "I didn't get a chance to talk to him this morning. But I'm keeping my fingers crossed."

"I hope my old goat isn't lame today. David riding Lucky in our class?"

"Umhum. Look." Penny pointed to the ring. "The judges have sent all the horses out but six or seven. Jane and Louise are still in. I wish Jane could get a place."

"She ought to," Mary said. "She's a beautiful rider and she has a good horse. You don't want her to win though, do you, Bob?"

She gave her brother a playful push and he retaliated by tipping her, chair and all, into Penny's lap. "Goof," he grinned as he loped off toward the paddock.

Mary righted herself and said good-naturedly, "He's gone to lift Jane tenderly from her horse."

"If she places," Penny laughed. "But if she gets the gate, he'll probably give her the dickens."

"And she'll be sweet about it—and then turn around and beat him in the jumping class. I hope she does."

"Oh look, the judges have decided." Carrol leaned forward and clasped her hands over the rail. "I do believe. . . . Oh!"

The horses were lined up, the judges gathered

in a little group comparing their score sheets. They walked away and the loud speaker blared.

"First, Paddy's Pride. Ridden by Mrs. Arnold Stayer."

"Jane didn't win." Carrol's shoulders slumped as Mrs. Stayer rode forward to receive her trophy; a silver bowl which was being presented by the general's wife. She was shaking hands with Mrs. Stayer, patting the horse and fastening the blue ribbon to his tossing head.

"Too bad. Sh . . ."

"Second, Clip Along. Miss Louise Frazier, up."

"Darn!" Penny sat back and beat with her crop on the rail. "She'll be so cocky!"

"Third, Miss Jane Carter, riding My Pal."

"Nice going, Jane!" Penny megaphoned into the ring. "Well," she said as she leaned back, "she got a place anyway. But I wish Louise hadn't beaten her."

"I do, too. And I bet Louise heard you yell for Jane." Mary made a face. "She'll be furious."

"I don't care." Penny scraped her chair back and stood up. "There comes my trusty steed. I'm in the class after this one so I'll have to warm him up. Why don't you go over to the tent and have a coke? This class is just for polo mounts." She pulled a bulky programme from her pocket and gave it to Carrol as they walked toward the refreshment tent. "You keep this one," she said, "so you can tell the horses. Mine is named Tango Dance, and I'll be the girl in the black hat with the number twenty-two on her back. Don't forget to cheer for me when I get the gate."

"Oh, we'll applaud every time you go by," Mary promised.

"And then, the judges will think you have such a big following that you must be good," Carrol added. "They'll have to give you the prize."

"Oh yeah?" Penny waved her hand and swaggered off. "See you later."

While Mary and Carrol were sipping their drinks, Jane and Louise and Bob came by. Mary hailed them.

"Congratulations," Carrol said to the girls. "You must feel awfully proud. May I see the ribbons?"

Mary gave Louise's shoulder a pat and hugged Jane. "Nice going. Have a drink?"

"We need it." Jane waved her ribbon proudly before she gave it to Carrol and leaned back against the counter. "It's as hot as the dickens out there." She pushed her hat back and began taking off her riding coat. "I'm boiling. How about you, Louise?"

"Melting." Louise carelessly tossed her ribbon to Carrol. "I'm disgusted," she pouted. "I don't think that Paddy's Pride horse is a bit better than Clip Along."

"Yes, but I told you, Louise," Jane turned to her in exasperation, "Mrs. Stayer gave a beautiful ride. The horse's gaits were perfect. I think Pal is just as good as Clip, too, but you must have done something better than I did, or you wouldn't have beaten me."

"But . . ."

"Oh, stop beefing," Bob said in disgust. "You've done nothing but cry ever since you left the paddock. The judges call it the way they see it—and it's nothing but a horse show, anyway. You'd think your whole life was at stake."

"Well, it is. Dad paid a lot of money for Clip Along."

"So what?" Bob took the yellow ribbon from Carrol and stuck the hook through his button hole. "How do I look?" he smirked at Jane. "Like it?"

"Ummmmm. I'm satisfied." Jane wrinkled her nose at him and reached for the bottle the attendant was handing her. "On to bigger and better things, that's me. Come on, let's go set a spell."

Carrol gave the red ribbon back to Louise who crumpled it up and thrust it in her pocket. They sauntered back to the Parrish's box, drinking their Coca Colas as they went. Several people stopped them to congratulate the girls, and by the time they reached their seats the polo trophies had been presented and Penny's class was coming into the ring.

Many of the riders were younger than Penny, a few were older; but they all rode well. Their horses were quiet, hands were held low, light yet steady on the reins. They walked around the ring, the judges looking at each one intently. When the order came to trot they moved out swiftly, still well spaced apart. Later they cantered. They walked, trotted, cantered in a circle, then reversed and repeated the gaits.

"Penny looks cute, doesn't she?" Carrol whispered to Mary. "She does everything as though her whole heart and soul were in it."

Penny, in the ring, was conscious of nothing but herself and Tango Dance. She maneuvered him along, heels down, head up, watching her distance from the horse in front of her. When the command came for the canter, she applied her legs to his sides, shifted her balance, and Tango went smoothly into a rocking-horse gallop, his right foreleg beating out the rhythm before his left.

"We were pretty good at that," she whispered. "But wait until we turn the other way and you have to lead with your left foot. You're not so hot at that, my man, so don't get cocky." Tango waggled an ear at her and the loud-speaker shouted:

"Walk—and reverse."

The horses slowed, made small circles, and moved out in the opposite direction. Tango kept his ears up, only flicking one back occasionally for Penny's whispered comments. Penny could feel trickles of perspiration running down under her white linen coat and she longed to wipe her hot face on her sleeve. She trotted for what seemed hours and was hardly conscious that she had put Tango into his left lead with certain sureness. At last, when they were told to line up in the center of the ring, she pulled thankfully into the long row of horses that faced the boxes, dropped her reins and searched her pockets for a handkerchief.

"Gosh, I'm hot," she said to the boy who was standing beside her. She took off her hat, shook her hair out into the air, fanned her face, and mopped. Tango stood like the silver horse on his block of marble. He looked with disdain up and down the line; at the other horses who were pawing the ground or making frantic nips at the grass. A judge, walking past them, smiled at the picture. Penny cooling herself, and Tango, the reins on his neck, staring haughtily about him.

"Look," he said to another judge, who had come up beside him. "The third pair—the little girl on the black— wouldn't they make a painting?"

The other judge laughed and nodded. "They would," he said. "And the kid's good, too."

They went off to confer and the long line waited patiently. Penny put her hat back on, disposed of her handkerchief, and she and Tango looked as though they had gone to sleep. Eventually, the judges walked across the ring toward the judges' stand. An officer hurried to them, took their score sheets, and after a quick glance called up to the waiting announcer. The loud-speaker emitted a few staccatoed chirps, as though loath to break the news, while the riders and the occupants of at least one box waited breathlessly. At last, with bumbles and buzzings, it found its voice.

"First. Miss Penny Parrish, on Tango Dance."

"Yahoo!"

The yells from the junior audience in the Parrish box were deafening. Carrol hardly saw the boy and the girl lined up beside Penny receiving their red and yellow ribbons. Her eyes were on Penny, red of face and grinning, as she accepted her trophy and clutched it to her. The horses trotted off and Carrol scrambled out of her chair and tore for the paddock.

"Oh, Penny," she cried as they met at the paddock gate, "you were wonderful!" I'm so proud of you, I think I'm crying."

"Nut." Penny hugged her, the silver vase digging into Carrol's back.

They were deep in their inspection of it when David strolled up to them. "Nice work, kid," he said, giving Penny's shoulder a brotherly hug. "Let's see your loot."

Penny gave him the vase and he walked beside them

along the path, carrying it proudly. When they came to the refreshment tent they were surrounded by the others, vociferous in their joy.

"How about a drink, Pen?" David asked, drawing her up to the counter. "Get that coat off before you explode. Have you got a handkerchief? Here."

He helped her out of her coat and Penny shook her wet shirt loose from her back. "Just let me sit down a minute," she said. "I thought we were going to ride around all day."

She sat on the ground, her back against a tree and her legs stretched luxuriously before her. David gave her a cold, iced bottle and turned to Carrol. "Drink?" he asked.

Carrol shook her head. "Thanks, we just had one."

"Boy, it's getting hot," David said to Bob. "When we get out there this afternoon we'll melt." He looked down at Penny. "Don't gulp," he ordered. "Drink it slowly or you'll have one sweet tummy-ache."

Penny bestowed upon everyone a large and impartial grin. "I never got so much attention in my life," she said, a tinge of awe in her voice. "If this is what happens when you win a class, be it ever so humble, I don't wonder people go nuts over horse shows." She crossed her knees and, one foot swinging, began taking dainty sips from her bottle.

"Good heavens, has Penny fainted?" her mother's worried voice asked as she tried to peer through the circle.

"Dead on my feet," Penny answered, looking up impishly. "Don't disturb me. I'm a heroine."

"Oh, Penny, you're so crazy," her mother laughed. "Let me see what you won."

Penny scrambled up and her mother hugged her. "I'm proud of you, honey," she said. "The children told me to tell you they are, too, but Woofy has got himself stuck under a bleacher and they've gone to pull him out. At least, they think he's stuck, but I suspect him of hiding in self-defense." She took the vase and examined it critically. "Just what I need for flowers," she commented.

"Oh, no you don't." Penny snatched the trophy back. "Over my dead body! This little pet is going in Penny's room and he's going to be shined every day."

"For how many days?" Mrs. Parrish laughed and turned to David. "You'd better go home and eat, now. Dad and I are invited to a luncheon, but I don't suppose he'll show up, so you might bring him over a sandwich. Why don't you all go over to our house?" she added as an afterthought. "Trudy has a baked ham and plenty of salad." Dick and Michael had come up to congratulate Penny and she included them in the invitation. Each accepted with thanks and enthusiasm, so she went back to her friends and they straggled homeward.

"Come in and I'll show you the trophies," David said as they walked into the shaded coolness of the house. He led the way to the piano where the remaining and finest trophies were still resting. "These big boys are for to-night."

They crowded around admiring the pieces of silver and reading the cards.

"Wow!" Dick said, picking up the horse. "Won't this be something for Dad to put on our mantel."

"Just a minute." David lifted the horse from Dick's unwilling hands. "That's my horse. It even has my name on it."

"Sure 'nough?" Dick leaned over and peered intently at the card. "I can't see it. Come here, fellows," he made a sweeping gesture. "Come here and see if you can find David's name on this horse any place."

They looked over David's shoulder, inspecting the card thoroughly. "I can't see it." Bob shook his head. "I can't either," Michael sighed, dropping the card. "Sorry, Dave."

"Dummies." Penny took the statue from David. "You're all looking in the wrong place. David's name isn't on the tag; it's right here on the silver plaque. 'Won by David Parrish.' There, now can you see it?"

They solemnly shook their heads. "I may be blind," Dick said, "but I still can't see it."

"Well, I can." David stroked the horse's head as Penny set it down. "It's my horse. It just has to be."

"Why?" they asked.

"Because, if you've got to know, Dad's so crazy about the thing. He's like a kid over it. And he's done most of the work for the whole show. He's so busy he can't ride —and so, I've got to win it for him."

"I hope you can," Mary said. And Dick added: "If you can't, they should give him one for putting the show on. No one else could do it as well as he does."

As they were talking the screen door slammed and Major Parrish dashed in. "Hi, kids," he grinned. "Help me get some of the plates and bowls for this afternoon. Here's the list of what I want." He tossed the paper on the piano and sprang for the stairs. "I've got to put on a clean shirt in nothing flat."

"I'll get you a sandwich, Dad," Penny called as he disappeared above.

"Fine. Where's Mother?"

"She's gone to a luncheon and she hoped you would come."

"Can't make it." There was the sound of drawers dragged open, doors slammed, and he was down again, tying his tie as he came. He snatched the thick slices of bread Penny held out to him and, through a mouthful of ham, mumbled: "Ready? Thanks."

David piled the prizes into his free arm, asking: "Don't you want me to take them, Dad?"

"No thanks. I'll just put them in the car."

"How about the horse, sir?" Michael asked with a grin. "Shall we take it over tonight or just keep it here for David?"

"I wish we could keep it here." Major Parrish took another bite from his sandwich and looked longingly at the horse. "It's a beauty, isn't it? Well, maybe David can get Lucky over the water jump and we can bring it back. Somebody open the door for me." Carrol ran ahead of him, held the door, and he was gone.

"Oh my," Penny sank into a chair. "That was a whirlwind!" She hopped up again to tell Trudy they were ready to eat and to help Williams with extra plates and forks and napkins. They gathered hungrily around the table, attacking the ham, prickly with its decoration of cloves, and the potato salad nestling, luscious and golden, in crisp lettuce. There were rolls and pickles and white mounds of cottage cheese.

"Let's take our plates out on the porch," Carrol suggested. "It's cool out there. I'll come back for the pitcher of iced tea and the glasses."

"Williams will bring them," Penny said. She started out, but stopped as she had an inspiration. "I tell you what let's do," she cried. "Let's fill my vase with iced tea and pretend it's a loving cup." She dashed into the hall and returned with the graceful little urn. "Somebody pour in the tea."

They clustered around. Bob took the vase and Carrol filled it carefully. As she finished and stepped back, Bob lifted it high in the air. "To Penny!" he cried.

"To Penny!" they shouted.

The cup went the rounds, toasts were drunk until, at length, it came to Carrol. She held it in her hands, looking into its depths as though seeing a picture there. She did see one. It was Major Parrish. Major Parrish, hurried, hot, his arms full of trophies, smiling at the prize he coveted but couldn't win—and trusting David to bring it home to him. She lifted the cup and, blue eyes looking straight at David, said clearly: "To David and the silver horse."

David smiled and squared his shoulders as she handed the cup to Penny who was the last to drink. Penny took it and caressed it. "I feel kind of like a speech," she said. "It sounds silly, but I feel like it. You all gave such nice toasts—about the show and Fort Arden, and me—and there is just one thing I can think of. It's sort of sentimental but . . . Well, we're bound to be separated pretty soon and, goodness knows when we'll all get on a post together again, so—I want to drink to us. To us and our friendship for ever and ever and ever." She took a mighty gulp of the tea and set the vase down on the table with a bang. "Now, let's eat." She looked at the serious faces around her and picked up her plate. "The last one out," she yelled, "is a tailless monkey!"

They snatched up their plates, dashing for the porch. They were embarrassed by the sentimentality of the last few minutes and yet, each felt that a bond, fragile yet enduring, bound them closer than they had ever been before. Even Louise seemed impressed, for she seated herself on a footstool without waiting to see what corner of the porch the boys occupied.

David was unusally quiet. He had a far-away look in his eyes and often he glanced at Carrol, then quickly away again. Finally he put his plate down, refused the chocolate cake Williams was passing, and stood up.

"Do you mind coming with me a minute, Carrol?" he asked. "I've something I want to talk to you about."

"Of course not." Carrol set her plate on a table, took a piece of cake in passing and followed him, munching it. "What is it, David?" she asked when they were in the hall.

"It's . . . Come out by the tennis courts where no one can hear us."

He stalked through the house, in the kitchen and out again, without even his usual joke for Trudy or a pat for the children who were having a noisy lunch at the table.

"What can he want?" Carrol wondered as she hurried along behind him.

CHAPTER EIGHT

DAVID'S PROBLEM

WHEN THEY were seated under a tree beside the deserted tennis court David picked up a twig and began breaking it into bits. "I've been thinking," he said at last, "about that darned horse. I can't win it, Carrol."

"Of course you can," Carrol encouraged him. "And even if you don't, it's the trying so hard that matters."

"No, it isn't. That horse has come to mean something to me. It's something I can give Dad. Something he really wants. There's never been much I could do for him before—not any gift I could give him, I mean, just socks and ties and things for birthdays and Christmas. But he's crazy about that horse. It's the first thing I ever knew Dad to really want."

"I know, but—if you can't win it, we could buy him one."

David shook his head. "That wouldn't be the same thing. It's going out there and winning it that counts.

And I can't win it. I know it, Carrol. You gave that toast, and I wanted to explain it to you. I'm not good enough yet to battle Lucky over that water jump." He flipped a piece of twig with his thumb nail and stripped off bits of bark. "I don't know why I'm so stirred up about it," he said at last as Carrol sat, silent, beside him. "It's got to be a sort of symbol I guess. It seems to me that, if I could win it and give it to him, I'd feel closer to him every time I looked at it."

"I know."

"Maybe it's my pride. Maybe I just want to feel cocky and say, 'Here, Dad, I got this for you.'"

"I don't think so, David."

"I don't either. I'd feel . . ."

"You'd feel just as happy if he could win it for himself, wouldn't you?"

"You bet."

Carrol leaned forward and clasped her hands around her knees. "Do you think he would have a better chance than you will if he could have ridden Lucky?" she asked.

"I know darn well he would."

"Then . . ." She too picked up a little twig and scratched it in the grass as she talked, her eyes intent on the marks it made. "If you can't win—you can't. You can try. And you don't have to worry about it. It's going to spoil the whole day for you if you do. And your father would feel much worse about that than he would about you losing the class. Now wouldn't he?"

She smiled at him and David covered her white hand with his big brown one. "I guess you're right," he sighed. "There doesn't seem to be anything I can do about it.

But there ought to be." He took the twig from her and tossed it into space as Penny's 'yoo-hoo' came from the porch. "On your feet, pal, let's go. I'll see how Lucky jumps this afternoon, and I'll do the best I can. We won't worry anymore and maybe he'll live up to his name. Maybe we can bring a 'lucky souvenir' home."

As they crossed the lawn the others were pouring out from the house. Dick stood on the bottom step waiting for them, his eyes following Louise who was clacking down the walk, her head in the air. "My, aren't you and Carrol somepin'," he teased, "going off for a little twosing."

"We had something to discuss. Thanks, Carrol." David took the steps two at a time, calling over his shoulder, "Wait a minute, Dick. I want to get my crop."

Carrol, laughing at her abrupt dismissal, hurried on to link her arm through Penny's and to join the others who were waiting at the curb. The sun, high in the blazing sky, was casting its white heat over the entire stadium so they found shelter under a tree above the boxes until the late afternoon shadows would make their chairs more comfortable. They lounged on the grass until something in the ring caught their fancy, and consumed cold drinks and endless candy bars.

"We'll all be dead tomorrow," Penny remarked complacently as she leaned forward to take a nip from a dripping ice cream cone. "I don't see why I go on eating, except that it makes me feel cooler."

Carrol, never as talkative as the others, had even less than usual to say. As the afternoon waned she looked more often at David who lay on his back. His felt hat covered his eyes, his arms were behind his head and one crossed leg swung idly. Suddenly he sat up and asked what time it was.

"Ten after four," Louise answered.

"Think we had better warm up?" David looked at Dick and Bob for confirmation.

"Wouldn't hurt." Bob got to his feet, pulled Jane up and turned to help Louise. Dick, leaning against a tree, held out a hand lazily. Louise took it and between the two boys swung to her feet.

"I hope Clip Along isn't as sleepy as I am," she yawned as she straightened her tie.

"Well, at least he isn't as full of junk." Dick looked down at David who had fallen back again and was staring at the sky. "Hey, you," he said. "You got the rest of us up, how about joining us?"

"Me, I don't feel so good." David grinned up at him and suggested, "You ride my horse for me."

"Get up." Dick gave him a none too gentle kick and David scrambled to his feet. "You'd as soon let Tippy ride that horse as me."

"Right you are." David brushed the grass from his riding breeches and picked up his coat. "Lead on," he said, "and let's get this over with."

"Seems to me you're kind of jumpy today," Dick ventured as they went toward the paddock. "Anything worrying you, Dave?"

"Nope. Not a thing."

"Not a thing," he thought, meeting his own reflection in the brown of Lucky's eye. "Just you and fifteen jumps and a few pails of water. Throw in a silver horse and Dad and a cock-eyed idea and everything is practically perfect."

He put his arm over Lucky's neck and stood looking out into the arena where a number of officers were competing for the most perfectly trained officer's mount. Horses remained calm under pistol fire, stood quietly while maps were opened and studied, and waited for their riders to drop the bars of an improvised fence. David watched his father lean over the rail of the judges' stand, an interested spectator. "He ought to be out there, too," he thought. "And by George, he's going to be!" He swung himself onto Lucky and his face was grim as he cantered around and around the paddock, waiting.

"Here they come," Michael said as he and the three girls hurried into the box. "The hurdles aren't very high so it should be a walk-away for Dave. Anybody want to make a bet with me?"

No one seemed eager but Mary finally succumbed. "All right," she offered, "I'll take Bob, but you'll have to give me some odds."

"Okay. I'll bet you two candy bars against one. Who do you want, Penny?"

Penny's reply was instantaneous. "I want David."

"You can't have him. I'm betting on him."

"Then I'll take Jane. Same odds, remember."

"Sold. Carrol?"

"What? Oh." Carrol turned to him with a start. "I was thinking about tonight," she explained lamely. "I'll take Dick, I guess, and Louise too; they're the only ones left in our crowd."

"That funny little guy Penny's so crazy about wouldn't be a bad gamble."

"Jimmy Peterson? I'll murder you for that." Penny lunged at Michael but he warded her off and grabbed her wrists. "I apologize," he laughed as he ducked her flailing elbows. "I should have said the guy who's so crazy about Penny."

"Well, that's better." Penny freed her hands and gave him a push. "You're a dope."

She settled herself in her chair again and pressed forward. The gates were opening for the first rider and the loud speaker was doing its duty. Horse after horse performed and cantered out followed by enthusiastic applause or sympathetic murmurs. David, waiting his turn by the fence looked speculatively at the hurdles. He was scarcely conscious of hearing his name, of taking Lucky into the ring. The gate swung to behind him and he and Lucky were breezing down the field. Rhythmically they cleared low fences, gates and walls as, twisting and turning, they wove their way through the maze.

"He's won it," Penny breathed. "Careful, David—just one more jump!"

Just one more jump. Thundering toward it, Lucky's ears came back for the command. He listened—and the voice that came to him was hoarse. "I'm getting off here, son," David muttered. "Take care of yourself."

The reins jerked in a choking pull; Lucky's head came back with a snap. He fought to free himself, to see the wall that loomed before him. Too late he glimpsed it. He crashed into it and his front feet climbed the painted blocks of wood, scattering them after David who was somersaulting across the grass. Quivering he backed out of the wreckage and peered over what remained of the barrier.

David picked himself up and grinned sheepishly. Grooms hurried toward him but he waved them back as he reached for the dangling reins and vaulted the debris. He soothed the frightened horse and as he swung himself into the saddle the derisive notes of a bugle blew an exit command. Satisfied, he cantered Lucky Souvenir up the field and out.

"Well, for heaven's sake!" Penny broke the hush that gripped the grandstands. "I can't believe it," she cried. "I never saw David do a thing like that before. What do you suppose happened?"

"I don't know." Carrol shook her head while Michael let out his breath in a long-drawn whistle. "Gosh," he said, "anyone could see that Lucky was all wrong the way he came into the jump. Boy, will I kid him," he grinned. "The great David, pride of the cavalry, falling off his horse!"

"Don't be too hard on him," Carrol begged, sending him a pleading smile. "He'll feel awfully badly about it, especially since he doesn't think he has a chance to win tonight." She felt Penny's elbow nudging her so she slid out of her chair and they left the box without waiting to see who would be the winner.

When they reached the paddock, David was loosening the cinch of his saddle. He grinned ruefully at them over his shoulder as he bent down to feel Lucky's forelegs, and said dryly: "I made a fine spectacle of myself, didn't I?"

Penny leaned over to put her arm around him and Carrol thought he winced as she pressed his shoulder. "Don't you mind, David," Penny consoled. "Everybody has bad luck." But in the same breath she added: "What happened to you? I never saw you ride like that."

"Too many ice cream cones, I guess." David turned Lucky over to a groom and took the girls' arms as his father hurried up.

"Are you all right, David?" Major Parrish asked anxiously.

"Fine, Dad. It shook me up a bit, but that's all."

Major Parrish looked at him searchingly. "Sure?"

"Sure. My head thumps a little but I'll be okay in a minute."

"Well, if you don't feel all right you had better get the doc to take a look at you. I have to get back."

He hurried away and the three walked back toward the boxes. Half way there they met David's mother, her face anxious and her voice quivering as she tried to seem calm and untroubled. "Are you hurt, David?"

"Undamaged, Mom."

"Thank goodness. I . . ." She stopped whatever words were trembling on her lips and contented herself with a barely audible sigh of relief. The girls went on in front and David and his mother followed, swinging hands. David was rattling off an explanation of Lucky's refusal and she watched him as she consoled him, looking for any sign of injury. Finding none, she gave him a pat and dropped off at the box where she had been sitting with her friends. David acknowledged their sympathetic comments on his hard luck, smiled and continued on his way. As he neared the Parrish box with its occupants buzzing about Dick, who was jubilantly displaying a piece of silver, his footsteps lagged. Dick's face was beaming, but seeing David coming toward him, he dumped the bowl into Jane's lap and rushed to meet him.

"Tough luck, boy," Dick said, throwing his arm around David's shoulder. "But thanks, anyway."

"Thanks, my eye." David's hand shot out to meet his friends'. "You gave as pretty a ride as I ever saw. Every jump was as clean as a whistle. I'm proud of you."

They came into the box and everyone asked him how he felt. "Fine," he answered, sitting down and taking off his hat.

"Are you sure, David?" Louise turned in her chair and put her hand caressingly on his knee. "Are you sure you aren't even a little bit hurt?" She leaned toward him, so close her hair brushed his face, solicitous and tender. "Let's go and have a coke to cool off," she suggested.

"No thanks. It was too much junk that put me to the bad." David tipped his chair back from her and rested both arms on the rail behind him. Louise regarded him a moment, a storm gathering in her black eyes, her lips compressed into a straight line. Then she drooped pathetically.

"I do have such hard luck," she mourned, long lashes downcast, her cheek resting on the arm that was still hanging over the back of her chair. "I'm such a poor rider I can't win anything but second-place ribbons."

No one answered. They were busy helping Dick slide his silver bowl back into its green flannel case.

"Dick?"

"Huh?" Dick tucked the bowl under his arm and looked at her.

"What's wrong with my riding?"

"Nothing. You ride all right."

"But Dick . . ." Louise lifted her head and looked at him. Her face registered all the emotions a young actress might try to express before the camera in a screen test—awe, devotion, hope, despair. And she said throatily, "You're the best rider of us all. Couldn't you help me? I don't know what I do that's wrong, and I feel so discouraged."

The girls looked covertly at one another as Dick rose nobly to the occasion. "You're all right, Louise," he said, embarrassment in his voice. "Ask Dave, he knows more about it than I do."

"But he fell off." Louise's eyes flashed at David, nonchalant in his corner. "You won. That proves you're the best."

Dick was squirming on the half of the chair he shared with Penny. He knew he was being baited, and he knew why. Louise, in her abject humbleness was very appealing and there had been days, and nights, too, when he would have given a great deal for the looks she was showering on him now—when he had done everything he knew to provoke them. He also knew that she was spoiled and vain and arrogant; that she lacked the character of Mary, the gay exuberance of Penny, or Jane's sweetness. But she attracted him. His greatest difficulty was to keep from hanging around her like a moth around a flame. He seldom asked her for dates and his gay banter was directed at her more often than at the others. Now, he turned to her and said in a matter-of-fact tone:

"Listen, dumbbell, you know you're good, so you aren't fooling me a bit. But come on and I'll buy you a drink. I'll tell you just how to win every class you're in so a large crowd will gather to admire me and my prize. I mean this, not you." He waved the green case as he pushed her out of the box, and as he followed her through the narrow door he turned and winked at the others.

"There goes the lamb to his slaughter," Mary remarked to the audience in general.

"She can't slaughter Dick," Michael retorted. "She can't even get his goat."

"What's all this about lambs and goats?" David put his feet on the chair Louise had vacated and shifted about on his own until he was sitting on one hip. Carrol, glancing at him, thought his face looked pale beneath its tan, but he grinned at her and she turned back to the others.

"Has anyone any idea," Mary inquired, "just why we're sitting here? The afternoon show, ladies and gentlemen, has been over for some time. In fact, it is after six o'clock."

"I wouldn't be knowing," Bob answered lazily, "except that I'm just too tired to move. I wonder if there will be any dinner in the Prescott mansion tonight since the old folks are going out."

"Of course there will," Mary exclaimed. "The children have to eat and I heard Mother ordering it. Let's all go over and see what we can find."

Michael said he had to go home, Jane wanted to get out of her hot riding clothes but David seemed strangely willing to accept. Penny, being eager to go anywhere with anyone, readily agreed and they pushed back their chairs and strolled out. Louise and Dick had disappeared so the five waved a farewell to Jane and Michael and strolled down the street.

The Prescotts lived in the same block with the Parrishes and on the same side of the street. Coming from the stadium on the opposite side, and laughing and talking, it was not until they had crossed, almost at the Prescott walk, that they saw Major and Mrs. Parrish hurrying along under the elm trees.

"Hi," they shouted in greeting.

Mrs. Parrish waved and clutched her husband's arm. "I got him out," she called victoriously. "I don't think I can keep him long, but at least I'm starting out with a date."

Carrol thought she had never seen Marjorie Parrish look so lovely. Her brown hair was gathered into soft bangs on her forehead, held by a perky green velvet bow. Her long dinner dress, too, was of a soft green, frothy and cool, and she looked much too young to be the mother of David. Major Parrish was resplendent. He wore the summer evening dress of the army; a tight-fitting white mess jacket, gay with gold epaulets, above straight black trousers and patent leather shoes. His white cap with its gold embroidered visor was set at the correct angle and his black tie smirked perkily above his white shirtfront and the yellow sash wound about his waist.

"Aren't we a handsome couple?" he asked, his eyes as wide and dancing as Bobby's.

"Wonderful!" Carrol was very nearly speechless. "I never, saw such grand people in all my life. I'm dazed."

"We are, too." Mrs. Parrish laughed and added, "We haven't been out together for so long I feel like the old woman in the nursery rhyme who said, 'If this be I, as I think it be, I've a little dog at home and he'll know me.' "

"Well, we won't be out together now if you don't hurry. I have to get back to the ring." Major Parrish caught her hand and she pattered off happily, waving back as she went.

Penny and Mary and Bob turned into the Prescotts' walk but David stood looking after his parents.

"What's the matter, David?" Carrol asked. "You look as though you'd seen a ghost."

"I have," he gasped. "Did you see Dad?"

"Of course. I talked to him, didn't I? Or did I? You've got me wondering."

"But did you see what he was wearing?"

"Umhum, and I thought he looked marvelous."

"He did, but—he had on *shoes*. Not boots and breeches. Shoes and trousers!"

"Well my goodness," Carrol looked at him and laughed. "What difference does that make? He isn't going to ride, is he?"

"Why—no." David came to with a start and hurried up the walk. "Of course he isn't. I don't know what made me say that."

Carrol looked at him curiously as he held the door for

her, and all during the hilarious meal her mind was more on David and his strange behavior than on her plate. When she and Penny were alone in their room she could hear him rummaging in closets and drawers and walking up and down the hall.

"What can be the matter with him?" she wondered. "He acts so nervous and so excited." She opened her mouth to speak of it to Penny, but left the words unsaid as Penny leaned toward the mirror, humming and trying her hair in different effects.

At last Carrol heard David clatter down the stairs, and standing in the fading light by the window she saw him busy at the Parrish car which was parked in the back roadway. He had the door open and was arranging what looked like the corpse of a man on the seat. A pair of boots leaned in floppy abandonment against the running-board and an officer's cap sat rakishly above his own grey felt. He glanced up and saw her, flung the boots and cap into the car and trundled hurriedly away.

"Well, of all things!" Carrol turned back to the room, to Penny and a possible discussion of her suspicions, but Penny was twirling and pirouetting as she called attention to the most treasured possession of her wardrobe—a short white taffeta petticoat edged with lace ruffles. It swished and rustled most satisfyingly under her white crepe de chine dress and she beamed on her reflection happily.

"I look quite cute for me, don't I?" she asked complacently.

"You look perfectly darling, Penny. I never saw you so pretty." The moment was lost and as she admired Penny from the sleek page boy bob to the spotless white sandals, she decided that whatever David was doing it was his own affair, and had he wanted her to know he would have told her. She took Penny's place at the dressing-table and asked with serious concern: "Shall I wear my yellow crepe or the pink cotton lace?"

"Oh, the pink." Penny forgot her own elegance as she dashed to the closet and brought out the frothy lace dress. She gave Carrol the slip and held the dress, ready to ease it over her cascade of blond curls. "You look lovely," she enthused as Carrol crushed the pale blue kid belt around her slender waist and adjusted a bunch of blue flowers on her shoulder. "Come on. If we don't knock 'em dead no one can."

They gave themselves one last admiring glance and rustled down the stairs.

CHAPTER NINE

THE SILVER HORSE

THE BAND was playing, flags fluttering gayly as the two girls came down the steps into the stadium. Penny, chestnut-haired and bubbling, skipped along in eager excitement; Carrol, patrician, almost ethereal in her fragile blond loveliness, made each step as unconsciously rhythmic as a dancer's. Mrs. Parrish, sitting in the box with General and Mrs. Carrington thought she had never seen a prettier picture than her own box framed. Bob and Dick and Michael, sleek and immaculate in white, were standing above the gay pastel blur of the girls; and towering above them all, the shining blondness of David in his white riding coat. Reflected lights from the ring bathed them in a soft, flattering glow, catching their happiness and youth like a flaming torch.

Wholly unconscious of the attention they were attracting, the nine in the box were trying to dispose themselves upon the six chairs the committee had provided.

Ordinarily, they would have settled themselves on steps, rail or ground, whichever offered the most comfort or convenience; but tonight, attired in their best, they became sedate and adult. Even the hoydenish Penny smoothed her silken knee with a surreptitious joy at the whispered purr her hand evoked. She huddled closer to Mary whose seat she shared, and eyed the boys as her chair was jostled.

"If anyone dares push me off," she threatened, "I'll murder him. This is my very best dress—except my new evening dress," she amended honestly.

Everyone laughed, and Bob said: "We'll respect you, Pen. In fact, you've suddenly become so glamorous we'll probably fall for you like a ton of bricks."

"Hmm," Penny commented, shrugging. "Thank you very much—but don't forget I'll be wearing my old blue linen tomorrow."

"You'll still have glamour. After tonight you can wear anything."

"Penny, the glamour girl," Michael teased. "How about a date, Pen?"

Penny threw back her head and laughed. "You can't tease me," she said. "I'm too pleased with myself." She clapped her hand over her mouth. "Oh my goodness," she said aghast, "do you suppose I'm going to grow up and get vain suddenly?"

They laughed, Penny the hardest of all, until Michael reached out to steady her chair. "Careful, glamour girl," he said, his eyes mirthful but warm, as they rested on her. "You're going to end on the floor."

"Cut the clowning, Pen," David, seeing the look,

leaned forward and glowered. "You're just a kid. Stay that way."

"Well, that's what I'm trying to do." Penny's retort was sharp. "And I'm not clowning: I'm really worried about myself. I feel quite vain and proud, and as Michael said, glamorous." She tilted her head and looked off into space. "If that happens," she said slowly, "I can't have any more fun. I'd want there to be ten in the crowd instead of nine. It just wouldn't do at all. I don't want to be as old as the rest of you."

"You never will be, Pen." Endangering their balance, Mary reached out and hugged her. "It doesn't hurt to be a little vain sometimes; but you couldn't change much if you tried."

"Maybe not." Penny's bewildered eyes cleared as she smiled at Mary. But later in the evening, when Michael called from the back of the box, "Want a coke, Pen?" she refused and thanked him, and leaned her arms on the rail, keeping her eyes fixed on the horses. "You dumb-dodo," she told herself. "Any other time you would have gone with Michael; now you've got all self-conscious and silly." Abruptly she got up and threaded her way through the entanglement of feet. "Hey, Mike," she called. "Wait for me."

"Sorry, pal," Michael said as he took her arm and pulled her along with him, "about the glamour girl stuff and the kidding. The crowd wouldn't be any fun if you grew up. Why, you're the balance wheel. You don't know it, but you keep the whole thing together and hold us down to the kid level that we need."

"Really, Mike?"

"Sure. And don't you change. You're darned pretty, I meant that—but you forget I said it. Now come on. Dribble a drink down the front of your finery and you'll feel more like yourself." Penny skipped along beside him, light of heart; but she was careful not to spill her drink.

Back in the box, David tried to keep his eyes focused on Major Parrish. It was difficult to do because he was in and out of the ring, among the spectators, up in the judges' stand and down, so fast and so often, that it was like a game of hide and seek. David was squinting into the lights in a vain attempt to spot his father's white mess jacket when he felt a tap on his shoulder and Dick's voice buzzed in his ear.

"You'd better get aboard now," Dick was saying. "I see your nag in the paddock."

"Okay." David put on his hat and sighed. "I wish I didn't have to ride," he said.

"Scared?" Louise's voice bore a decided taunt.

"Not scared. I just don't feel so hot."

"There's nothing wrong, is there, Dave?" Dick's chair scraped as he leaned toward his friend.

"No, nothing wrong. I just feel punk." David got up and turned to Carrol. "How about walking along with me?" he asked carelessly. "You haven't really seen how the show is run."

"I'd love to." They went out of the box together and both heard Louise say clearly:

"I never knew David to alibi before."

They smiled at each other, and in the dim light each noticed that the other was forcing a rather sickly grin.

"Don't mind her, David," Carrol said as she preceded

him along the narrow path. "Don't you really feel well?"

"No."

His abrupt answer surprised her and she stopped to face him. "Why, David! I thought you were only joking."

"Well I wasn't—and I've got a job for you."

"For me?"

"Yeah. I want you to go and find Dad and tell him I can't ride."

She looked at him so searchingly that he hurried on. "I'd go myself, but I think he went into the judges' stand and I can't make him understand before all those officers. Just ask him to come over to the paddock a minute."

"Did you hurt yourself when you fell this afternoon?"

"A little. I bruised a rib or maybe cracked it, I don't know. Anyway . . ."

"And so you aren't going to ride?"

"I guess not."

"David!" Carrol stared at him, her eyes wide and dark with disbelief. "After all you said about winning the horse for your father. You can't quit . . ."

"I am, though." David started her forward with a gentle push and added as he followed her: "You just find Dad and ask him to come to the paddock. I'll wait for you by the car."

"Is the car in the paddock?"

"It's just outside, over there behind those trees." David guided her through a maze of horses into a small wooded spot where a sedan waited in dark loneliness. "I'll sit on the running board and wait for you."

"David." Carrol stood looking down at him as he sat.

She thought of his fall; of his strange behavior; of the car parked behind the house—and like a puzzle the bits fell into a completed pattern. "David Parrish, you're amazing!" She peeped in the car window at the riding clothes spread so carefully over the seat, then she laughed. "You're not hurt any more than I am."

"I am, too." David frowned at her with his eyes and tried to scowl with his mouth, but ended in a grin. "Get going," he commanded. "And hurry as fast as you can."

"Okay, boss." Carrol started to run but stopped to say over her shoulder: "Please forgive me for doubting and acting so Louise-ish."

Everything looked different from the other side of the stadium and she felt as though all eyes were upon her as she mounted the steps of the judges' stand, where she had no right to be. Major Parrish was deep in conversation with an officer as she stood on the top step and tried to catch his attention. At last, after futile waiting, she ventured a timid "Major Parrish" and he turned toward her.

"Hello, Carrol," he said in surprise. "What brings you here?"

"It's David," she answered in a small voice, so unlike her usual calm that she could hardly hear herself. "He says he can't ride Lucky."

"David?" Major Parrish hurried over to her. "What's wrong?" he asked.

Seeing his anxious face Carrol longed to assure him of David's safety; instead she said: "I think he has hurt his rib."

"Good heavens, why didn't he say so!" Major Parrish

motioned, "Be back in a minute" to the time-keepers and the judges and propelled Carrol down the stairs.

He hurried her around the outside of the ring, and, as she tried to keep up with his long strides, she said breathlessly: "He really shouldn't ride, Major Parrish."

"Of course he shouldn't. And I'm grateful you came and told me so that I can stop him."

"But he'll be so disappointed. He wants Lucky in the class so badly."

"I know he does, but it can't be helped. Where is he?"

"Over there." Carrol led him across the outskirts of the paddock and pointed to the blur among the trees. "He's sitting by the car."

"The car? Why did he bring the car? Is he too badly hurt to walk?" He broke into a run and by the time Carrol had felt her way through the darkness, he was looking down at David with concern.

"Sorry to trouble you, Dad," David was saying as he got slowly to his feet. "I got a little busted up this afternoon."

"So Carrol said. You'd better get up to the hospital as fast as you can."

"But I can't, sir. I've got a class coming up."

"Never mind the class. Just hop in the car and let Carrol drive. I'll come as soon as the show is over."

"But, Dad, I can't go. I've entered Lucky in this class and he's got to be in it. I thought perhaps you might ride him for me."

"Why, David, I can't ride him." Major Parrish put his hand on the door handle and motioned Carrol in.

"Please, Dad. It means an awful lot to me."

"I know it does, son, but . . ." He looked at David's pleading face and shook his head. "I'd like to help you out, and I would if I could—you know that. But the class is starting. I couldn't get home and change and back again to save my soul."

"I know you couldn't—so I brought your riding clothes over here. I've got 'em in the car."

"You've got my clothes in the . . ." Like Carrol, Major Parrish looked in at the neat array on the seat. "Good Lord!" Under frowning brows he stared at them a moment, then turned to David and asked sternly: "What made you bring them?"

"Well, I thought—you see . . ."

"He thought it would save time, Major Parrish." Carrol came bravely to David's aid and added her pleas to his. "Oh, couldn't you do something quickly?" she begged.

Major Parrish looked from one tense face to the other. His eyes rested long on David's as the precious seconds ticked away. At last a smile tugged at the corners of his mouth, and he asked: "Do you think I can ride Lucky to suit you?"

"I think you can win on him, sir." David's answer was so positive that his father laughed. "I certainly don't promise that," he said. "But I'll have a try at it for you. Now get away so I can hurry."

He disappeared inside the car and Carrol and David walked to the paddock. "Do you think he suspects?" Carrol asked, when they were a safe distance away.

"I don't know, but I wouldn't be surprised if he does. When he was staring at me I felt just like I used to when he caught me in some mischief. Dad can learn an awful lot from looking."

"Well, he's going to ride. That's the main thing."

"Yep." David glanced back at the car where Major Parrish was struggling with his boots.

"The young fool," his father was thinking as he tugged. "He might have broken his neck. I've a darn good hunch . . ." He slipped into his blouse and opened the door. "Carrol?"

"Yes, Major Parrish?"

Carrol hurried to the car and as he stepped out, he asked: "David planned this, didn't he?"

"Why—I think . . ."

"I do, too. But why?"

"Oh, Major Parrish, he wants you to have the horse so badly. And he knows he couldn't win it for you."

"And he thinks I can?"

"He knows you can."

"Well, I don't, but I'll do my best for him." He walked beside Carrol toward the lights and as they neared David, he whispered to her: "He's a pretty swell son, isn't he?" Then, without waiting for an answer, said aloud to David: "Here I am—but don't count on too much from me."

They went over to the horses, and the groom watching for them, drew Lucky Souvenir to the rail. Several riders looked around in surprise as Major Parrish began adjusting the stirrups and prepared to mount.

"Didn't know you were riding, Dave," one officer called.

"The boy had a little accident and I'm taking over for him," Major Parrish answered, gathering up his reins.

"That's a tough break for us." The officer laughed and rode on.

David patted Lucky's sleek flanks and stepped back. "Hope you break your neck, Dad," he said, grinning up at his father.

"Why, David!" Carrol stared at him, aghast. "What an awful thing to say." She glanced quickly at Major Parrish, but he was laughing and answering, "I hope I do," as he rode away.

"That's the cavalry's way of wishing him luck," David explained, enjoying her amazed expression. "We're superstitious about saying good luck. Haven't you ever heard it before?"

"Goodness, no." Carrol laughed, too. "But I suppose it's all right. What do we do now?"

David thought a second. "I don't think I want to go to the box," he said. "There would be five thousand explanations to be made about why Dad is riding instead of me. Let's hide."

"That suits me perfectly," Carrol agreed. "Only let's hide some place where we can see."

"Oh, we will. I know a place."

David led the way to a spot near the judges' stand, at the end of the grandstand which had been erected for the enlisted men. The hillside was dotted with soldiers, cool and comfortable as they lounged on the grass, and ardent in their cheers or booing of the riders. They had their favorites among the commanders of the different troops and, as Carrol and David found an inconspicuous place among them, were rooting violently or poking fun at their friends who had backed an unfortunate officer.

"How is it going?" David asked a clean-cut boy in uniform, not much older than he, as he and Carrol sat down.

"Not so good. Some woman from away from here has it won so far. She took every jump like a breeze, but her time wasn't so hot."

"Have many ridden?"

"About ten."

"Thanks." David turned to Carrol who was absorbedly watching a rider. "The one who goes around with the fewest faults, in the fastest time, wins," he explained. "Dad ought to be along in a minute. I was to ride twelfth."

The officer who was in the ring at the moment, finished the course, leaned over, patted his horse and trotted out. As the gate was held open, the announcer's voice came through the loud speaker:

"Captain Seagram. No faults. Time: One minute forty and four-fifths seconds."

A cheer went up from the soldiers and Carrol leaned over to whisper: "Was that good?"

"Darned good. The next should be Dad."

They watched the gate eagerly as it opened. Lucky Souvenir trotted out, ears up, eyes on the ring.

"He's looking at 'em," David rejoiced. "That's the way he ought to come in." They leaned forward, tense and staring. "See? He's tending to business. Watch Dad."

"They're perfect together!"

Major Parrish was trotting Lucky in a circle, as was allowed before he began the course. He gave the horse a signal, picked up a light canter, rhythmically finished his arc, and turned toward the jumps. The starter's red flag came down, and they were off.

Down the field they tore, over a light brush, with a sharp turn toward a gate. They cleared the gate, and even in the air Lucky seemed to turn, ready for a diagonal thunder toward a broad jump five feet high. Around the end and onto a high square box, which was called a "table." Lucky lifted his fore-feet, and before his hind had touched the grass, was down and away.

"He—he isn't galloping as fast as the other man," Carrol stuttered breathlessly.

"Oh yes, he is. You watch Dad. He cuts every corner just as short as he can. That's what counts. You've got to cut your corners to save time, and yet get straight for the next jump—if you can do it. It doesn't look as though Lucky's legs move so fast because he has such a long stride. Oh gosh!" Lucky had cleared a high bank, topped with a red and white striped pole, and was tearing along directly under them. "It's the water jump! Pray!"

They crouched forward, scarcely daring to breathe as the horse's flying hooves passed them. Major Parrish, legs taut against Lucky's sides, was giving every ounce of strength and help he could. Lucky's ears came back, listening, then up, watching. He slowed, faltered; felt the stinging contact of digging heels and iron will. His stride shortened until he churned the ground. Then the heels came in again and, with a mighty grunt, he heaved himself into the air. Forward, over his neck, Major Parrish lifted him over the last few inches needed to bring his feet onto solid ground. Turf flew as they landed, but no water, and they were on to other hazards.

"Did you see it? Did you see it?" David's fist beat on Carrol's knee.

Her breath, held so long, came out with a rush and she gasped: "He did it! Oh, David, he did it!"

A mighty roar went up from the whole stadium as Major Parrish jumped off Lucky at the paddock gate. David stood up and shrieked a loud, "Wahoo!" The time-keeper's voice boomed into the excitement and they listened with bated breath.

"Major Parrish. Riding Lucky Souvenir. No faults. Time: One minute and twenty-two seconds."

"Wahoo! Wahoo!" yelled David again, jumping up and down like a mad-man.

Carrol tried in vain to catch his flying coat-tails. "Was that good time?" she had to ask the soldier.

"Practically perfect, ma'am. Major Parrish is sure one swell rider."

"He is, isn't he?" Carrol swallowed hard. "I think my heart is going to burst," she thought, "it's pounding so." She leaned back and closed her eyes. David looked down and saw her.

"What's the matter, pal?" he asked.

"I never was so excited in my life. I'm just—shaking." She held out her trembling hands and David laughed.

"It was a bit unnerving," he admitted. "But you will have to shake a while longer. There are more to ride; it isn't won, yet."

"But the soldier said . . ."

"Don't believe the soldier. There's no record that has ever been made that hasn't been broken. That one little shuffle Lucky made at the water jump could lose the ribbon for him by about a second."

"Not really! Oh, David, I'll be a wreck before it's over."

"So'll I, but here comes another horse."

They sat tensely on their hill, watching horse after horse—some good, some retired in certain defeat. "It's all right," David kept saying. "None yet as good."

Every time a horse left the ring they stared at the loud speaker until its voice quieted their fears. At last, only one rider was left mounted in the paddock. "If he beats us," Carrol said, shivering, "if he beats us, I can't stand it." The horse came in, pranced about a moment, and rearing up on its hind legs, refused to take even the first jump.

"That's that. Come on, quick!" David grabbed her hand, dragging her to her feet. "We want to see Dad get the trophy."

They tore around the stadium, scrambling through the band at the far end, their eyes on the incoming horses. Both were gasping for breath as they stumbled into their box, too exhausted to answer the questions that were hurled at them.

"I'll tell you all about it," David panted as he shook off Penny's clutching fingers. "I've got to see this."

The horses were lined up, the first three places, and General Carrington handed Major Parrish the silver horse. The crowd burst into applause as the two men saluted each other. They shook hands and the General turned to pin the blue ribbon on the bridle of Lucky Souvenir. Lucky looked at the ribbon, sniffed it, then arched his neck and received it graciously. After it was securely fastened he turned his head and watched his defeated rivals accepting lesser awards. He looked haughty and very proud of himself.

"The old pup," David muttered joyfully. "He couldn't bluff Dad." The horses trotted off and the buzzing questions began again.

"What under the sun happened, David?" Penny was not to be denied.

"Nothing. I just hurt a rib this afternoon and Dad rode for me, that's all."

They crowded around him and the rest of the show was lost as he answered or tried to evade their questions.

"There are some shenanigans going on around here," Bob exploded. "But I'll be darned if I can figure out what they are."

"Why?" Mary asked.

"Well, first, David rides like a nit-wit. He falls off. He and Carrol go into a huddle. He and Carrol disappear. His father shows up in riding clothes—when we saw him, not ten minutes before, all dressed up. His father wins. David . . ."

"Oh, shut up." David gave him a playful punch. "You think too much. It was just one of those things that happen and Dad came through for me. Here comes Mom."

Mrs. Parrish came flying up. "Oh, David!" she cried. "Wasn't it wonderful? Dad actually got his horse. But tell me, how did he happen to ride instead of you?"

David began his explanations again but his mother

stopped him. "You go straight home," she ordered, "and get the car and drive over to the hospital. I want that rib X-rayed. Now hurry!"

"Okay." David was unusually meek as he obeyed her. Dick offered to go with him, and not until the two had left the box did she turn away.

Penny still wore a furrow between her brows and still seemed puzzled. "Let's go home," she said to Carrol as the last class ended and the band began its final march. "I want to see Dad when he comes in."

Major and Mrs. Parrish were already on the dark porch by the time they had convinced the crowd that they did not want milk shakes at the Post Exchange, that they did not want to go to the club and dance to the radio, that they simply could not spend the night with Jane. Muffled voices came out to them as they opened the screen door, and a car drew up to the curb. David got out and came up the walk.

"Just cracked," he called. "I knew that was all."

The Parrishes got up and came to meet him. "Did they tape it, David?" his mother asked.

"Yep. Feel me." He banged the door shut and grinned while his mother made her inspection.

When she had satisfied herself he dropped his coat and his father's arm closed around his shoulder. "Son," Major Parrish said, "let's go inside and dedicate a statue."

On the mantel, as much a part of the room as though it had always been there, stood the silver horse, and beside it lay the blue ribbon. Carrol felt tears sting her eyelids as David said:

"Congratulations, Dad."

Major Parrish's arm tightened on the boy's shoulder and he touched the little statue gently. "It's ours, David," he answered. "Ours, together. And we'll never look at it, either one of us, that we won't feel a bond, closer even than father and son. I'm the proudest father in the whole world tonight."

David's eyes flashed to his father's face. "He does know," he thought. And his heart pounded as he answered: "I'm proud, too, Dad."

"Then let's shake on it." Major Parrish held out his hand and deliberately winked. A slow grin spread across his face but he shook his head. "You're going to get yourself in trouble sometime," he said. "It's a good thing for you, young fellow, that you're going to be in West Point until you grow up."

It was meant for a reprimand, and David knew it. But the wink had taken out the sting so he laughed as his father ordered:

"Now get to bed, all of you. Late as it is, my beautiful wife and I are going to a party." He pushed Mrs. Parrish toward the door but she hung back, calling:

"Be sure to eat. There's plenty in the refrigerator."

As their footsteps left the porch the three inside looked at each other. "Let's eat," David said simply. "I'm starved."

As they followed him to the kitchen, Penny thought: "I suppose I'll get an explanation when I get in bed. In the meantime . . . ." She listened to her dress swishing as she walked and hoped the refrigerator would contain fried chicken.

CHAPTER TEN

PENNY AND THE GOOD FAIRY

"Are you as bored as I am?" Penny looked out from the heap of pillows in the swing and dropped her magazine on the floor.

After the excitement of the horse show, the affairs of the crowd had settled into their usual calm, and the days had been filled with swimming and movies and sessions around white tables in the soda fountain. To Carrol, it had been enough. She enjoyed her daily ride on Ragamuffin, was proud of her progress in swimming and delighted with the tan that was steadily deepening, day by day. She was always pleasantly hungry, ready for bed or eager to be up again. Screen doors still banged and at regular intervals the telephone crackled with plans. Rest periods were short, and while there was nothing very thrilling to be done, time tore relentlessly on until June was past its half-way mark. So she looked up from the letter she was writing to her grandmother and asked:

"What do you want, Pen? You haven't been in the swing ten minutes."

"I know it." Penny laughed as she swung her feet to the floor and gave the glider a violent push. "I feel all restless."

"Want to swim?"

"Nope."

"Take the bikes and go over to the P. Ex.?"

"No, I don't want that, either. I want something different. What became of that moonlight picnic David was talking about?"

"I don't know." Carrol shrugged her shoulders as she began addressing an envelope. "I suppose he's been busy studying again and no one else has thought about it."

"Well, it's time someone did." Penny thumped the pillows and scowled at Carrol. "Do you realize that in less than two weeks you'll be gone? Your visit is half over and what have we done? Just a scavenger hunt and a horse show."

"Why, Pen, we've been busy every minute. We ride and swim and . . ."

"Oh that, pooh! I mean big things."

"Well, they're big to me, Penny. I never get to do things like that at home. It's just because you're used to them that they don't seem important to you."

"Maybe it is." Penny leaned back in the swing with a sigh. She flung one leg in and lay down again, stubby brown oxford pushing rhythmically against the floor. There was no resemblance between the young lady of the swishing taffeta petticoat and the little girl whose white shirt, instead of being tucked neatly into her shorts, was tied in a knot on her stomach, and whose tumbled hair was tossed back over the pillows. "I wish," she said at last, staring at the ceiling, "that something perfectly thrilling could happen to me every day. I wish I could have as many adventures as a gangster or a spy or a movie star, or something. Don't you?"

"Don't I what?" Carrol looked up as she licked the flap of an envelope. "If you'll just wait until I put a stamp on so that I can catch the postman when he comes by I'll listen to anything you ask me." She lifted the lid of her writing portfolio, found a stamp and stuck it on her letter, then dropped it into her lap and leaned back. "All right now, fire away. Don't I what?"

"Don't you wish you were a movie star or something?"

"Good gracious, no. What made you think of that?"

"Oh, it would be so exciting. I'd like to be as beautiful as Hedy Lamarr and as devastating as Bette Davis. Or perhaps I'd rather be Priscilla Lane, she's so cute. Which one would you choose?"

"I don't think I'd care for any of them, thanks." Carrol straightened the belt of her white play suit thoughtfully. "I think I'd just rather see what I can make out of Carrol Houghton. That ought to be a good, lifetime job."

"Yes, but . . ." Penny leaned on an elbow and peeked out from among her pillows. "Suppose there really was a good fairy. And she came walking by, or was sitting in the bushes or something, and she saw us up here—and she said to herself, 'My, those girls look bored. I'll have to stop in and give them some wishes.' So, in she flew, all gauzy and beautiful, and sat down—on that rose, maybe. Suppose she gave us each a wish. Just one wish! One lovely, grand wish—anything we wanted. What would you wish?"

"Well," Carrol thought for a moment, then she looked at Penny and laughed. "You started this game," she said. "Suppose you tell first."

Penny rolled over on her back and stared out at some

puffy white clouds that were wandering aimlessly across the sky. "It's kind of hard," she said at last. "I didn't think it would be . . . but just one wish . . . Maybe I'd better wish for a million dollars. If I had that I could get most anything else I wanted."

"No you couldn't, Pen. I don't think that's so good." Carrol shook her head as she answered. "You might have the million dollars but your family might think you were too young to go off and be a movie star. Suppose they'd say 'you have to go to school,' then where would you be?"

"Dad could retire and they could all go with me."

"But suppose he didn't want to? What if he and your mother should say 'We'll go on living just as we always have, thank you; the rest of us like it here'?"

"Then I'd buy myself a car."

"And where would you go? Your family already has a car and they won't let you drive it."

"Well," Penny's brow was pleated as her proposals met with such prompt counter-attacks. "I could get myself a chauffeur."

Both girls burst into laughter at the picture of Penny riding around the post on the back seat of her limousine. "You would be something!" Carrol said at last as she wiped the tears from her eyes. "Is that the best you can do with one wish?"

"Well it isn't so good, I can see that," Penny reluctantly admitted. "But it's the best I can do on short notice. See if you can top it."

"It shouldn't be hard, although . . ." Carrol shook her head. She opened her portfolio again and took out some pieces of paper. "Look at these," she said, holding them like a fan in her hand. "You wanted a million dollars. Well, look at these checks. My father has the million dollars, several of them; and I could buy us the car and the chauffeur, and we could ride around or smash it up, and he wouldn't care or even know it. If we got hurt he'd just have his secretary telephone the hospital every few minutes and would send more checks and a deluge of flowers. Money doesn't make happiness, Pen."

"No, I s'pose not."

"It makes things easier of course, but . . ." Carrol stopped and looked thoughtfully at the blue and white bundle in the faded swing. "I've been happier here than I've ever been in my life. I know it sounds strange to say, and perhaps ungrateful, but when I'm at Grandmother's I feel as though I'm too young and too noisy and too—too —well, as though I *should* enjoy having tea with Grandmother and going to concerts with a governess, and dancing lessons and shopping. But I don't. I'm just rebellious inside. And then I go to visit Daddy, or he comes to see us, and I can't reach him. He's so cold and polite and—I can't tell whether I bore him to death or whether he doesn't like me."

"Oh, Carrol," Penny sat up straight, her face a worried pucker. "Of course he likes you! Fathers . . ."

"I know." Carrol smiled in reassurance as she tried to erase the unhappiness from Penny's eyes. "I didn't mean it to be so awful as it sounds. I do think Daddy loves me. I have to think that or I'd be perfectly miserable. But if I could just have a chance for him to really know me, and not be all mousy and frozen every time he sees me; if I could loosen up like I have this summer and could be jolly with him as I've been with your family; if we could get to be pals . . . I guess that's my wish," she finished ruefully. "Just to have a chance to know my own father. It's a crazy wish, isn't it? Maybe yours is better."

"It is not!" Penny threw herself out of the swing, stumbling over scattered pillows as she dived for Carrol. "It's a swell wish. And it's going to come true." She nodded at Carrol earnestly. "I'll add my wish to yours," she vowed, "and then it has to come true. Look up here at me."

Carrol's blue eyes came up meet her brown ones and both held a twinkle as Penny struck a grotesque, but dramatic, pose. "I, Penelope Parrish, the greatest actress of all times, do speak," she proclaimed. "How's that?" She cocked her head and Carrol nodded.

"Perfect."

"That from this day forward, for better or for worse, in sickness and in health . . ."

"Aren't you getting a little mixed? That sounds like a wedding ceremony."

"So it is." Penny snapped her fingers. "But it's the only thing I know except 'Now I lay me down to sleep', and that doesn't sound like much of a promise. Take it or leave it."

"I'll take it."

"Sold."

"But I don't want to marry my father, you know, and I'm not keen about the sickness part."

"I'll take care of that. Just wait a minute. Now I'll have to start over." Penny resumed her pose. "For better or for worse, in sickness and in health . . ."

"For heaven's sake, what's going on?" Marjorie Parrish appeared inside the hall door. "I thought someone was getting married."

"Mums, listen." Penny made a dash for her.

"The neighbors thought so too; the windows are full of them."

"I've got an idea!" Penny dragged her mother toward the swing, capering as she pulled.

"I know. You want to be an actress." Mrs. Parrish breathed a sigh of relief as she made safe contact with the swing and shook her head. "That's just today, darling. Tomorrow you'll want to be an acrobat."

"Oh no, you're wrong." Penny threw herself down beside her mother and the glider rocked on its standard. "We're going to have another guest."

"Another *what?*" Both her mother's face and Carrol's showed dismay.

"Another guest. Carrol's father. He's coming to visit us."

"Carrol's fa . . ." Mrs. Parrish looked as completely knocked out as a boxer who hears the referee counting ten above him, and Carrol sprang up.

"Don't you believe her, Mrs. Parrish!" she cried. "She's just being crazy."

"I am not. I'm going to invite him myself and Mummy's going to write to him, too, and he's going to come. So there!" Penny's eyes flashed. "Why, it's practically settled," she exploded into the silence with an airy wave of her hand. "I'll just borrow some of Carrol's paper . . ."

"Wait a minute." Before she could bounce up Carrol pushed her back. "This is my fault, Mrs. Parrish," she said. "I told Penny that I had never got to know my father and that I wished I could be as free with him as I have been here this summer. I said too much about it, and now she . . ."

As Carrol talked Mrs. Parrish looked from her troubled face to Penny's silent pleading one. A gleam passed between them and she interrupted Carrol. "But I think it would be wonderful to have him. I don't see why I didn't think of it myself."

"But, Mrs. Parrish . . ."

"Wait a minute. I can plan almost as fast as Penny. Suppose we ask him to stop by for a few days on his way back from California? Then he could take you home with him. When did you tell me he would be leaving there?"

"He said about the twenty-fifth, but . . ."

"Why, that's perfect! I'll dash upstairs and write a letter now so that we can post it."

"But, Mrs. Parrish," Carrol dropped to her knees before the swing. "I think you're the sweetest people in this whole world. You have been so wonderful to me, and I couldn't, in a million years, ever thank you enough— but I can't dream of letting you invite my father, too."

"But we want him, my dear." Mrs. Parrish bent over and stroked the bright curls. "Don't you understand? We want him. I don't see why I was so stupid that I didn't think of it long ago. He can take you home with him and I won't have to worry about your traveling alone."

"And I'll scribble him a line, too." Penny jumped up and began chanting, "Thirty days has September, April, June—oh dear!" she broke off. "By the time he gets here he'll have to start right off again."

"Perhaps Carrol's grandmother could postpone their trip for a day or two. We can ask when we hear from Mr. Houghton."

"Oh, Daddy would fly." Carrol's eyes, catching their fervor, began to dance. "It would be fun, wouldn't it?"

"It would be elegant!" Penny, halfway across the porch, spied her father on the walk and danced to the door. "Hey, you're going to have a pal," she called. "Carrol's father is coming to visit us."

"Fine." Major Parrish came inside, kissed his wife and beamed on them. "When is he coming?"

"We haven't even asked him yet," Mrs. Parrish laughed. "Penny always gets so far ahead of herself. We just thought of it."

"Well, he's coming anyway." Penny was rifling Carrol's portfolio as she answered. "A fairy told me so."

"Good for the fairy." Major Parrish turned to Carrol. "Does he ride?"

"Yes, he rides a lot. He keeps some horses on his place in Connecticut."

"Golf?"

"Umhum, he won a cup once."

"Then I can see I have got a pal."

As they talked about her father Carrol felt proud. She could see him, tall and athletic, riding with her, sitting on the side of the pool while she swam for him, calling up the stairs to her—then common sense returned, and a lump came into her throat. "I really don't think he'll come," she said. "He . . ."

"Oh, he'll come." Penny was positive in her interruption. "You don't trust that fairy one bit, but I do. Thank goodness, I do." She took Carrol's paper and pen and marched into the house. "Don't disturb me for a while," she called. "I've got important business to attend to."

Alone at her mother's desk, she scowled at the blank sheet for some time. Composition had never been her forte. And now, with so much at stake, she felt like a fisherman luring a wary trout with a gaudy and artificial fly. The good, plain angleworm of truth would have been easier, but Langdon Houghton did not sound like a man who cared to nibble at the plain fare of life. So she tried to bait her hook and to cast it at him with the neat snap of an expert, but only succeeded in covering a sheet of paper with blots and unfinished sentences.

"Darn," she muttered, as she rummaged about in a drawer for a scratch pad and a pencil. The room was hot, her hair was plastered damply to her forehead and beads of perspiration stood on her lip. She removed her shirt and hung it over the back of her chair and kicked off her shoes.

"Dear Mr. Houghton," endless sheets began. Eventually, from writer's cramp, she omitted the salutation and pitched in. "We are perishing for you to visit us . . ." Rip, went the sheet. "Carrol is very lonely . . ." With a plop another page hit the waste-paper basket. It was not until crumpled papers began to spill out onto the rug that she breathed a sigh of relief and sat back to consider what might be a masterpiece, or a failure.

"It's the best of the bunch," she thought, preparing to read it aloud to herself. "It may be all wrong, but it might just do the trick." She propped the pad against a lamp, twined her legs around the slender spokes of her chair and leaned forward, elbows on the desk.

Dear Mr. Houghton: (she saluted for the hundredth time)

I hope you will have read a polite letter from my mother asking you to visit us, before you open this envelope, because I am starting right off with a bang.

Do you know you have a daughter who saves all the checks you send her like an autograph hunter because she thinks you are more wonderful than President Roosevelt or Clark Gable?

Do you know she was as lonely as a princess in a tower before she came to Fort Arden to visit, because she was always with old people and no one ever laughed with her and she never had a chance to have any fun?

Do you know she is so beautiful it almost hurts you to look at her?

Do you know that another girl's father thinks she is perfectly beautiful and says she will be a knock-out someday and that she is the most attractive girl he ever saw, right now?

Do you know that the Good Fairy offered her a wish and the only thing she asked, the only thing she wanted, was that her father would come to see her at Fort Arden and might learn to like her?

Do you know these things, Mr. Houghton? I don't think you do, because you sound to me like the kind of man who would do something about them if you knew.

If you are offended please don't blame your daughter. And please don't blame the Good Fairy. She promised that she would bring you here but I always get mixed up in things too.

Sincerely and hopefully,

Penny Parrish (secretary to the Good Fairy)

P.S. When you come please don't mention this letter to my family. They don't know all these things either.

P.P.S. Will you please accept the invitation by telegraph? I don't think we can stand the suspense very long."

When she had finished she pursed her lips and sat scratching her knee doubtfully. "It sounds pretty awful," she told herself. "And it isn't at all what I intended to say, but it's just what he deserves. And it's going to take something like this to get him here, I know it will. Maybe even this won't bring him."

She sighed, shrugged her shoulders, and appropriated a piece of her mother's monogrammed stationery. Laboriously she set to work and after a few slight catastrophes, turned out a finished product that satisfied her. She hastily sealed it into an envelope, and, lest she change her mind, rerobed herself and clattered down the stairs with it. She bore with her the waste paper basket and its damaging evidence, and made a trip to the trash can behind the house before she delivered her letter to the front porch.

"Well, for goodness' sake, I thought you were upstairs," Carrol exclaimed.

"I was, but I went outside a minute." She laid her

work of art on the table and asked: "Where is everybody?"

"Your father got a brief case and went off and your mother is back in the study. She said she looked into her room but you were muttering so she was afraid to go in. What did you write?"

"Little girls mustn't ask questions." Penny shook an admonishing finger. "I just wrote. And I'm so hot I'm about to bust. What d'you say we go swimming?"

"All right." Carrol got up, then rushed over to Penny and hugged her. "Oh, Pen, I'm so excited!" she cried. "You are the most wonderful people—and do you think he'll come?"

"Of course he'll come!" Penny spoke with confidence, but she felt as though she were swallowing her heart when she thought of the letter. So she spun Carrol around in a dance that was a cross between a shag and the latest thing in jitter-bugging, and the floor was bouncing with their steps when her mother came out.

"Here's my letter," she said. "Is yours ready?"

"Right here." Penny collected the letter Carrol had written her grandmother, tapped it against her own, then thrust them both out. "Stick 'em with yours on the mail box," she said. "The postman usually gets here around three and they can make the afternoon mail. We want to go swimming."

She dashed inside with a quick glance at her mother who was tucking the letters behind a mail box, hung beside the front door. She was tempted to snatch hers back, to try again. "I tell you what I'll do," she told herself as she took the stairs two at a time. "If the postman hasn't been here by the time I come down I won't send it. I'll do it over."

She dawdled so over her undressing that Carrol who was ready and waiting, looked down at her in surprise. "I never saw you so slow, Penny," she said. "Shall I go on down and get our beach coats and towels?"

"Oh no, relax and wait for me." Penny, deep in a chair, slowly untied first one shoe and then the other. "What time is it?" she asked.

"Five after three. Thanks for reminding me. I nearly forgot to take off my watch."

Carrol laid her watch on the dressing table and tossed Penny her bathing shoes. Penny put them on and wandered to the window. She searched both sides of the street but no old soldier with his leather pouch was to be seen. When there was nothing more she could do to herself, a bathing suit being a very simple contraption to adjust, she followed Carrol down the back stairs to a closet where robes and bathing towels were kept. They selected what they wanted, girded themselves in the silent kitchen and dug their bicycles from under the porch. As they pedaled around the walk Penny stopped and rested a foot on the side steps. She could see into the porch. A magazine protruded from the box—and the letters were gone.

"Well, that's that," she thought. "I don't know whether I'm glad or sorry."

She considered it for almost a block, then being Penny, she dismissed it. Her mind jumped the intervening days. "I hope he brings a bathing suit," she panted as she chugged up a hill.

"Who?" Carrol, behind her, leaned forward.

"Your father, silly. Have you forgotten about him?"

"No," Carrol answered, "but you were staring so hard at that soldier we passed I thought you were going to hit the curb."

They both laughed, and as they leaned their bicycles against a high wire fence that surrounded the pool, Penny spied her crowd by the diving platform. "Hey," she called as she skidded along the wet cement, "Carrol's father is coming!"

"Do tell." Dick, sunning himself on the high diving board looked down at her and grinned. "You certainly look all pepped up about it."

"Yes, doesn't she?" Louise, beside him, swung her feet lazily and shrugged. "I can't imagine getting so excited about an old man."

Penny made a face at her and turned to the others who were sitting along the edge of the pool and asking eager questions. "It's just marvelous," she was telling them as Carrol came up bearing the towel and cap she had abandoned in her rush. "He's going to be here several days. And he's a marvelous golfer and rides like a cavalryman and swims . . . Oh, he'll be loads of fun; and he's coming by plane. Isn't it thrilling?"

"It's wonderful." Mary looked up at Carrol and smiled. "We'll have to rally our parents around, too. I'll bet he's good-looking."

"Oh, he is!" Penny took charge of the conversation again. "He's as handsome as Tyrone Power or Cary Grant, or even Robert Taylor. Why he . . ."

"Penny, you nut." Carrol made a dash for the jigging

Penny in a vain attempt to clap a hand over her mouth.
Penny side-stepped neatly and the clutch Carrol gave her
was one of self-defense. They wabbled together on the
side of the pool, balanced, hovered, and with a sly push
from Bob, went in with a splash.

"You—you . . ." Penny gurgled as she came up. "I'll
get even with you, Bob Prescott. I know you pushed me."
She headed toward the ladder with long powerful strokes
while Carrol diving, caught her by the legs. They began
a water battle that was cheered from the side lines and as
they crawled up the side of the pool, exhausted, Penny
was spluttering. They lay on the cement, dripping like
wet seals, too spent to shake the hair out of their eyes. At
last Carrol sat up and caught the bath towel Jane pitched
her. She bent over and was rubbing her hair with it when
Jane said:

"Good grief, we forgot to tell them. Roll over closer.
We're going to have a dance."

"No!" Penny sat up and she and Carrol scrambled the
few intervening feet. "When did you hear it?"

"Just now. Michael brought the good tidings from his
father. There are so many things going on at the club
that it has to be tomorrow night. We'll have to do some
hurrying."

"Oh boy!" Penny wiggled with excitement and looked
up at the diving board. "Come on down," she called.
"We're talking about the hop." Receiving no answer but
a wave of the hand from Dick, she spied David parking
his bicycle by the fence and yoo-hooed to him. "Come
over here," she called. "There's going to be a hop tomorrow night."

David was threading his way through the small children at the shallow end of the pool and Penny glanced up at the diving board again. Louise, as Penny knew she would be, was swinging down the ladder so that she and David arrived together. Everyone was talking at once. "The colonel says we'll have to use the second orchestra . . . it's just as good, Williams plays in it . . . the invitations will have to be sent in to the town kids tonight . . . I think I'll wear my blue . . ." And Louise stood by, waiting patiently until there was a lull. Then, standing close to David, she asked in a voice that was low but clearly audible to everyone:

"Are you sending me flowers, David?"

"Flow . . . What do you mean?" David looked at her, frowning.

"A corsage, stupid. The last time I had to change my dress because you sent red roses. It's just easier to mention in advance that in case you're sending them, I'm wearing pink."

"Oh."

Louise sat down by Mary while David's miserable eyes sought Carrol. Dick had come down the ladder and was tapping her on the top of her head. "Date?" he was asking. She laughed and nodded, and David walked to the side of the pool. For an instant he poised there, then his body shot forward and he dived.

"Who are you going with, Mary?" Louise asked carelessly into the silence.

"Chuck Carstairs, I guess. He asked me the other night for the next hop." Mary returned the dig of Jane's elbow with her own, meaning, "I got the point—and so did David," and began gathering up her towel and cap.

"It's nice to have a date in advance." Louise motioned toward Penny and Michael who had moved to the edge of the pool and were dangling their feet in the water. "Glamour girl seems to have got herself one, too. Going home?" she asked, tilting her head up at Mary.

"Yes, I always seem to start the trek. But it's nearly five and Mother and Dad have some people coming in to tea. Send Bob home, please, in time for dinner."

She wandered off and Jane hopped up. "Let's all take a quick dive and go," she suggested. "We always get home so late that it might be fun to give our families a shock. Okay?"

They began scrambling up. Michael and Penny rolled off into the water, someone discovered a ball, and such an exciting game of water polo was begun that the only shock their families had was the relief of seeing them when hope had been abandoned.

CHAPTER ELEVEN

THE HOP

THE FOLLOWING evening, due to Penny's repeated pleas to hurry, the girls were dressed and waiting a full half hour ahead of time. Mrs. Parrish had arranged for the three, Carrol, Penny and David, with their dates, to have dinner at home at half past seven; and she and Major Parrish had departed for the movies. Bobby and Tippy, aided and abetted by Penny, had begged so hard for an exciting jaunt out into the forbidden night that their parents had succumbed and they had been whisked away, too.

"Peace," Penny said as the car drove away. "Blessed peace."

She and Carrol trailed their skirts down the stairs and were undecided whether the occasion warranted a decorous waiting in the drawingroom or whether they might take to the usual vantage point of the front porch.

"Oh pooh, let's sit on the porch," Penny decided.

"We can be careful." She spread the red and white candy-stripes of her organdy carefully about her and looked at the trailing yellow chiffon of Carrol in the swing. "We do look elegant, don't we?" she sighed. "Do you like this rose stuck up on top of my head? I took it out of my corsage."

Carrol smiled at the red rose that was tucked into Penny's soft curls. It nodded and bounced about with every head shake and Carrol wondered if all the pins and the perky velvet bow could make it last the evening. It was quaint and it suited Penny, and as she told her so, Penny threw back her head in laughter and the rose gave up the struggle and plopped off.

"Heck." Penny picked it up and began punching it back into place. "I knew it wouldn't stay on me."

"Let me fix it." Carrol came over to her and was busily at work when David came out.

Penny, head bent, saw the lower half of him coming. "My, you look mad," she said peeking up at him.

"Well, who wouldn't be." Regardless of his white dinner jacket David flung himself into a chair. "For two cents I'd not show up."

"I think Louise is mean." Penny pushed Carrol's hands away and sat up. "That's good enough," she said, shaking her head experimentally. "It won't stay on anyway. I think she's the meanest girl that ever lived. Didn't you really ask her?"

"Of course I didn't ask her." David's eyes followed Carrol going back to her place in the swing. "You know Louise."

"But, David, you must have said *something*!"

"I didn't. I took her to the last hop—and I didn't send her any flowers by the way, that was months ago—and I took her home and left her at her front door and said goodnight. She said, 'It was lovely, David,' and I said, 'Yes, it was.' She said, 'I hope we have another one soon,' and I said 'I do too.' And that was that. If you call that a date I'm crazy."

"Of course I wouldn't call it a date. But Louise would."

"Well, I'll take her—but I'll be darned if I'll dance with her." David stuck his jaw out and looked at Carrol. "I was going to ask you," he said bluntly.

"Were you?" Carrol smiled at him and Penny bounced up.

"I'm so mad," she spluttered. "I'm so mad I feel like not letting her in. When I think of the fun we could have had at dinner, the four of us! And now she's going to get Trudy's good fried chicken and the ice cream and the cake—and the rest of us will just sit there and glower at her and can't enjoy it. She's ruined it all!"

"Maybe it won't be so bad. She's pretty popular and I won't have to bother with her at the dance." David sighed and got up. "I'd better trundle along and get her."

"Are you going to walk?" Penny realized for the first time that the car was gone.

"Sure. How else would I get there?"

"Why didn't you ask for the car?"

"Because I didn't want it. We'll all go over in Dick's. I like it better that way." He grinned at Carrol as he passed her.

Penny sat down again, thinking how like old times it was to have David discussing his troubles with her. One half of her mind was thinking that and the other half was worrying about a smudge on the hemline of her skirt. David's voice brought her up with a start.

"Pen?"

"Yeah?" She looked up and David was standing by the door.

"You remember what I told you the other night at the horse show about getting ideas and growing up? Well, don't you forget it!"

"Why, David!"

"I mean it, Pen." He walked back and patted her shoulder awkwardly. "You're just a little girl and you stay that way. Listen to Carrol. She's got the right slant on things, and she'll tell you." He gave her shoulder another pat then dashed out the door and down the steps.

"Isn't he priceless?" Penny looked at Carrol, and holding her rose, shook her head. "He certainly has become brotherly all of a sudden."

"But he's right, Pen. You're so cute and so much fun. David is really serious about it." She got up and came over to Penny. "Everyone loves you," she said, straightening the ruffles on Penny's shoulder, "because you're so sweet and true and funny."

"And everyone," Penny answered thoughtfully, "loves you and admires you because you're so beautiful and so good. I love you, but . . ." She looked up impishly. "Couldn't I be sort of grown up just for one night? I look so nice."

Carrol laughed and was about to answer when Penny sprang up. "Here they come," she cried, "Dick and

Michael." Unmindful of her curls she stuck her head out into the breeze as a car door slammed and the two boys started up the walk. "You're five minutes early," she shouted. "Go back and ride around the block."

"Like fun we will." They came on, Dick immaculate in white linen and Michael a dark duplicate of David in white dinner jacket, black tie and trousers.

The girls were properly admired before they seated themselves in a decorous little group, as attractive as any magazine advertisement. Small talk was beginning to give way like a defeated army in a battle with hunger, and Williams' head was peering around the door in plaintive supplication, when Penny finally gave vent to her feelings.

"I don't see any sense in Louise's being so late!" she stormed. "I'm perfectly furious. Do you suppose she's coming?"

The telephone shrilled as she spoke and she dashed inside to answer it. There was a silence, then her voice floated out to the porch. "Dick," she called, "it's Louise. She says she can't walk over and wants you to come and get her."

"Tell her I'm busy." Dick leaned back in his chair. "Tell her to hot-foot it over here or we're going on and eat. I should go and get her," he said to the others. "She's not my date, thank goodness."

They laughed and Dick looked pleased with himself. He looked proud too, and serene, as he moved over into the swing beside Carrol. Penny came out again, trouble written on her brow.

"It's five minutes to eight," she said plaintively. "And

the dance starts at half past. I do want to be there on time."

"Well, tell Trudy to get the food on and we'll dash in and eat the second they come. It won't be long."

Penny nodded to Williams who was again hopefully blocking the door and he disappeared with relief. A car drove up to the curb, chauffeured by Louise's father, and David sprang out to open the door. Louise's face looked as though a thunder storm had crossed it, but she turned on the sun when she saw the group on the porch.

"I'm so sorry to be late," she cooed, "but Mother simply wouldn't let me walk in these slippers. I didn't dream that David wouldn't come in a car, and I did so hate to disturb Daddy. The post really should have a taxi service."

She fluttered in, appropriated the spot by Dick which Carrol had left vacant at her arrival and was about to seat herself and to lure Dick down again, when Williams announced happily and with gusto, "Dinner is served."

The chatter and dawdling which should accompany a formal dinner, the bouncing back and forth of a conversational balloon, was noticeably lacking. Penny wanted to be at the club for the opening dance, and Williams knew he had to be. Hers was desire and his was duty, so between them, courses were whisked on and whisked off again so rapidly that shrimp cocktail tasted like fried chicken, and peas and potatoes and salad were washed down with ice cream. Hurry, hurry, hurry was donged in the ears of the guests like the voice of a barker before a circus tent. Before they knew it finger bowls vanished from under their very fingers and napkins were already in the soiled clothes hamper. They found themselves in the hall with Penny half way out of the door.

"We can just make it if we hurry," she called back.

"If you say that word once more," Louise answered her, "I'm going to sit down here and not go."

"Well, sit then. You spoiled dinner anyway by being so late." Penny's eyes were flashing as she whirled around. "Who wants to go to the hop with me?"

"We all do." Michael, close behind her, collided with Carrol and Dick as he signaled them to follow. David was on his way, too, and Louise, who had sat down got up again.

"All right," she said with a shrug. "You don't need to get so upset about it. We're all going." She trailed them to the door and stood looking at the car. "Are we *all* going in that?" she asked as David held the screen door for her.

"I don't see any other way to get there, do you?" He leaned against the screen and waited.

"No, I suppose not." Louise looked pained, but she shrugged again and strolled down the steps. "Penny shouldn't give way to her temper," she remarked. "After all a guest . . ." She finished the sentence with another eloquent shrug that outdid all the others and stepped on Michael's toes getting in the car.

"She'll have Saint Vitus dance if she doesn't give her shoulders a rest," David growled silently as he crawled in after her.

Someone shut the door and Dick gave a cheerful blast

of the horn. "We're off," he shouted as he charged away from the curb.

"We'll be in—in the guard house, if you don't slow down to the allowed twenty miles per hour," Penny cautioned him. "Take it easy."

Dick took it easy, as easy as he could with the first notes of swing music floating over the golf course. He swept a wide arc to the club house door and urged them out so he could park the car.

The dressing room was empty when the girls came into it, with the exception of two little things in a corner, stiff and nervous in their first long dresses. The band was blaring, trombone sliding, saxophone wailing as, with a jab at the powder jar, the three passed through like a breeze.

At the door into the ballroom Penny stopped and looked back. "What's the matter?" she asked the two behind the coat racks. "Don't you want to come out?"

They looked at each other and giggled nervously so she went back to them. "Come on," she coaxed. "I'll take you. I know lots of little boys out there your age."

She shepherded them along and at the door saw Michael. The others had gone on to dance but he was waiting by a stag line that, to Penny in one brief glance, looked like the answer to a maiden's prayer.

"I thought you were the hurry up gal," he said.

"I was," she explained, "but I found myself a couple of young charges. Be a lamb and see if you can pry two of those little boys loose from the orchestra."

Michael laughed and went away and Penny stood talking to the little girls who looked up at her, big-eyed and adoring. She tapped her foot to the music and made them laugh while she watched the dancers. Annoying and butting little boys of twelve steered sedate little girls of eleven among the eighteen-year-olds, and big sisters found time to help little brothers plow their way about. Big brothers were bent over little sisters as though flirting with seniors in high school. It was the way of the army and no one seemed to find anything odd about it.

Carrol noticed it, too, doing intricate steps with Dick. She watched for Penny; saw her in a corner introducing a foursome that probably fought battles and ate bread and jam together during the week; saw her sort them out, give them a push, then swing onto the floor herself, her red rose bobbing. After that she lost her. The dance, called by the parents and the committee "the children's hop" was to Carrol the most novel thing she had yet discovered in Fort Arden. There were no formal programmes. Someone asked you for a dance—and away you went. When the first encore began it was sink or swim, for anyone could cut. If you were popular you danced joyfully from one pair of arms to another and if you weren't, you probably went home and cried yourself to sleep. The stag line moved as though on an escalator and conversation were merely "hello" and "I'll be back." A few parents, in formal dress too, sat on comfortable divans in a fringe, admiring their children. Now and then they wandered out onto the wide veranda where they sipped limeades and even danced among themselves.

Carrol lost Dick, of course, on the first encore; exchanged tall boys for short ones, short ones for tall again, in a never ending marathon. Between dances a water cooler outside did a gurgling business because the younger children hovered six deep around the punch bowl. It was after the third dance, when she was leaving the water cooler, that David touched her arm.

"My dance?" he asked.

She nodded and turned to the boy at her side. He thanked her for the dance, drifted off into the dark and she and David were going through the broad doors into the lighted ballroom.

"Having fun?" David asked as he began a smooth and rhythmic tango.

"Loads." Carrol smiled up at him and added: "Are you?"

"Not much, so far. Louise trouble," he explained briefly. "But business is picking up now."

He swung her in an arc. They dipped and swayed and for a few bars were too busy to talk. Then David slowed his steps, held her at arms' length and went on with the conversation. "Louise and I danced for a few minutes, then she decided she wanted to go out by the fountain. We went out—and she put on a swell act about no one understanding her. Said I had insulted her by making her walk; that you and Penny had flowers and she didn't get any; and—oh, a lot of stuff. I tried not to listen and that made her so mad she flounced in again, and I don't know what became of her."

They both glanced around the room and at the same moment their eyes discovered a cloud of black hair above a pink dress dancing with Dick. Feeling the pull, Louise turned her head before they could look away. She whispered something to Dick, he bent his head, then they both laughed and whirled away.

"Poor dub." David shook his head sadly. "Dick has so much sense I can't see why he is always falling for the line she feeds him. She can throw him away and yank him back like a kid with a toy on a string. I wish he'd wake up."

"I do, too." The music stopped, there was a burst of applause and the orchestra began its encore.

"This is the end of me," David prophesied. "At least for the time being. But I'll cut back."

And he did cut back, again and again. They all cut back; and it wasn't until the evening was half over that Carrol had time to realize that she hadn't seen Dick since the first few dances. David was standing with Penny so she excused herself to her partner and walked over to them. "Have you seen Dick?" she asked.

"No, haven't you?"

"Not for ages."

"Well, that's funny." Penny looked around the ball-room. "David and I were just talking about it. We don't see Louise either."

"It doesn't matter." Carrol turned back to the boy who was patiently side-stepping the bumping couples. "I just wondered."

"I'll cut in in a minute," David called.

Carrol nodded and went on dancing. In a few minutes she heard his voice saying, "May I break?" and they were whirling off together.

"Of course it's Louise making more trouble," David said smiling down at her. "But it's my good luck. Miss Houghton, I think you have changed partners."

"That's all right," Carrol laughed. "I like dancing with you better."

"Really? And you don't mind if Louise got in some dirty work at the crossroads?"

"Not a bit. But I am sorry," she said seriously, "that she doesn't like me and that she wastes so much time trying to hurt me."

"But she doesn't hurt you? That's the main thing."

"No, she doesn't hurt me. She only hurts herself, poor girl; and she'll keep on hurting herself more and more if she doesn't watch out. She has worked herself into such a state about me, because I have money and because I'm visiting you and Penny that—well, she just can't bear it."

"If she doesn't do anything worse than this I don't mind. It's a swell break for me, but . . ." David looked worried. "I wonder if I ought to speak to Mums about it?"

"Oh please, David," Carrol's hand tightened around his, "please don't say anything to your mother. We don't want parents mixed up in it. It will straighten out—and after all, just going off with Dick isn't anything."

"But it is. Dick's your drag. And most girls would be roaring mad. Why aren't you?"

"Because I'm having fun." Carrol's eyes laughed into his and her one desire was to steer him away from an open quarrel. "Let's just pretend we didn't notice it. If they don't come back we can go home together and say we thought the exchange was a good idea—and if they do, we can pretend we didn't miss them. It's really quite simple."

"It is, at that." In a corner, safe from the chaperone's

watchful eyes, David assayed a little jitter-bugging in his exuberance. "You're a honey," he said, as flushed and laughing they sank into chairs.

The evening flew by. Penny flitted about, candy-striped ruffles flying; her rose a long-dead pulp under the sliding feet. Carrol danced from one to another with scarcely the loss of a beat, and it was not until she and David were beginning the last dance to the soft strains of Home, Sweet Home, that Louise and Dick stepped up to them.

"I'm awfully sorry," Dick said with an embarrassed gulp. "Louise tore her dress and . . ."

"Oh, hello." Both Carrol and David turned smiling. And David looking down at Carrol, asked: "Shall we give them part of this?"

"I think so." Carrol's dimple flashed as she turned to Dick.

"Well, I don't." David's arm tightened as he spun her away, and he grinned at Dick over his shoulder. "Sorry son, but you lost your chance," he called. "Thanks, so much."

"What made you do that?" Carrol asked when they were across the floor and she could see Louise and Dick standing where they had left them, arguing heatedly.

"Well, for several reasons. First, she planned it. She wanted to leave you alone all evening, stranded and dateless, and then at the last minute—hand you back Dick and march off with me. And second, also third, fourth and fifth, I like it better this way."

Carrol considered for a moment. "You know, I do, too," she said truthfully. "I've had a grand time."

They both laughed and David caught her arm. "Come on. Let's suggest a sandwich at The Halfway House."

Penny and Michael were saying goodnight to the chaperones, and Carrol and David stepped into the long line that was making its farewells. As they finished and turned away Penny clutched David's coat and pulled him aside. "They've gone," she hissed. "At least, Louise flew out the door with Dick sort of tagging along behind. Mike's father is outside and he told us we could take his car."

"How about The Halfway House?" David reached over and drew Carrol into the group. "Will Mums let you go?"

"She will if I telephone her and tell her you're going. Oh, David," Penny looked at him adoringly. "Can we *really* go there? I've always been dying to."

"Well, go on and telephone. All right with you, Mike?"

"I'd like to go." Michael took Penny's hand and they slid across the deserted floor.

"Hi, Williams!" Penny cried, peeking over the velvet-curtained rail at Williams who was tucking his big bass viol into its case. "Swell music!"

"Thanks, Miss Penny." Williams beamed. She and Michael disappeared into an office and David looked at Carrol. "Alone, at last!" he said dramatically, grinning.

Carrol laughed and sank down on a divan looking ruefully at her feet. "Are you just dead?" she asked.

"I feel as though I'd walked a million miles. Someday I'm going to get me a pedometer." He sat down on the arm of the sofa and they waited in complete and relaxed silence until the door flew open and Penny bounced out.

"I can go!" she shouted. "I can go!"

"Well, come on." David pulled Carrol to her feet and Michael told them where the car was parked.

When they reached The Halfway House, a small white building midway between the post and town and famous for its chicken dinners, it was crowded. A radio was blaring and an overworked waiter was rushing about with sandwiches and cold drinks. It was completely occupied by the older crowd from the hop and Penny felt very important as she came in. She tried to look unimpressed, but she whispered to Carrol as they struggled through the mob to a table in a corner:

"I never got to stay out and eat after a dance before. David talks about me not growing up!"

"Well, if you must know," Carrol whispered back, "I never did either."

They both laughed and slid into chairs the boys held for them. They ordered chicken sandwiches and milk, and David impressed Penny greatly when he said carelessly, "I'll have a cup of coffee." Her brown eyes were sparkling and she waved to anyone who so much as looked at her.

"Boy, I'm glad we lost Louise," she said through a large bite of sandwich. "You never would have suggested coming here if she had been along, would you, David?"

"You can bet I wouldn't!" David answered. "The dinner was bad enough without dragging it on here."

They laughed and talked, called nonsense to their friends, and after a few avid bites, Penny only nibbled at her sandwich. "Go on and eat, Pen," David urged, pushing her plate toward her as though she were a puppy. "Mums will be walking the floor pretty soon."

"I'm trying to make it last." She took another bite and sighed. "You're going to make us leave as soon as I've finished, and I want to stay awhile."

Michael's white teeth flashed in his lean brown face as he threw back his head and laughed. "You're priceless, Pen," he said. "We won't hurry you." Then he turned to David. "Do you realize, Dave," he asked, "that this is the last time we may be down here for at least a year and a half? We're going to be shut up in those grim, grey walls."

"You sound as though you're going up the river to Sing Sing," Carrol told him.

"Well, it isn't Sing Sing, but it's up the same river. And from all I hear the first year is something like a 'stretch'. We don't get home next summer—not until the following Christmas."

"And we don't get home then," David broke in, "unless we're good little boys and don't lose our furlough."

"Tell me something about it," Carrol begged, leaning forward, elbows on the table.

"Well, we have to be there on the first. You know that because you've seen Mums running around and moaning. She used to moan because she thought I couldn't get an appointment from a congressman to enter, and now she moans because I'm going. We go in and get our uniforms, and then the grind begins."

"Yeah," Michael interrupted. "But before we even start to commence to begin, the upper classmen haze us."

"What is that?"

"Oh, they make us do silly things; like sitting for hours on infinity—that means without a chair. And they don't have to speak to us if they don't want to, and we can't go to the dances and . . ."

David glanced at Penny. "Come on, we have to go," he interrupted. "The kid's gone to sleep in her milk."

"I have not!" Penny looked at him indignantly. "I was only feeling sorry for you."

"Well, you don't need to." Michael patted her on the back. "We're just about the two happiest lads in America, aren't we, Dave?"

"Sure. Hurry up." David moved Carrol's chair back for her and hustled Penny around the table. "I'll tell you about it some other time," he said to Carrol as he stopped to pay the check at the cash register. "I know Mums is lying awake waiting for us."

They went out into the night and the drive home was all too short. Michael walked to the porch with them and they stood on the steps.

"It's a heavenly night, isn't it?" Carrol said, looking up at the stars.

"Yes, it's a shame to have to go to bed. Well," Michael put out his hand to her, then to Penny, "thanks for the evening, and thanks for the dinner, Pen. It's been grand. So long, Plebe." He saluted David and went whistling down the walk.

"What is a plebe?" Carrol whispered as they tip-toed through the dim hall.

"It's what David's going to be," Penny mumbled with a yawn. "Next year. A freshman. Gosh, I'm sleepy."

David turned out the lamps and they groped their way up the stairs and through the hall. "Goodnight," they whispered at the door of Penny's room. David gave Carrol's hand a squeeze as it rested on the banister. "Good sport," he said softly. Then the doors were closed and Penny's slippers were sailing across the floor.

"Oh, bless Louise," she yawned as she lay in bed and watched Carrol hanging up her dress. "She got me to The Halfway House—and if she doesn't do anything worse than she has . . ." Her eyes drooped down. "Talk in the morning," she mumbled. "G'night."

CHAPTER TWELVE

ANXIOUS WAITING

PENNY ROLLED over and blinked at a sunbeam that filtered across the floor. Someone had closed the curtains, and except for the exploring little ray of light, the room was cool and dusky. Her feet felt like bruised knobs and she pulled one out from under the sheet and inspected it, surprised that it bore no cuts or blisters. She gave a mighty yawn and sat up, fumbling for the clock on the bedside table.

"What time is it?"

The voice from the other bed startled her so that she almost dropped the clock she was holding. "Oh hello, are you awake? It's . . ." She stared, unbelieving, at the hands. "Why, it's after eleven o'clock. Do you suppose this thing is right?"

"It must be. I've been awake for ages."

"Why?"

"Oh, I don't know." Carrol stretched and put her

hands behind her head. "I just woke up and have been lying here thinking."

"About the hop? It was grand, wasn't it?"

"Marvelous."

They began talking of their partners, clothes, what this one said and how that one danced. They made a few half-hearted attempts to get up, only to fall back onto their pillows and go on talking.

"I wish I weren't hungry," Penny was saying when the door opened and her mother's voice called, "Good morning, darlings." She came into the room carrying a large tray, Trudy close behind her with another.

"Sit up, quickly," she ordered. "Breakfast is being served in style." There were exclamations of joy and pillows were plumped into fat roundness. "We only have one bed-tray," she went on to explain, setting the legs of the tray across Carrol's lap, "so you'll have to be careful, Penny, how you balance yours. Perhaps Trudy can put some books under the ends." Between them, Trudy and Penny got the tray anchored so there would be no danger of accident.

"It looks heavenly," Carrol said, attacking grapefruit chilled in ice. "I never knew bacon and eggs could smell so good."

Trudy opened the curtains and Mrs. Parrish sat down on the foot of Penny's bed. "Did you have a good time last night?" she asked.

"Wonderful! Penny waved her fork so wildly that her mother leaned over to steady the tray.

"Were there many there?"

"All the usual crowd. And Mums. . . ." Catching Carrol's warning eye she left the sentence unfinished and said instead, "Do you know what? Carrol's father ought to get his letters today. Did you send yours air mail?"

"Yes, did you?"

"Umhum. I wonder if he will wire us. I bet he will."

They discussed the probabilities of a telegram, and when the last crumb of toast had disappeared with the final account of the hop, Mrs. Parrish took the trays and set them in the hall while the girls threw back their covers.

"I think we had better stick close to home," Penny said, as upside down she fumbled for her mules. "We might get that telegram."

The day, what remained of it, scuttled by like a meek little person trying to make way for bigger and more important ones. The telephone hummed with discussions of Louise's treachery, and Dick, late in the afternoon, sidled in with a large box of candy. He was embarrassed and, for Dick, unusually quiet. When Penny and Carrol seemed more interested in his candy than in his halting explanations he became himself again and did his share toward littering the floor with small crinkled bon-bon containers.

A movie filled the evening and David made a point of laying his books aside and driving the girls over in the car. When Louise attached herself to the end of the long row, heads turned stiffly like a line of clothes pins nodding in a breeze, then jerked back to the screen.

Alone in their room again, Carrol said: "Well, that passed off painlessly."

"It wasn't so bad," Penny agreed. "But I don't see

how we can keep it up. Louise can't go on indefinitely doing mean things and being forgiven. Something's bound to bust loose."

"Not from me it won't."

Carrol was brushing her hair and Penny flopped into a chair. "I can't understand," she said, looking blankly at the wall, "why we didn't hear from your father."

"Did you ask him to wire?"

"Well, I sort of suggested it. I should think . . ." She sighed and picked up her shoes, tossed them absent-mindedly into the closet, their shoe-trees after them.

Day followed day in a tense and unvaried pattern. The sun rose and sank like a curtain on a play whose actors knew their lines but whose plot was dull and boring. The telephone rang, but when the Parrishes raced each other to snatch at the receiver, said nothing of importance. And Carrol and Penny gave up hope.

"Eighteenth, nineteenth, twentieth!" Penny made angry little jabs at the calendar. "Ye gods, the man could have written a dozen letters and sent 'em by freight."

"I told you not to worry, Pen. I really didn't think he'd come."

"He'll come." Penny clamped her lips together. "He's got to come. Oh, look! The telegraph boy!" She was down the steps and on the curb before the soldier could kick down the standard of his motorcycle. "I'll take it," she shouted above the roar of his motor. She seized his stump of a pencil, scratched into his book and was tearing open the yellow envelope as she ran back up the walk. At the steps she stopped to read, sank down and began to cry.

"Penny! Penny, darling, it doesn't matter." Carrol, who had been afraid to move, afraid to hope, dashed down the steps. Their arms went around each other and their tears dripped down together, onto the yellow paper, as they stared at it.

"He sounds so cold and—horrid—and unfeeling," Penny sobbed. "I don't see why he has to answer like this."

It was just as well perhaps, that she couldn't see, although Penny, being Penny, might have been undaunted by Langdon Houghton's mood of the morning. She certainly would have reacted to it better than did his secretary, who stood so meekly by, his pencil hovering above a waiting pad, his forehead creased into a frown and his ears ringing from the explosion.

"Why haven't I seen this letter from Mrs. Parrish?" The great Mr. Houghton was shouting. "Why wasn't it given to me? Can't I have any of my personal mail? Must I miss all my invitations because you are too stupid to do your work? Take a telegram."

Before the harassed little man could reply that, for three days the letter had stood propped conspicuously against an inkwell, his pencil began hopping in strange hieroglyphics across the page. He tried to keep up with the words that were flung at him and, like a stooge for a knife thrower, caught them as best he could.

"Mrs. David Parrish, Fort Arden. Greatly regret that due to previous engagements I cannot accept your kind invitation to visit you. Stop. Suggest Carrol proceeds by train as planned. Stop. Letter follows. Sign it and get it off."

"Yes, sir." The secretary juggled his note book and hustled out.

Langdon Houghton shoved the papers back on his desk and sat staring at Marjory Parrish's letter. "I should go," he thought. Then his mind pictured the trip into the mountains that had been planned, the trip which would clinch a business deal and meant the keen bracing talk of men around a camp fire. He spread a thick salve on the rough edges of his conscience by telling himself, "Carrol's all right. Lord, she's got everything a girl could want. And she wouldn't have much time for me anyway. Of course, if I'd known sooner . . ."

The ill humor of a few moments before vanished and he leaned back in the ivory and gold nest that was serving as a desk chair. "I haven't done much of a job with Carrol," he thought, his eyes wandering over the pampered setting of his hotel suite. "If her mother had lived . . ." He rubbed his fingers across his forehead, sighed, and turning back to his papers, plunged again into work.

Time sped by as, deep in reports, he went from one business matter to another. His brain, quick and keen, sorted facts and leaped to decisions. With machinelike rapidity he made notes, and it wasn't until he was exchanging one stack of papers for another that he saw the second letter. He pushed it to one side as he went on with his work and the letter fell with a soft little plop onto the thick rug at his feet. An hour later he leaned back.

"Carson!"

"Yes, sir?" The bedroom door opened and the baldish secretarial head popped in.

"Order me some lunch."

Langdon Houghton got up, ran his hands through his hair, his mind still filled with steel and railroads and bonds. He walked to the window and stood for some time, staring down into the street. Then he came back to his chair, picked up the letter at his feet, and sat tapping it on the desk. "It will work," he told himself. "It is the exact solution." He leaned back, satisfied with his decision, and became conscious of the envelope he held. Idly he lighted a cigarette, crossed his legs and opened it. At the first few lines a puzzled expression came into his eyes, but he sat up straighter as he read. Then he began to smile. When he had finished, he read it again, more slowly—and very, very thoughtfully. After the third reading he shouted:

"Carson!" There was no answer. He jumped up, threw open the bedroom door with a roar. Carson!"

"Yes, sir." The little man at the telephone put down the receiver. "I was just ordering your lunch, sir."

"Forget the lunch. Get Fort Arden on the phone. Get Mrs. Parrish." He slammed the door only to fling it open again. "And while you're waiting for the call I want a plane schedule to Kansas City and a reservation for the twenty-fifth."

"The little rascal," he thought as he stood waiting for the ring. "Lord, but she's clever. And she's right. That's the worst of it—the kid is right." He checked a sigh and shook his head. "I hope," he thought, "that I can learn to know Carrol as easily as I think I can this funny Penny."

While he waited, two thousand miles away another phone was ringing. Penny, the first to reach it, was clasping it to her stomach and screaming. "It's California!" she shrieked, "Carrol! Quick! It's California."

There was the pounding of many feet. Down the stairs they came, across the porch, with the shuffle of Trudy's slippers through the pantry . . . "Hello, hello," Penny was saying as David and Carrol hung over her shoulder and Bobby and Tippy squeezed in from the side. "Mrs. Parrish isn't here. This is her daughter; will he speak to me?" There was a wait. "He will? Oh, thank you." She turned to the others and grinned. "I think . . . Oh, hello. Yes, this is Penny. You are? Really? Oh, of course we want you!" She rolled her eyes and nodded her head until Tippy, catching her excitement jumped up and down and shrieked.

"Sh!" Carrol whispered, clapping her hand over Tippy's mouth, while Penny strained to hear.

"Yes, the Princess is right here. Oh no, she isn't in

the tower now. Would you like to speak to her? Umhum, I have the time and our airport will watch for you. Thank you for coming. Here's the Princess."

"Go on," she said, handing the instrument to Carrol who looked shy as she took it. "Say something."

Carrol's voice was quivering as she took the receiver and spoke. "Hello, Daddy," she quavered. There was a pause, then her eyes shone and Penny hugged herself in her excitement. "Oh yes, I'm so glad you're coming. Yes, I'm having a wonderful time. You'll like the Parrishes so much." Then her silence grew so long, punctuated only by her nods, that Penny longed to snatch the phone herself. At last Carrol said, "All right, I'll tell Penny. I don't quite understand, but I'll tell her. No, I don't need any money. We'll be watching for you. All right, Daddy. Goodbye." Penny punched her back and she added, "Penny says to tell you goodbye for her, too."

"I want to tell him goodbye. I want to tell him . . ." Tippy began climbing the table and Carrol hastily held the phone down to her. "Goodbye," she called. "G'bye, g'bye, g'bye." Penny pulled her away and Carrol spoke into the mouthpiece once more. "That was Tippy. We are all awfully happy, and we'll see you soon. Goodbye." She laid the telephone back in its cradle and Penny grabbed her around the waist.

"He's coming, he's coming, he's coming!" she chanted joyfully. "What did I tell you?"

She dragged Carrol to the divan and they fell on it in a tangled, laughing heap, with Bobby and Tippy on top of them. David sat on a chair, patiently waiting for them to become sane, and Trudy inched in. "Set up, Miss

Penny an' act natural," she begged. "I wants to know, does he likes chocolate chiffom pie?"

"He *loves* it!" Penny peeked out from under the pile. "He even eats it for breakfast. We all love it. Go on and make me one right now."

Trudy shuffled out and Penny fought her way to an upright position. "What did he say," she asked Carrol, "when you said 'I don't understand but I'll tell her'?"

"He said," Carrol pushed Bobby and Tippy off and looked at her, frowning. "You wrote something funny, Penny Parrish, because he said, 'Tell Penny the Good Fairy is a great old girl.' Now what did you write—and why did he call me 'Princess'?"

"I didn't write anything." Penny doubled up laughing. "I just . . ."

"Come on, out with it." Carrol jumped up and shoved Penny back into the pillows, holding up her chin. "Come on. Tell."

"I didn't . . ."

"Yes, you did. David?" Carrol turned to David who was only too willing to get into the fray. He held Penny's arms above her head, and as she wriggled to get free Carrol sat on her chest and tickled her.

"Somebody help *me!*" Penny panted. "Bobby! Tippy! Kick 'em or bite 'em or . . ." But Bobby and Tippy joined the winning side and she bit and kicked alone.

"I'll tell," she finally gasped through Tippy's curls. "Get off of me and I'll tell."

"Promise? Scout's honor?"

"Scout's honor."

They let her go and she sat up pulling her clothes into

place. "I said . . . Now Bobby, the fun's all over so go and sit down." She gave him a push and laughed as he knocked Tippy down like a ball with one ten-pin. "I said —oh, do I really have to tell?"

"You do!" David half stood and Carrol's hands slid toward her throat. "All right, but it sounds so silly. I said that Carrol was like a lonely princess in a tower and that the Good Fairy had asked me to help bring him. That's all. It sounds silly, doesn't it?" she said again.

"*Silly!*" David looked at her as though she had an empty swimming pool where her brain should be. "Ye gods!" He threw up his hands and staggered as he went out the door.

Carrol laughed. "It may be silly, pet," she said. "It really doesn't sound quite bright, you know; but it's bringing him. No one but you would ever think of such a thing." She looked at Penny in awe. "Maybe you're a genius," she concluded.

"Why, maybe I am." Penny began to feel herself, arms, legs, even the top of her head. "Does it show? Is anything sticking out of me?"

Bobby and Tippy crowded close to her, their faces worried little puckers. "Is anything wrong, Penny?" Tippy squeaked. "Are you broken some place?"

Penny scooped her up. "No, I'm not broken, sweetie," she consoled her. "I'm just a very wonderful person. I'm a genius."

She stood up and deposited the still doubtful baby on a chair and turned to Carrol. "Madam," she asked with a deep bow, "will you go walking with a genius?"

"I should be charmed." Carrol got up, completed the

formalities with a curtsy and accepted the arm that was offered her.

"And shall we celebrate our good fortune by the quaffing of liquid refreshments, madam? A tasty ice cream soda, shall we say?"

"By all means. Let us go in our coach and four."

They were halfway across the porch before Bobby came out of his daze to ask, "Can we go, too?" and for David to lean out of the swing and call, "Hey, where are you going?"

"Off on a little important business," Penny answered as they got their bicycles from beside the big tree and pedaled away. "We'll be back in a few minutes."

CHAPTER THIRTEEN

THE GREAT DAY DAWNS

"ONE MINUTE I wish the time would zoom and the next I want it to crawl. It just seems . . . Ouch!" Penny scowled at her finger where a drop of blood was oozing out. She stuck the finger in her mouth, sucked it, then retrieved her needle from the end of a long thread that was attached to a pucker in a bathing suit.

Carrol got up from the divan and went over to her. "Give me that thing," she said. "It's the darndest looking job of mending I ever saw."

"Why, Miss Houghton, you are becoming as slangy as I am." Penny handed her the bathing suit without protest and without shame, and hitched her legs over the arm of her chair. "As I was saying before my accident," she continued, "I can hardly wait for your father to get here—and yet, every day that goes by just brings the time nearer when you'll have to leave. That sounds sort of contradictory," she added, "but I guess you can figure out what I mean."

"Yes, I guess I can." Carrol sighed and began ripping out the maze of stitches that zigzagged around a very small hole. "I'll hate to go."

She searched about in the mess that was Penny's sewing basket for a spool of yellow thread while Penny watched her idly. "I made a list," Penny said at last, reaching into the pocket of her sport shirt, "of all the things we can do while he's here. I left some time for Mums and Dad, and sort of took him for ourselves at odd moments. I hope he won't think he's running on schedule like a train. I'll read it to you, shall I?"

Without waiting for Carrol's nod she scowled at the paper as she unfolded it, trying to decipher her own handwriting. "Let me see. Plane arrives two twenty-five. Meet with car. Only adult members of family included. That eliminates Bobby and Tippy," she explained emphatically. "Conducted tour of the post; one hour. Arrival home. Introduction of Trudy, Williams, Bobby and Tippy; fifteen minutes. (That means so he'll get to know 'em.) Guest room, luggage, and bath if he wants it; twenty minutes. I suppose," she looked up doubtfully, "he might want a bath. And so, as I don't know how long it takes him, I left ten minutes with nothing to do. We can just sit and talk to him if he gets through before time. Four P.M. . . Tea. Older friends of parents invited; Carrol and Penny to pass things. Carrol to wear blue dress and ribbon in hair. I want you to look pretty," she said with a serious nod. "I want you to simply stagger him."

Carrol answered, "All right, I'll try," her head bent so far over the bathing suit that Penny asked:

"You aren't near sighted, are you?"

Receiving only a negative shake in answer, she looked dubiously at the screen of curls, then went on with her reading. Six o'clock; guests depart. Family gathers on front porch. Conversation. Seven o'clock; dinner. Carrol to sit beside father. Eight o'clock . . ."

A giggle made her look up. Carrol was holding the bathing suit over her mouth and stifled explosions were coming from behind it. "I'm sorry." She looked at Penny's blank face and began again. "I tried—not—to—laugh," she sputtered, "but the part—the part about my father taking his bath . . ." She was off again, and this time Penny joined her.

Mrs. Parrish, curious about the cause of such merriment, leaned over the upstairs banister to ask what was so funny. And it was with the greatest difficulty that they made her understand. "Penny, you absurd child," she said, coming down the stairs, "don't you know you can't time everything to the minute? Can't you see Carrol's father looking at his list and figuring, 'now I have fifteen minutes for my breakfast. If I eat an egg I'll run two minutes overtime. If I skip it . . .' "

"I didn't mean it to be so exact, Mums." Penny looked up appealing for understanding. "It's only that the time is so short and . . ."

"I know it is, honey." Mrs. Parrish sat down on the divan and poked a pillow comfortably behind her back. "We will have to plan the big things, but we'll let the time in between wander along for itself, just as we always do. That is what we really want, you know; so that he can relax and be with Carrol."

"Okay." Penny tore the list into small pieces and popped them back into her pocket. "But what can we do for the big things?" she asked, still undaunted.

Carrol and Mrs. Parrish glanced slyly at each other and Mrs. Parrish shook her head. "You're a hopeless planner, Penny," she said. "What do you want to do?"

"Well, I'd thought of a tea."

"I've planned that, too. Now what?"

"Well . . ."

"Have you thought of a picnic?"

"My stars, no! Wait a minute." She jumped up, ran to the door that opened into the back hall and basement stairs, and shouted, "David! Come up here!"

Sawing continued from the cavern, so she shrieked again. "David! *Call* for you!"

"Why, Penny, you fibber."

"I am not. He'll think I meant telephone—but I didn't say it. It's the only way to get him."

She flattened herself against the wall as she listened to pounding feet on the stairs. As David turned into the hall she made a pounce for him. "I'm the call," she said, pinning his arms behind him. "Come over here."

"Why, you little bum." David shook her loose but she clutched him again and said quickly, "We want a picnic."

"A what?"

"A picnic. The moonlight picnic you promised us."

"Oh." David, seeing his mother curled up on the divan, realized that plans really were in the air, gave Penny a shove and went to drape himself over the back of a chair. "Fire away," he invited. "I've got to get Tippy's table finished before I leave, so make it snappy. When do you want the picnic?"

"Well . . ."

His mother opened her mouth to speak but he silenced her by making the plans himself. "I leave on the twenty-seventh," he said, "so let's make it the night of the twenty-sixth and have it a big farewell bust. I'll get the grooms, Penny and Carrol can invite the crowd and, Mother, you can plan the food. You and Dad and Carrol's father and the Prescotts can be the chaperones— and also do a little cooking. Okay?"

He turned away but his mother at last got a word in. "That's all very fine," she said. "But if you think I'm going to ride a horse, you're mistaken. I . . ."

"That's all right. I'll borrow the McNiel's trap and tandem; Dad likes to drive it. Now can I go?"

"Oh, for heaven's sake, go on." His mother laughed and called after him, "Thank you very much, kind sir."

"You're welcome," he returned as he clattered down the stairs. "If you want anything else come down to my shop."

"Let's go down," Penny said to Carrol an hour later when plans had been made and everyone on the post between the ages of fifteen and twenty knew the Parrishes were giving a moonlight picnic. "We can sit around in his shavings and talk."

They wandered down and spent the afternoon munching chocolate bars, and running up and down the stairs for telephone calls and cookies and milk. The hours sped away and all too soon it was dinner time, then bed time; and then the sun rose majestic and hot over the low hills.

"This is the day," Penny said, sitting up and squinting into the light. "Only this one more morning to wait."

"Pen?" A small voice came from Carrol's bed. "I just thought of something. Do you suppose his secretary and Mathews will come with him?"

"Who is Mathews?"

"He's Dad's valet; I never knew him to go any place without him."

"Oh my soul!" Penny bounced up and onto the foot of Carrol's bed. "Wouldn't that be something? You don't really think he'd bring them, do you?"

"I don't know. It just occurred to me."

They stared at each other in consternation, then began to giggle. "Can't you see the post?" Penny laughed. "To say nothing of Mums and Dad. What would we do with them?"

"Let's not mention it. If they *should* come I can whisper to Daddy to send them to the hotel in town. Oh, I hope . . ." She threw back the sheet and went resolutely about the business of dressing. "Surely he won't bring them," she thought as she took a dress from its hanger. "It's an awful way to feel, but I wish he weren't coming." She could hear Penny splashing in the bathroom and she leaned her head against the door frame. "Oh please, God," she prayed, "don't let it be too awful. Please make Daddy be nice." Penny pattered out from her shower and she straightened up and made a feeble attempt at humming.

"Don't sing before breakfast," Penny admonished. "It's bad luck."

The morning departed to join all other forgotten mornings, and after lunch Carrol had a reserved seat at a pre-view entitled The Parrishes Prepare To Meet a Plane. It was all very much as Penny had described it to her on the train, but it was even more hectic because more people were involved and because the guest was such an important one. Williams, either from awe or from Trudy's constant reminders, had outdone himself on the car, and it actually stood before the door ready and shining—except for the blue paint of its fenders which Bobby was rapidly transferring to the seat of his white trousers. Tippy, roused early from a nap that had only been a marathon around the sides of her crib, sat on a chair, round-eyed and plotting. Trudy, voluminous of apron, stood at the foot of the stairs, an eye on Tippy and head cocked toward the kitchen where Woofy had got himself by strategy.

"If you leave Tippy," Mrs. Parrish called, "if you leave her for an instant, we'll never find her when we come back. Where is David?"

"He's apoundin' in the basement. Shall I fetch him?"

"No!" Mrs. Parrish ran down the stairs as Trudy moved. "You stick to your post; I'll get him. And while I'm down here throw Woofy out."

"Yes'm." Trudy picked up Tippy, and while Mrs. Parrish pleaded from the basement stairs, she tried to entice Bobby away from a baseball team that had discovered the Parrish lawn to be an ideal diamond.

The girls came down starched in dotted swiss; Penny in pink and Carrol in the desired blue. They seated themselves sedately, but Penny winked as her father rushed in. He flung his hat on the divan and scattered crop, gloves and papers on various tables as he breezed through. His wife dashed in to speak to him, saw only the trail he had left and made a helpless motion to Penny.

"We'll never make it," she kept saying as Penny set the room to rights. "Did you hear a plane?"

Everyone rushed out, peered into the sky, and came back to sit down again. Mrs. Parrish went to the stairway and called, "Dave, are you sure they understand at the airport?"

"Sure, honey." His voice came back so muffled they could see him tugging at his boot straps. "Colonel Arnold phoned they have had a notice that the plane has left Kansas City."

"Well, hurry then. We've got to get off."

"Coming down."

David was called again; the girls were urged to sit in

the car, and Bobby was forcefully shoved inside the screen. Mrs. Parrish ran down the walk, climbed into the car and leaning over, began punching ear-splitting blasts from the button on the wheel. "We'll just *have* to start," she wailed with every toot. "A plane isn't like a train— it can arrive any old time it likes. Go get them, Penny."

Penny trotted obediently into the house in time to collide with her father coming out. "Can't wait for David," he shouted, buckling his Sam Brown belt as he ran. "Thought I heard a plane."

Penny hurried behind him and, as the purr of their motor mingled with a roar from the sky, David took the steps in a flying leap. He jumped on the running board, inched himself inside and closed the door.

"Someday you're going to get left," his father told him, peering up through the windshield as he drove. "I don't know whether we can make it this time, or not."

The big plane was taxiing across the field as they pulled up beside the hangar. "We did it again, by heck," Penny exclaimed as she climbed out. "You can't beat the Parrishes."

It was with a thankful sigh of relief that Carrol looked into the cabin of the plane. Only two figures were visible: the pilot who was pushing back an imitation glass covering, and the tall man who was preparing to climb down. "I should have known," she thought as she ran toward him. "I should have trusted him more." She held up her arms and waved and the others crowded around her. The pilot cut his motor and her voice was very loud in the sudden quiet as she called, "Hello, Daddy."

She received a quick kiss. "A kiss," thought Penny,

"that hovered between being a kiss or a handshake, and was surprised when it turned out to be a kiss." When it was her turn, after her elders had been blown upon by a chill wind, she put out her hand and searched the close-clipped sentences of greeting for some resemblance to the jolly voice she had answered over the telephone. She could find none; so she turned away to watch David seizing the luggage as it was swung down to him.

There was so much noise and confusion that Mrs. Parrish waited until they were walking across the turf to inspect the lean giant beside her. Trotting to keep up with his long strides, she looked up, up, up at his profile and felt as awed as when she had first craned her neck to see the Empire State building in New York. "Even though I'm so hot I'm melting," she thought, "he makes me feel that I should have worn a coat."

Major Parrish, in spite of his six feet, was looking a little up too, and his courteous remarks sounded as though he might be mentally thumbing through a book on etiquette; searching for a chapter entitled "How to converse with the deaf and dumb." David, bringing up the rear, only wished he owned the plane.

"I told you," Carrol whispered, "that he's simply impossible to know."

Penny looked at the back of the politely nodding head and compressed her lips. "Pooh," she answered, "he looks as frozen as the Arctic Ocean but I'll bet he'll be all right if we can get him thawed out. I'll see what I can do with him when we get home."

She spoke with such confidence that Carrol, whose spirits had sunk to zero, began to take hope, although she was very quiet in the car and left the burden of the conversation to the Parrishes. They struggled with it gallantly, but for all they could do it was not a success. The post seemed very small and grey as they toured it, and when they drove up in front of their own quarters the house looked as though it had shrunk.

"Why, the poor thing," Marjorie Parrish thought. "It looks as if it's hiding." She tapped up the walk ahead of the procession and glared at the two little faces pressed against the screen. "You're a nice house," she scolded mentally, "so stand up and behave yourself. We're nice people! And that awful clothes-horse is nice, too. I'll make him be."

She kissed the children, introduced them, and after one brief moment on the porch, when everyone seemed waiting for the executioner's axe to fall, walked resolutely inside. Penny made a dash and waylaid her in the hall.

"Gosh," Penny whispered, "he's even worse than Carrol said he'd be, isn't he? What'll we do with him?"

"Do?" Her mother stared at her, then shrugged. "I suppose," she said, "we'll do like the Hindoo, the very best we kin do." She looked at Penny's gloomy face and laughed. "Don't take it so hard," she advised. "He'll be all right." She went on to the kitchen to announce their arrival to her staff. Carrol took her place.

"Oh, Penny, it's awful," she whispered.

"I know." Penny nodded toward the door. "What are they doing now?"

"They're sitting. Even Bobby and Tippy are sitting. Your father, bless his heart, is rattling a mile to the minute."

"Isn't your father talking at all?"

"Unhunh. He only nods his head up and down every now and then and says "really? Oh yes. Really?' "

"Well," Penny drew herself up and swept the folds of an imaginary cape over her shoulder. "Here goes General Penny into the fray." She saluted smartly and caught Carrol's hand as she passed her.

"What do you think of your daughter?" she asked gayly as they came out on the porch. "Did I do her justice in my letter?"

"I don't believe you did." A little of the ice began to thaw in Mr. Houghton's eyes.

"Just a baby iceberg," Penny told herself as she appropriated a stool beside him. She looked at Bobby and Tippy who were welded solidly together in a chair, their eyes as big as saucers and their mouths, for once, looking as though they had zippers on them. "Scat!" she ordered. "Go find Woofy."

With evident relief they slid away and she was surprised to see the puzzled look on Mr. Houghton's face as his eyes followed them. "They are quiet little children, aren't they?" he remarked.

"Oh no!" Penny threw back her head and laughed. "Ask Carrol. They're just on their good behavior because you're strange. After you have been here a little while they'll climb all over you and you'll want to murder them; won't he, Dad?"

"He will, and I shan't blame him much if he does." Her father smiled and added, "We're fond of them, though."

Silence settled like a thick cloud of smoke. At last

Major Parrish fought his way through to ask, "Did Williams take in Mr. Houghton's bags?"

"He should have by now. Mother probably had to shake him off that cot he's fixed himself in the basement." Penny turned to the silent man beside her and grinned. "The service you get here will be remarkable," she confided, "remarkable for its absence. I know that, in books, they always usher the guest right upstairs where his clothes have been put away by a magic hand, so he can rest. Yours will be put away eventually, when Trudy gets around to it, but you don't want to rest, do you?"

She prompted him with an advisory shake of the head and received a reassuring shake in return. "That's good," she went on, "for we've asked some people in to meet you—later on, of course. They all want to know you, don't they, Carrol?" She turned to Carrol, adroitly drawing her into the one-sided conversation and was rewarded with a mute smile and a nod.

"I declare," she said in desperation, with a glance for her father who was sneaking off under pretext of speaking to David, "you two are the most tongue-tied people I ever saw! Why, if I hadn't seen Dad for months and months I'd be right there in the swing beside him." She sighed at their muteness and added coaxingly, "Go on over, Carrol. Go on!"

Carrol blushed, but she got up and went over to the swing. Her father put out his arm and she settled into it self-consciously.

"Does that suit you better?" he asked.

"Well," Penny surveyed them judicially, "it's better.

I think," she hesitated and looked at him shyly, "I think I'd better take the other side."

They slid along the cushions and Penny seated herself beside them. "*This*," she said with emphasis, "is the way I thought it would be." She sighed again, this time in apparent pleasure, and added: "This looks like we sounded over the telephone."

Langdon Houghton laughed. He laughed so freely and with such enjoyment that both girls looked at him in surprise. "You won't let a fellow be shy or stuffy, will you?" he asked.

"Not if I can help it." Penny turned and studied him thoughtfully. "You know, I'll bet you are shy," she said at last. "I thought you were haughty at first. But now, I think you're like Carrol—just quiet because you're shy. I am too, sometimes."

Both of her listeners teased her so hard she blushed. "I am; I really am," she defended. "I was awfully shy about sitting down here and talking. But I knew I had it to do. I knew we'd waste an awful lot of time getting to be friends if I didn't. And now, look at us. We're practically . . ."

"We're practically buddies," Mr. Houghton interrupted.

"That's right. And I expect we had better begin telling you about the things we do before the family comes back. Then you can enter into everything better." She leaned across him to Carrol who nodded.

"Where do you think we ought to start, Penny?" Carrol asked.

They were chatting away when Mrs. Parrish told herself that, as a hostess, it was her duty to go out. Penny's voice and Carrol's were mingled and a deep rumble was asking questions.

"What are you three talking about?" she asked, unable to believe her eyes or her ears.

They stood up and she noticed that Mr. Houghton had Carrol drawn to him with his arm about her shoulder. Happiness was painted on Carrol's face in glowing color.

"We're just gossiping," he said, and his eyes actually held a twinkle. "These are delightful daughters that we have."

"I wouldn't trade them for any others in the world." Marjorie Parrish smiled at the group. "But perhaps you would like to go up to your room. I think the confusion indoors has subsided and your bags are in."

"I'll take him." Carrol reached eagerly for the hand on her shoulder. "But he'll have to hurry because we want to show him our bikes before the guests come."

She led him away, and at the door looked back and grinned at Penny. "I believe," she teased, "that I can hold him to less than the twenty minutes you allowed."

As they disappeared Mrs. Parrish sank into a chair and leaning her head back, looked at Penny. "What happened?" she asked. "What did you do?"

"I just talked to him. I told him he was shy and to snap out of it."

"Well, I can't believe it," her mother said incredulously, "but the man is thawing. He was as cold as the frozen north. And now, he's actually thawing. Come here, sweet, and give me a kiss."

CHAPTER FOURTEEN

THE MOONLIGHT PICNIC

To THE impatient Penny the thawing process of Mr. Houghton was a slow affair. "He's like an electric refrigerator that you waited too long to defrost," she told Carrol as they dressed for the picnic. "You just get him dripping nicely and then the ice is so hard and sticks so tight you almost have to take a chisel to him. I had him going fine yesterday."

"I know you did." Carrol tossed her jodhpurs on a chair, then absent-mindedly sat down on them. "At the swimming pool everybody was crazy about him; but coming home he didn't say a word."

"And at the movies . . ." Penny sighed and shook her head. "Mums says he's all right when they go out and Dad thinks he's swell. I don't see why he gets these funny spells when he's with us." She ran a comb through her hair. "You'd better get dressed," she suggested, her chin in the air above the tie she was knotting. "The orderly is out back with the horses."

"I'm nearly ready." Carrol got up, shook her head over the wrinkles she had put into her breeches and began to pull them on. Penny at the door, listened to the chatter from below. The Prescotts were arriving, excited over riding in the trap; her father's voice was booming instructions, and Mr. Houghton was helping Williams with the hampers.

When the girls hurried down the walk an old-fashioned conveyance with its tandem of black horses was the center of an enthusiastic audience. Most of the neighborhood children surrounded it, and those who had been detained by their supper were streaking across the lawns. A colored soldier was alternately flapping his hat at an assortment of dogs and trying to point out to Major Parrish that there was a step by which the ladies were supposed to mount.

As the girls pushed their way into the crowd Tippy discovered it was her family that was preparing to drive away in such style, and turned herself into a flying pinwheel. Attached to Trudy's firm hand she made grabs for the bright red wheels and shrieked at the top of her lungs.

"You can't go, baby," Mrs. Parrish called down from her precarious perch on the high seat. "Although," and she turned to Langdon Houghton beside her, "for five cents she could have my place. I get dizzy every time I look down."

"It is a bit wobbly," he conceded. "But we'll even up better after the Prescotts get aboard."

Major Parrish was testing his reins like the gear shift of a strange car, and presently they jogged off, the audience falling in behind. Tippy's tears changed to smiles as she shouted "hep, hep, hep," with the others, and Trudy's face was a mirror of pride. The girls shooed off the last of the dogs and turned as David's irate shout reached them.

"Hey," he called. "Are you two planning to go?"

"We're coming." Penny caught Carrol's hand and they raced around the house. "We didn't mean to be late," she apologized, giving her beautiful Tango a pat. "But it was such fun watching them get off. I wish you could have seen Mum's face! And that big Saint Bernard of the Drake's trotting along in front made it look as if Dad had three horses."

"Well hurry." David tested the girths of both saddles and helped the girls to mount. When their stirrups were properly adjusted he took Lucky Souvenir from the groom and swung himself into the saddle. "I'll take care of the horses, Stewart," he said. "You won't need to come back."

"Thank you, suh." Stewart's broad face beamed as he watched the trio move off. "Sho' nice ge'm'an, Mistah David," he told the garbage cans and Williams' dilapidated car. "He give me fo' bits, too." Following along behind, he saw them turn the corner and pull into the crowd on the parade ground. Then he went his whistling way to the barracks.

"All set?" David called as Lucky stepped over the curb and broke into a hurried shuffle in his eagerness to reach his stablemates.

"You're a swell host!" Dick turned sidewise in his saddle as the horses rubbed noses. "We're all here and Mary has been threatening to go home."

"What's the matter, pal, scared?" Penny rode over to Mary who sat on a dejected animal.

"Scared? Me? Ha, ha, ha!" Mary wagged her head in attempted bravado then gulped and clutched the saddle. "I'm scared stiff," she whispered. "I'm miserable, and my clothes don't fit (I borrowed them from everybody on the post) and the horse doesn't trust me."

"Why, that's Robin," Carrol laughed, riding up on her other side. "Good old Robin. You don't have to worry about him."

"Oh, don't I?" Mary withered her with a glance. "He's rickety. He almost unjointed himself getting up here from the stables." She forced a sickly grin to show her ill humor was against the horse and not the girls, and clutched her reins tighter as David's voice rose above the others.

"We're off!" David called. "Fall in any way you like and take the road to Little Neck Canyon. Dad will lead the way."

"Off, is good," Mary muttered, wiggling herself more firmly into the saddle. "Where's Tubby gone? She isn't much happier about this than I am and she promised to poke along with me."

"I'll find her." Penny trotted into the milling mass of horse-flesh, routed Tubby out and joined Michael who was waiting conveniently near.

"Why, fancy seeing you here," he said, as his horse

fell into step beside hers. "Would you happen to be going my way?"

"I might—if I knew which way you're going." Penny laughed, then drew herself up. "I don't believe," she said primly, "that we have been properly introduced."

"Tut, tut, what an oversight!" Michael frowned with concern. "I do beg your pardon. I'm Lord Michael McMichael, and this is my horse, Sir Donald McDonald."

"How do you do, Lord Michael, and Sir Donald." Penny inclined her head gravely. "I am the princess Penelope Pasterdash. My horse, alas, bears the simple name of Bill."

"Princess." Michael halted a courtly bow, and with his hand to his mouth, said out of the corner of it, "How about it, kid; shall we can the phony titles and join them guys up in front?"

They laughed and rode away and Carrol, with a last call of good luck to Mary, moved her horse forward, too.

"Hold up a bit," David said, motioning her back. "I'll get them started and you and I can bring up the rear."

"You can't do that," Mary called going by in a jouncing trot. "Tubby and I've got it."

"Like fun you have," David jeered as Robin hopped off the three inch curb with a bounce that brought a shriek from his rider. "She'll go where Robin decides to go," he told Carrol. "Only I hope it won't be back to the stables."

The last of the riders paired off and Carrol and David jogged along behind them. At the outskirts of the post the cavalcade crossed a highway and turned into a dirt road that wound over vast acres of government reservation. There were rolling plains, bare but for the tangle of grass and wild flowers; deep, unexpected canyons, tree-shadowed and dark where the last glow of the sunset failed to reach; and now and then, high shelves of rimrock on which the riders were outlined like silhouettes against the sky.

"It's beautiful," Carrol breathed, looking up at the still rosy sky that was fast deepening into night. "And there's our moon."

"Yep. There's our moon." David laid his reins against Lucky's bobbing neck. "I suppose it will come up tomorrow night just like this. And I won't be here to see it. It's strange to think that I'll be on a train somewhere and Mother and Dad and Penny, and you, will all be here—just like we are tonight. I wish I weren't going."

"Oh, David, you don't!" Carrol wrenched her gaze from the moon to shake her head at him. "You're glad you're going. Why, you've waited years and years just to go."

"I know it. But," he looked shyly at her, "after having waited years and years—I'd like to wait three more days."

Carrol smiled. "I wish you could," she said lightly. "But as you can't, you've planned a wonderful finale. Listen, they're singing up in front."

"I suppose you might call it that." David grinned and gathered up his reins. "Perhaps we should add our melodious voices to theirs."

They pushed their horses into a trot and as they pulled in behind the long column, were singing with the rest,

"Shine on, shine on harvest moon." Songs, begun at the front of the line swept back in growing volume or were drowned in competition from the rear. When the horses trotted there was added the good creak of leather and the clang of metal as stirrups rang against stirrups.

After one last sprint they halted for the descent into Little Neck Canyon. Mary and Tubby huddled desperately to one side, peering down into its black depths as David explained where the camp fire would be. A few of the more eager were disappearing down the steep hillside and Mary looked after them piteously.

"I don't see," she begged, "why Tubby and I can't go around by the road like the carriage did. You're going clear up to the other end and all we'd have to do is walk down a nice little hill that's got a road on it."

"You can't do it because no one else wants to go that way, Mary," Bob answered in exasperation. "You might get lost and someone would have to come out to find you and it would be a mess. I told you I would hold your bridle until you got down the cliff." He sighed and turned to Jane. "You take Tubby. Now hold on to your saddles, and if you feel the horse slip, grip with your legs and lean back."

There came wails and moans as the foursome disappeared over the rim into blackness and the others waited until Bob's call told them the way was clear and that no prostrate bodies blocked the path. They wound through the black and silver stillness and were surprised when the glow of the camp fire lighted their small world in red. They were more surprised when Mary pranced up to them.

"Welcome," she shouted as she ran about, stretching up a hand to each new arrival. "Welcome to my new home. I'm here, and here I stay. I'm going to eat grass and berries, and nothing is ever going to get me out unless it's a derrick."

The trap was drawn into the circle of firelight. In the shadows, its horses were unhitched and tethered on a rope that had been strung from tree to tree for a picket line. Williams, aided by two soldiers who had bounced out with him in the car, was trekking up and down the hillside and was important and busy as he lugged the heavy hampers. There was the fragrant odor of wood smoke, the cool dampness of a summer night, the gay voices of happy people, and over it all the white radiance of the moon shining through the trees.

Carrol, turning Ragamuffin over to David, looked at it as one looks at a beautiful picture, never to be forgotten. "June moon," she thought, gazing up through the feathery branches, "please go on shining; don't ever, ever stop." Then she spied her father, long-legged on the ground beside Mrs. Parrish and she walked around the fire to them.

"It's fun, isn't it?" she asked, dropping to her knees beside him. "Aren't you glad you came, Daddy?"

"Very glad." His lips smiled but his eyes turned to Mrs. Parrish again and he went on talking of a summer he had spent in the Canadian woods. Carrol waited, the light dying out of her face, then she scrambled to her feet and joined a noisy crowd around Major Parrish and a box of frankfurters.

"I'll give you each one," he said, "but you can't do

any roasting until the boys finish cutting the sticks. It won't be long, so you might get your plates and start on the salad and rolls that Williams is putting out." He doled out his supply and dived into the carton again.

"Daddy?" Penny stuck her head down into the box beside his. "Could you sort of call your pal over here and put him to work? I can see Mums having the fidgets because Mrs. Prescott is cutting our best cake all crooked."

"Sure. Hey, Lang." Major Parrish beckoned pleadingly. "I'm being mobbed. How about giving me a helping hand so I can rake up the coals?"

"Coming over." Mr. Houghton unfolded himself and held out a helping hand to Mrs. Parrish. "We're off to work," he said. "You take the high road and I'll take the low."

They went their two ways around the fire; she to lay a cloth on the battered table that had stood under the trees for years, he to his relief job at the hot dog stand. Halfway there he was stopped by Louise, flushed of face and bearing a long forked stick on whose prongs two dripping wieners hung.

"One's for you," she said, her long lashes sweeping upward. "I have a roll for it, too."

"Why, thank you." Langdon Houghton smiled down at her from his great height. "It's very kind of you to be so thoughtful for us older folk, but we have a bit of work to do. We want you young people to enjoy yourselves. We'll catch a bite later on."

He patted her shoulder and strode away leaving her clutching her stick and conscious of the eyes she knew to be boring in her back. With an angry tightening of the lips she bounced one of the frankfurters into the grass, clamped the other in a buttered roll and strolled over to the crowd around the table.

"Just doing my good deed by the aged," she remarked, reaching for a plate. "After all, they get hungry, too."

Penny and Jane, watching the bit of by-play, turned to each other and winked. "I know what she wants," Jane said. "Her mother told me today that, though it's breaking her heart, she is going to send her darling east to school this winter. The Houghtons live on Park Avenue —and Park Avenue is a swell place to spend your weekends."

"Oh Jane, she wouldn't! Not after the way she's treated Carrol."

"Wouldn't she! You watch her. She'll be sweet to Carrol tonight."

"Meow, meow." Dick's curly red head rubbed against Jane's knee and he scratched at her boot.

"All right," she said leaning down and clouting him none too gently on the ear. "Let's all be cats together. Spft, spft. You're a snooping cat."

"Not me." Dick set back on his haunches and doubled his fists into paws. "Didn't hear a word, didn't listen; but kitty can see."

"Well, kitty sees too much—or not enough." Jane started to give him a push, changed her mind and gave him a pat instead. "Kitty go and get himself a nice bowl of milk," she said as she took Penny's arm and marched her off. "Dick's a nut," she laughed as they stood in line for their plates, "but I like him."

"I do, too." Penny took her plate, selected what she

wanted and made her way to a group sitting on a fallen log.

The boys, who had inherited the sticks from the girls and the job of roasting themselves as well as the frankfurters, were grouped around the fire. Frequently there was a spluttering hiss and jibes would follow an unfortunate as he returned to the box that held an inexhaustible supply. Gradually the blazing logs crumbled and fell apart, and fewer and fewer weighted sticks were tempting the licking flames. Conversation lagged as boots stretched toward the fire and heads rested against gnarled trees or in cupped hands. There was a restless stamping of the horses and the chirp of crickets, brave in the unaccustomed light, as the moon rose higher and higher in the heavens.

A group was singing "There's a long long trail awinding," and Penny, lying with her head on her arm, thought, "It's so peaceful. It doesn't seem that people could ever be mean or horrid. Maybe we wouldn't be if we did this sort of thing oftener." She began to hum softly and was conscious of someone stepping over her.

"Sorry," Louise said. "Hope I didn't kick you."

Penny lifted her head to answer and was surprised to see that Louise was not speaking to her, but to Carrol, who sat a few feet away and was tuning the strings on Dick's mandolin. Shamelessly, she rolled nearer to listen.

"I had good news today," Louise was saying. "I'm going east to school this fall."

"Really?" Carrol thumped a string and smiled. "I know you'll love it."

"I suppose I shall. I get awfully bored here." Louise

leaned against a tree and looked at the fire. "But I suppose I'll get lonely, too. Couldn't you come up and spend a week-end? I'll be quite near New York."

"I'd love to," the mandolin twanged softly as Carrol, too, looked into the fire, "but you see, I'll be at Grandmother's. I don't live in New York."

"You *don't*? Why, I thought . . . Oh, Mr. Houghton. Please come here." Louise turned, shoulders lifted in appeal, as Carrol's father came toward them. "I'm going to be near New York next winter and Carrol and I could plan such wonderful times—only Carrol says she won't be in New York."

"Well then, I imagine she won't." Mr. Houghton looked from Carrol's embarrassed face to Louise's disappointed one. "Carrol certainly knows where she's going to be."

"But you could make her come, Mr. Houghton. We could have such grand week-ends together, and could go to theatres and lovely places to lunch."

"In New York, you mean?"

"Of course—and I mean at school, too."

"You'd like to visit Carrol?"

"Why, I'd love to! And I'd want Carrol . . ."

Mr. Houghton interrupted her and his eyes were cold. "Did you ask her to visit us, Carrol?"

"Oh, Daddy," Carrol dropped the mandolin and jumped to her feet. "I—I—" she stammered in confusion, looking helplessly from her father who was waiting, impassive, to Louise, who was striding away. The lump in her throat prevented her saying more. Blinking back her tears she stooped down and picked up the mandolin.

"Carrol?"

"Yes, Daddy?"

"Never mind." Langdon Houghton turned on his heel and left her standing there.

"Hi, Carrol, I've been looking for you." David slipped his arm through hers and Penny, who was halfway up lay down again. She knew that David could do more for Carrol than she could.

"Where have you been hiding?" David asked, taking the mandolin and dropping it into Dick's lap as they passed him. "I got so tied up helping Williams move that kicking mule of a Clip Along that I thought I was never going to get back. He's a nasty brute."

He chatted on as they walked around the circle and Carrol gulped down her heartache as she pretended to straighten the open collar of her shirt. "It's his last night," she told herself. "Don't make him unhappy."

"Stand still." David stopped her fumbling fingers and laid the collar neatly over her coat. "There. Let's sit down where we aren't so close to the fire."

They dropped down on the soft grass and David picked up a twig. He twirled it in his fingers and laughed. "This makes me think of the day we discussed Dad's famous ride. Remember? I'll bet I scratched up a bucket of dirt deciding what to do."

"You were pretty much upset." Carrol drew up her knees and clasped her arms around them as David rolled over on his stomach and broke the twig in two.

"See these people?" David asked. "This is me and this is you. Here I am at West Point," he stuck a twig into the ground, "and here you are in New York."

"But I won't . . . Humhum, I see. Now, what do we do?" She leaned forward as she asked and the little twig that was in New York began to move.

"Why, you come up to see me. Maybe in a car or maybe on the bus that brings all the other femmes up for week-ends. And we have a grand time—and then you have to go home." The twig went slowly back along the way it had come and David turned his head with a grin. "And *then*," he said with careful emphasis on each word, "there is a big football game in New York. And all the cadets come down. Ping!" The taller twig jumped the intervening space and both hopped about so wildly that it was evident they were registering joy.

Carrol laughed and David rolled over on his side and looked at her. "You will come, won't you, Carrol?"

"You know I will, David. If I'm in New York, of course I'll come."

"And you'll write to me? You'll write often?"

Carrol laughed again. "I'll write as often as you do," she promised. "How often will that be?"

"Oh boy, oh boy!" David went from his side to his back. "That'll be just about five letters a day. Five letters and a post card."

"And when are we supposed to study?"

"We aren't. We just write letters. Gosh, you're beautiful in the fire-moonlight." His head came up and he rested on his elbow staring at her so fixedly that she blushed. "You wouldn't like to have your picture hanging in my locker, would you?" he asked suddenly.

"David." Carrol shook her head and looked down at him. "I never saw this side of you before. You're more like Penny or Bobby, or even Tippy." She reached down, picked up the twigs and rolled them between her fingers. "You, you sort of embarrass me."

"Do I?" David grinned but continued his staring. "You know," he said, "I'm kind of fussed, myself."

They were still laughing when they became conscious of a general flurry. The singing had stopped, the horses were being harnessed to the trap and Williams was throwing water on the fire.

"Are you two going home tonight?" Mary called. "And have you seen my sweater?"

"Sure, we're going home," David answered as he and Carrol scrambled up. "But I thought you weren't."

"Oh, yes I am." Mary nodded. "Tubby and I are going in the car with Williams, and the soldiers are going to ride our horses. I wish I could find my sweater."

She disappeared into the gloom and Carrol and David walked to the picket line. There was a crowd around the trap and only a few horses were being saddled. Louise was there, checking Clip Along for cuts or bruises, and she looked through Carrol with a long, hard stare. Carrol would have gone to her, to explain as best she could, but David was beside her, putting Ragamuffin's halter shank into her hand.

"Hold him while I get his bridle on," he ordered. "We'll let him wear his halter underneath, then he'll be all ready for bed when he gets home."

He whistled as he put on the saddle and Carrol, patting Ragamuffin's soft muzzle watched Louise mount Clip Along. She wished there were something she might say.

"Okay." David dropped the saddle girth and held out his hand to her. "Come on, I'll boost you up."

No one could ever say just how it happened. One moment Carrol was in the saddle, searching for her stirrup, with Ragamuffin placid and sleepy; the next, Clip Along was whirling. His heels lashed out at Ragamuffin who reared and plunged to escape those vicious hooves. Carrol lay on the ground, very white and still, and blood was trickling slowly down her forehead.

CHAPTER FIFTEEN

HAPPINESS IN THE NIGHT

"How is she, Penny?"

"I don't know."

David pressed his face against the white frame of the door as though his eyes must pierce the wood into that small hospital room where Carrol lay. "Can't you go in and ask?"

"I can't, David; they sent me out." Penny began to sob and David left the post he had guarded for an hour to go to her.

"Don't cry, Pen. She's all right." He stroked her hair as she leaned against him and as her sobs broke out afresh they clung to each other in frightened misery.

"It's all my fault," David muttered, his eyes still on the door. "If anything happens to her I'm to blame."

"Oh, no, David."

"Yes, I am. I knew that beast of a Clip Along—and I

243

knew Louise. I should have led Carrol's horse away from them."

"Oh, David, you don't think Louise would *deliberately* try to hurt Carrol, do you?"

Penny's tear-brimmed eyes looked up at him and he shook his head. "I don't know. But if she did!" He tightened his lips and pushed her roughly away. "Try to get in again. Sneak in. *Do something!*"

"All right." Penny went to the door and laid her hand on the knob. As she turned it the door opened and her mother came out. Her face was haggard, but she nodded and smiled.

"She's all right," she said, her voice shaking with emotion. "She's going to be all right." She leaned weakly against the wall and as they rushed to her she held her finger to her lips. "The X-rays show that no bones were broken," she said quietly, "and she's conscious now. That's what frightened me. She was unconscious so long."

"You're sure, Mums? You aren't trying to pretend?"

"I'm sure, David. Let's go down to Colonel Babcock's office; he said there would be coffee; and your father is waiting there."

She drew them along with her and although David glanced longingly at the closed door, he put his arm around her and said gently:

"Poor little Mums, we've given you a bad night, haven't we?"

Behind the door the light was dim and there was only the sound of a nurse's starched skirt rustling. Carrol's head turned slowly on the pillow and her eyelids fluttered.

"There you are, little girl. Feel better, now?"

The deep voice above her blurred into a kindly face as the doctor took her limp hand and smiled down at her. "You had a very nasty crack, but all you have to show for it is a plaster on your head." He patted her hand, touched his fingers lightly to her wrist and turned away. "Right as rain," she heard him say.

There was a low murmur of voices at the door, the nurse bent over her, and Carrol's eyes drooped down again. She tried to remember what had happened to her, why she was here. There was the picnic and Ragamuffin; David had saddled Ragamuffin—then there was a blank. A long blank that had brought her here. She heard the nurse tip-toeing to the door, rustling as she slid through. She turned her head and winced with pain. "It hurts," she told herself plaintively, since no one was there to hear. "My head hurts."

"I know, Carrol."

The voice that came from beside the bed was low and tender, the hand that took hers as it fumbled among her curls gripped it firmly.

"Daddy. Oh, Daddy."

"There, there, dear." Strong arms gathered her close and gentle fingers wiped away her tears. Her father's arms held her and he was murmuring, "Don't cry, honey. Don't cry."

"I won't."

She reached out a weak hand to stroke his face.

"You're all 'frowned up,' as Tippy says. You mustn't worry. Smile."

To please her he managed a feeble smile which spread into a real one as she smiled with him. His arms tightened and he looked down at her tenderly. "I think I'll always keep you here," he said, "just like this; then you couldn't ever get hurt."

"I'd like to stay," Carrol sighed. "I wouldn't even mind being in bed if I knew you were coming home every night."

"You wouldn't? Oh, my little girl, I've been such a rotten father."

"No, you haven't, Daddy. It's only that we haven't been together very much."

"I know. And that was my fault, too." He smoothed a stray curl back from her forehead and spoke to her soberly. "There is nothing that I can ever say to you, Carrol, that will change the past. I've been selfish and thoughtless, and I've been lonely, too. I wanted you with me after your mother died but I listened to your grandmother because it didn't seem possible that I could care for a baby and make her happy. I thought I was doing the right thing."

"I think you did. I've always been happy with Grandmother. The only thing . . ." Carrol dropped her hand to his coat, running her fingers along the smooth flannel lapel. "It's—it's rather hard for me to say, but—well, I didn't think you loved me."

"Carrol, dear, I always loved you. But I saw you so seldom. Even when you were a baby I didn't know what to say to you. Why, I didn't know fathers were meant for anything but to write checks and send presents until I came here and saw Dave Parrish. I've tried to act as he does, but you see, I've had a good many years to overcome, and I wasn't sure that I was copying him very well. Tonight, when you didn't want Louise to visit you—and said you wouldn't live in New York . . ."

"Why, Daddy, I didn't mean that!"

"You didn't? I thought you did. And I almost asked you after Louise had stalked off."

"Oh, my poor Daddy." Carrol sighed. "What a lot of things we have to make up to each other." She hugged him tighter to her and whispered, "Here I was, thinking you didn't like me, and you were thinking I didn't want to be with you. You were trying to be like Major Parrish and I was wanting you to be like yourself. I'm so glad we're straightened out at last."

"So am I, dear. I suppose there will be many times when I'll seem cold or shy, or engrossed in business; but I want to be a good father, Carrol, and I want to make up to you for all the love you've missed. It often takes a very severe lesson to bring a man to his senses." He caressed her cheek and added, "Speaking of senses, I think my knees are slowly breaking through the ceiling of the room below."

Carrol laughed. She laughed freely and happily, now, and even lifted her head to watch him rub his aching muscles. "I feel fine," she said as he sat down on the bed beside her. "Couldn't we go home?"

"Not yet. The doctors want you to spend the night here, what's left of it, and tomorrow. Just to be safe, you know."

"But I can't. David is going away tomorrow. He'll be so worried about me and I'll have to be at home so he can go away happy. He'll think it was all his fault."

"But we know it wasn't. It doesn't matter whose fault it was; if it has no ill effects it was a blessing in disguise. Now, if you will lend me your ear I have a plan. I have to whisper."

Carrol pushed her hair back above one ear, a look of surprise on her face as her fingers encountered the patch of adhesive tape. "My goodness," she said, "I didn't know I had that. And I'm bald in one spot."

"It's where they shaved your hair for the little cut." Her father took her hand and laid it on the covers. "I'm treating you as though you were about two," he said with a shame-faced grin, "but you are to me, tonight. You'll be an old lady before I catch up with all the years I missed."

"I hope so." Carrol snuggled down comfortably and her eyes sparkled as he whispered to her. From time to time she nodded and when he finished exclaimed, "Oh, Daddy, it's perfect! When can we tell them?"

"Right now, I think, from the voices I hear outside the door. I'll find out."

Outside, David and Penny had returned to their watch. "I don't see why we can't go in," David kept muttering. "If she's all right you'd think someone would go in or come out, or something. Do you think Mums told us the truth?"

"Of course she did." Penny reduced to sitting on the floor from sheer exhaustion looked up at his endless pacing. "Do you suppose she'd be sitting downstairs calmly drinking coffee if Carrol weren't out of danger? You have to stop being so nervous."

"But it was my fault. How would you like it," David flung at her over his shoulder, "if you took a girl out and let her get killed or scarred for life? If I'd gone to Mums when I wanted to and told her about Louise this wouldn't have happened."

"Oh, but David, it would. And Mummie says it's just a small cut. Besides, you wouldn't know that Clip Along was going to act the way he did."

"I should have." He paced the length of the corridor and back and stopped before her. "I can't go tomorrow, Pen."

"You have to, David."

"I can't, I tell you. Carrol's the swellest girl I've ever known. I'm not going to let her get all bashed up and then go off as if I didn't care. Gosh, she might be crippled for life."

"David, she isn't going to be crippled. Mums told you so." Penny, seeing her parents coming up the stairs at the end of the hall, got stiffly to her feet. "Dad," she cried, running to meet them, "tell David that Carrol is all right. Tell him again what the doctor said. He's got himself so worked up he says he won't go to West Point tomorrow."

"I won't, Dad." David went to meet them, too. "Louise has done rotten things to Carrol ever since she's been here, and we've let Carrol take 'em. But I won't go off with anything like this hanging over me."

"All right, son, now wait a minute." Major Parrish

sighed as he put his arm around David's shoulder. "I know how you feel. Louise has behaved rottenly, I'll grant you that. But don't let's say that this accident to-night was anything but an accident. Louise was pretty much cut up about it—she's been downstairs with her father, crying. If this was an accident—and you must admit Clip Along is a hard horse to handle—and you make an issue of it, you may be branding a girl for life, for something she didn't do."

"No, I wouldn't." David's jaw was stubborn. "I stood right there—and I saw it."

"David. Please." His mother turned him to face her, her hands holding his elbows. "Will you do something for me? Will you promise not to say anything to Louise or to Carrol until Carrol speaks of it to you? She knows what happened. Let her be the one to place the blame if there is any. I think she will talk it over with you."

"All right." David patted her cheek and turned away. "But I won't go tomorrow."

Major Parrish looked at his wife and sighed, then walked over to the door and lifted his hand to tap gently. As the others stepped up behind him, hoping for a glimpse inside, the door opened and Langdon Houghton said with a smile, "Come in."

Behind him Carrol was propped up on pillows, her face pale but happy above the coarse white hospital gown. She kissed Penny then turned to Mrs. Parrish, holding the outstretched hand. "I'm so sorry to make so much trouble," she apologized. "You all look so tired and worried."

"We aren't tired, dear." Mrs. Parrish leaned over and

kissed her, too. "And we aren't worried now. We're relieved and happy."

"You gave us a scare," Major Parrish said from the
foot of the bed where David was hovering. "But your
white plaster is very becoming."

"Is it?" Carrol touched the white patch gingerly. "It's
right where I can cover it with a flower or a ribbon." She
smiled at them, then her eyes rested on David. "I messed
up your last evening terribly, David, didn't I? No, please
don't say anything; I know I did. And because I did, we
have a lovely plan we want to ask you about. Come here,
Daddy."

Her father came obediently around the side of the
bed and took her hand. "Shall I tell them, or will you?"
he asked.

"Oh, you."

"Shall I tell it the long way, or shall I just pop the
question?"

"The long way. You tell it so nicely, and they won't
mind ten minutes more when they're already so sleepy."

"Very well." He sat down on the side of the bed and
the others perched at the foot or found chairs where they
could watch the complete happiness in Carrol's eyes.

"Well," he began, "this is the scheme Carrol and I have
been in here concocting, when she was supposed to be
resting. I don't think it hurt her. In fact," he patted the
hand he held, "I think it healed another hurt that needs
a lot of mending."

Mrs. Parrish smiled. "I think I know; and I'm awfully
glad."

"Thank you, so are we. Well, the point is, that after

we had had our little talk, I realized we had some plans that needed changing. Carrol was going to the sea shore with her grandmother but she has agreed to give that up and to stay with me in New York. I have some business there that must be attended to. As Carrol can't travel for a few days, and as I must be in New York on the first, and as David, I believe, has an appointment with his government, we thought the three of us could fly east together. How does it strike you?"

There was a silence when Mr. Houghton finished speaking as his audience tried to grasp his words. Then Penny jumped up and threw her arms around David. "There you are," she cried. "You're all fixed. And you aren't going tomorrow. Oh, isn't it wonderful?"

"Why, yes, yes it is," her mother answered vaguely, unable to realize that her son was to have three days grace at home and would be whisked away in a plane. "What do you think, Dave?"

"I think it's swell." Major Parrish held out his hand to Langdon Houghton. "I don't understand why I didn't think of it myself. David got upset tonight and vowed he wouldn't leave tomorrow. I was so worried I never thought of sending him by air."

"But you aren't sending him. That's the point of our scheme. I'd already chartered a plane for the thirtieth, and we're all going in it like a house party. You borrowed my girl all summer, now I'm going to kidnap your boy."

The two men grinned at each other and David came around the side of the bed. "Thank you, sir," he said. "I don't deserve it after my carelessness of Carrol tonight, but there's not a chance of me refusing."

Mrs. Parrish stood up. "We must go now," she said decisively. "We've tired Carrol and she needs rest." She leaned over to smooth the pillows and whispered: "Would you like me to stay, dear? I'd love to sit here beside you."

"Oh no." Carrol thanked her and looked up at her father. "This is the happiest day I've ever had, and I just want to lie here and think about it. I'm really not sick, you know," she added. "Even my head doesn't hurt any more."

She waved at Penny who, unable to get close, was blowing kisses and making signs that she would be over early in the morning. "I'll miss our room," she told her, "but I'll be back in time for dinner. Goodnight, Major Parrish. Goodnight, Daddy."

Her father bent over her, his cheek pressed to hers. "Goodnight, little girl," he whispered. "We're going to have a wonderful time."

David was the last to leave. He stood looking down at her as the others filed from the room. "Carrol," he ventured at last.

"Yes, David, I know." Her level gaze met his. A long look passed between them, then she held out her hand. "Thank you for taking me to the picnic. You don't know how much it has meant."

"Good. See you tomorrow." David gave her fingers a squeeze. "Same good sport," he said as he turned away.

As the door closed behind him it opened again to admit the stiff rustle of a disapproving nurse. "I had no idea you were awake," she scolded. "The colonel gave you a sedative and only your father was to sit with you. You weren't to have company."

"They weren't company." Carrol tossed off the reprimand happily. "They were the dearest people in the world, and I shouldn't have slept a wink if I hadn't seen them."

"Well," the nurse bustled about adjusting windows and tidying the room, "it doesn't seem to have hurt you, but you must go to sleep now. It's after two o'clock."

"I will." Carrol lay on her pillows watching her coat and her jodhpurs and her white shirt, covered with blood, being folded neatly and laid on the closet shelf. It seemed such a little while since she had put them on, laughing and chatting with Penny. So much had happened since. And now, they were folded away—and she wouldn't see them again until they were clean.

"Oh, nurse." She raised herself on her elbow. "Would you mind letting me have the coat for just a minute?"

"Of course not. Just the coat?"

"Yes, please."

She watched while the coat was brought to her, reached into the pocket and said shyly: "There was something I wanted to take out." Her hand came out, a stubby little fist. "Thank you."

"That's all you want?"

"Umhum, thanks. That's all."

The nurse, with but a normal curiosity, folded the coat again and wondered what the closed fingers held. But she only said: "Shall I turn out the light?"

"I can do it, thanks." Carrol reached up to show that she could touch the chain and they said goodnight.

As the door closed she bent above the night table that stood beside her bed. Carefully on its white porclain surface she laid two little twigs. Then she snapped off the light and lay smiling in the dark.

CHAPTER SIXTEEN

HAPPINESS AT HOME

"It's almost time to bring Carrol home, Penny," Tippy sang out from the bottom of the stairs. "Daddy says are you going with them?"

"Of course I'm going." Penny clattered down the stairs and gave a leap from the landing. "And don't you touch anything in my room. I've worked all morning putting it in order and fixing flowers and things. And don't you let Woofy in there." She turned in the doorway to make the direst threat she could imagine. "If you do," she said, shaking her finger, "I'll take back the doll I gave you."

"I won't, Penny. I won't touch a thing. An' I won't let Mummy touch anything, or David or Daddy or Woofy or Bobby. Could Trudy touch something, Penny?"

"No, Trudy couldn't touch something either." Penny

was halfway across the porch and Tippy was left asking herself questions.

"I don't think," she said solemnly as she inched through the screen and seated herself on the top step, "that Penny wants anyone to go into her room. I mustn't let them."

After a time the responsibility began to weigh heavily on her. "Here, Woofy, Woofy, Woofy," she called. But no familiar puppy peeped out from under the bushes. "I s'pect he's gone into Penny's room," she told herself. "I'd better go and see."

She trotted up the stairs, calling Woofy as she went, and at the door of Penny's room which was unexpectedly closed, she felt a twinge of doubt. "Woofy pushed it shut," she said, reaching for the knob. But inside there was no sign of Woofy. Everything was in order as Penny had said it would be. The lacy pillows were freshly pressed, crisp curtains swayed gently in the breeze, and on a low table beside the chaise longue stood Penny's silver vase filled with flowers.

Tippy walked about the room looking for Woofy. He wasn't in the closet or in the dresser drawers or among the shining crystal bottles on the dressing table. By the time she finished searching she was sprayed liberally with perfume and was wearing Penny's best hat.

She had decided to abandon the hunt, having exhausted all the interesting places, when the vase of flowers caught her eye. Feeling that since she was in she might as well see everything, she skipped over to inspect it.

"Pretty roses," she admired, lifting the vase to smell

them. Unfortunately for Tippy and the rug, the vase was filled with water. When she had finished sniffing it was not so heavy to hold and she looked with dismay at the puddle at her feet.

"Oh dear." She set what remained of the floral display on the table and hurried into the bathroom for a towel. Nothing she could do dimmed the damaging evidence of her mishap, and as all her aids lay in a crumpled heap in the bath tub, she made one more trip for the bathroom rug. This, to her great satisfaction was pink, and although it was a soft woolly mass of looped string she laid it carefully over the spot and hoped it might go unnoticed.

Like a criminal repairing the scene of his crime she wiped the table off with her dress and decided to take the vase down to Trudy for reconditioning. She clasped it to her stomach and tiptoed toward the door. Carefully she closed it and carefully she tiptoed down the stairs. Halfway down she bethought herself of something and tiptoed up again. Sitting in beruffled state on the window-ledge of her own room was Georgia, her doll. She pushed the vase farther under one arm and scooped up the unwinking creature with the other.

She had no idea where Georgia might hide until the fuss blew over—for that there would be a fuss she had no doubt. "I was very naughty," she said, kissing the round pink cheeks. "But I'll hide you."

The problem was, where? She had great faith in Penny's powers of persistence and there was no place Georgia could go that Penny couldn't follow—not if Georgia was to come back looking like anything.

She was standing in the lower hall, at a loss for a hideaway, when she heard voices outside. Like magic her mother appeared on the stairs, Trudy blocked the diningroom door and David had the basement stairs. She was trapped, so she stood like a cherub, her doll in her arms and the roses under her chin.

"Tippy, darling!" Carrol cried, as she came in with her father. She held out her arms and Tippy hurried into them.

She was thankful for the temporary shield they made and tried to hide from the voice that was calling from the porch, "Wait till you see our room, Carrol." It would be a brief haven she knew, but hoping to make it a good one while it lasted, she held up the vase of flowers and chirped;

"I got you these."

"Bless your heart." Carrol took the vase and kissed her on her quivering chin. "They're lovely." She held them up and her father's arm tightened around her.

"Do you know," he exclaimed, "I was so frightened about you that I forgot to send you flowers!"

"So you did!" Carrol clutched him around the neck, roses and all. "Oh, Daddy, that's the nicest thing you ever said to me!"

Everyone gathered around them and Penny, half in half out, saw the roses. "I knew it!" she shrieked. "I knew it! Where is that child?" She dashed through the house, but Tippy, fleet of foot, was gone.

Trudy shook her head. "Fine doin's," she said. "Here's Miss Carrol jus' come home, and all these ruckshuns takin' place. I wouldn't blame her if she went right back where there's peace an' quiet."

"Oh no, Trudy." Carrol went obediently to the divan and settled herself against the pillows Mrs. Parrish was arranging. "I like ruckshuns. I promised I'd lie around all day today, but tomorrow I'm going to make a few myself."

"Well, it'd be the first time you ever did." Determined to have her say, Trudy folded her hands over her white apron. "You's the bes' child in the world. Now, what's that?"

"That" was a series of shrieks from Penny's room. David went to the foot of the stairs and his mother looked up anxiously as Penny shouted from above. "I wish you'd see it," she screamed. "It looks like the end of the battle of Bunker Hill. It's a mess!"

"Well, come on down and stop stewing," David called. "Carrol has seen it when it looked worse and you won't find Tippy until dinner time."

Penny came down the stairs her arms full of towels. "Just look at these," she groaned, dumping them on the floor. "I picked out all the prettiest ones—and now look at them. It must be a joy to be an only child."

"If you'd like to get rid of Tippy," Mr. Houghton offered quickly, "Carrol and I could find room for her in the plane."

"You know I wouldn't." Penny grinned at him as she picked up the towels and stuffed them into Trudy's waiting arms. I don't suppose I'll even get rid of Georgia."

She shoved Carrol's feet aside so that she might sit by her. Trudy bore the towels away and Mrs. Parrish remembered some last minute purchases she must make at the Post Exchange. Mr. Houghton offered to drive over with her and after careful instructions to Carrol not to tire herself they departed. David sat down on an ottoman and looked at the girls.

"The calm after the storm," he said. "So much has happened that it seems like a let-down, doesn't it?"

"It seems grand to me." Carrol stretched luxuriously and Penny asked David:

"Aren't you going to the train with Dick and Mike?"

"They're coming by here first and I'll go down with them."

"You're sure you don't mind being left behind, David?" Carrol asked. "Now that the time has come to leave?"

"Mind?" David lifted his eyebrows. "After what I told you last night? Does that sound like I minded?"

"What did you tell her?" Penny sat up, ears cocked.

"You're so curious I don't see how you ever wait for Christmas," David told her, going to the door. "I hear guests arriving.

"Hi, there," he called as a car door banged. There was a clatter on the walk and Dick burst in. He was trailed by Michael and Bob, while Jane and Mary stopped on the porch to talk to David.

"Welcome home, partner," Dick said, dumping a box of flowers into Carrol's lap. "You don't look hurt to me."

"I do, too." Carrol slipped the cord from the box. "If I don't show traces of suffering I'm not going to fall off of a horse any more. Oh, thanks, Dicky, they're gorgeous."

"Just something my old man paid for." Dick watched her pin the corsage on her white dress before he was pushed aside by Michael, with Bob's head crowding him completely out.

"Sorry about the tough luck, Carrol," Michael said. "But you can munch on these while you're out of circulation." He gave her a box of candy and she looked up, surprised.

"Why, it's like a birthday," she exclaimed. "I'm overcome."

"Don't I get anything?" Penny's lower lip curled out and she sniffled.

"You can get the dishes, pet, before the ice cream melts." Mary, carrying a dripping cardboard bucket was followed by Jane with an evil-looking baker's cake.

"It's a party," Jane called as she hurried through to the kitchen. "It's a reunion and a farewell all at the same time."

While they were gone Dick sat down and studied David. "Aren't you somepin'!" he jeered. "Mr. Gotrocks flying to the Point. Well," he shrugged his shoulders, "we'll all look the same, Senator, when we get dyked out in those grey flannel shirts."

They laughed, as he meant they should, and a moment they had dreaded was safely passed. The ice cream was brought in, and the cake which tasted worse than it looked was crumbled over plates. No one mentioned that one member of the crowd was absent.

"I must say something," Carrol kept thinking. "If I don't, if I don't speak of Louise, they won't—and it will be awful." She listened to the chatter, and when there was a lull looked around the group. "Why didn't Louise come with you?" she asked. "It really isn't a reunion unless we're all here."

If she had cried "fire" there could have been no greater panic. They looked ready to flee for their lives and it was only David who managed to say sanely:

"Oh, I forgot to tell you. She went with her mother to Yellowstone this morning."

"She did? Then I won't see her until fall." Carrol's eyes sparkled and she said: "You know, I'm going to live in New York this winter, with Daddy."

"Really? How marvelous!"

The girls surrounded her and Dick yowled with delight. "That fixes me up," he gloated. "My date problem is settled for the winter."

"Oh, no it isn't, pal." Michael shook his head. "Sorry to spoil your plans but don't forget I'm in there pitching, too. And I don't imagine David, with the last say so in New York, is going to be left out. You'll have to take your turn with the rest of us."

"Very well." Dick arose like a hero. He extended one hand to Michael, the other to David. "May the best man win," he cried. Then, as an anti-climax, "Gosh, we've got to go."

The confusion that the boys' departure caused dragged Carrol from her couch and she followed them to the door for last calls of good luck. As they backed down the steps, David shook his head at her.

"Don't stand there," he said. "Go in and lie down. Penny, you make her." He waited for Mary and Jane, and when he saw Carrol go back into the house, called over his shoulder, "I'll come back with Dick's folks."

"Well, they're gone." Penny sighed as she heaped Carrol's pillows around her. "It's going to be mighty dull around these here parts."

"Didn't you want to go to the station with them, Pen?"

"No! I don't like seeing people go away." She gathered up the plates, chattering as she worked. "You know," she declared on one of her return trips from the kitchen, "I like the boys on this post. They're lots of fun and they think of me that way too. Michael said . . ."

The ringing of the telephone interrupted her and she went to answer it beside the broad landing. "Hello," she said. The silence that followed was so long that she leaned against the newel post as she listened. And her brief replies of "yes, umhum, I hope so" were so far apart that she finally sat down on the bottom step. At last she said goodbye and slowly cradled the receiver in its hook.

"Who was that?" Carrol asked idly.

"It was Michael."

"Michael? Why, what . . .?" Carrol looked at her dazed face and burst out laughing. "The boys on this post just think of me as fun," she teased. "What did he want?"

"He just wanted to say goodbye again and to tell me he was sorry I didn't come to the train and—well—well, he just wanted to ask me to come up to West Point. Gosh, you could have knocked me down with a gesture."

She replaced the telephone on the table and came slowly across the room. "It was funny about Mike's telephoning," she said thoughtfully. "But it was kind of nice, too. I feel important."

"Of course you do, Pen. People need to feel important. It doesn't matter if it's a boy who likes you or another girl; the main thing is to have people like you. And the ones who say they don't care what other people think are crazy."

"I guess so." Penny reached into the candy box; and she and Carrol were having a most interesting conversation when the family began to gather.

"This is to be a celebration," Mrs. Parrish called gayly as she and Carrol's father came in laden with packages. "We've been all the way to town and we have paper hats and everything. Carrol, your father got away from me and he has favors for everybody. Isn't it exciting?"

She flew to the kitchen to be sure Trudy used one of the best table cloths and returned with a soiled and sobbing Tippy behind her. "This is what Williams dug out from under the back porch," she said, displaying the dejected little figure crying into a doll's wad of yellow curls. "Isn't she a sight?"

"Oh, Tippy. Darling!" Penny was down on her knees with Tippy hugged to her. "Penny didn't mean to frighten you so. Come on, we'll have a nice bath."

She carried Tippy upstairs and Mrs. Parrish sat down and laughed. "I think she's had her punishment," she decided. "After all, two hours under the back porch wondering what Bobby was up to must have nearly killed her. Which reminds me, where is Bobby?"

From then on the confusion equaled that of Christmas Eve. The dining room doors were closed, with David on guard, and whispering and laughing leaked through them. At last Williams threw them open, and the impatient family had a glimpse of fairyland. The table was covered with flowers and candles, bright hats and balloons. Flowers lay at every plate, corsages for the ladies, boutonnieres for the men, and even Tippy had a wreath to wear on her curls.

"Suah is a nice party," Williams kept muttering to himself as he passed the dishes. "Suah is nice." Faithfully he recounted everything to Trudy busy at her stove, and was rewarded by her happily nodding head. When she had given him his last plate of dessert and was preparing for a peek herself, his head popped in the door again. "Miss Carrol's papa says you come in there quick," he called. "He wants me, too."

Mr. Houghton was standing when she got there and beside him, on his chair, was a large cardboard carton. "Because you have all been so swell to Carrol and me," he was saying, "I thought we should each have something to remember this summer by. Just some little thing that, when we look at it, will make us think of this time."

"Do you mean presents?" Tippy asked, eagerly leaning forward.

"I mean presents. I really didn't ever expect to see Georgia again," he said with a twinkle at Penny. "So fearing that you might be a lonely mother I tried to find you another child. As it turns out, Georgia will have a little sister."

"Oh!" Tippy took the doll in its long white dress. She cuddled it tenderly then insisted on being put down to bestow a kiss of gratitude. "Thank you," she said as she ran around the table.

"Thank you, Tippy. Thank you for showing me how

cute little girls can be." Mr. Houghton lifted her up to kiss her then set her on her feet again and turned to his box.

"There is another member of the family," he said, "who has given me quite a kick. He's taken me back to my own boyhood, and all the things I used to do; and I've noticed that one piece of his equipment is a bit the worse for wear. Bobby?"

"Yes sir!" Bobby was on his feet and halfway around the table as he spoke. His thanks were tumbling out before he had seen his gift and were only stopped by his whistle of delight. "Gee," he breathed, "a new knife. Thanks, Mr. Houghton."

"And thank you, Bobby." Langdon Houghton turned to the others. "I'm afraid," he apologized, "that I shall have to thank each one of you. You have each given me something that I had forgotten existed. I don't want to make a speech every second," he laughed, "and as I have four gifts all alike, I'll skip the ladies for a minute. It's your turn, Dave." A little box sailed across the table, and as Major Parrish caught it, he said, "For a sportsman."

"Gosh. How did you know I'd been wanting these?" Major Parrish looked up and grinned as he displayed a pair of white gold cuff-links made like a bridle bit. "I've had my eye on those darn things for a month."

Penny ran around to slip them into his cuffs; and Mr. Houghton was deep in his box again. As he came up, both hands were behind him and he looked at David. "Carrol told me a little story about this summer, David," he said. "And while I don't think any of us will ever forget it, still, it sometimes helps us to make a difficult decision if we have a visible object on which to concentrate." His hands came out and on each palm stood a small replica of the silver horse. He looked at them thoughtfully, then held one out to David. "One is for you, and the other one is mine. I imagine I'll need mine much worse than you will."

"Oh, Mr. Houghton," David swallowed hard as he answered, "there isn't anything I'd rather have."

"I know it. There isn't anything I'd rather have either, except perhaps this." He looked down at Carrol and smoothed her hair. "Yours is a selfish gift," he told her sheepishly. "Your mother always had one around somewhere. I thought I'd like to see it this winter."

Carrol was puzzled as she took the package. She lifted the lid and peeked inside. "Why, it's a knitting bag!" she exclaimed. "It's a knitting bag with pink wool in it. Oh, Daddy, you sweet, funny darling."

She caught his hand and laid her cheek against it, and he bent over to kiss the plaster on her head. "The next four mementos," he said, "if my daughter will unhand me, are all alike, as I told you. They vary of course, but the idea is the same. Faithful to the faithful. Trudy; Williams; Penny," he passed the little boxes, laying one on the table beside him, "and Marjory."

"Glory, Hallelujah!" Trudy's voice rang out above the rustle of tissue paper. "It's a watch!"

In the joy of the four recipients he was mobbed. Williams and Trudy pumped his hands while Penny had him around the neck. "I can't believe it," Penny kept repeating when she had calmed down enough to compare hers with Carrol's. "They're almost exactly alike!"

It was a long time before Williams could blow out the candles and clear the table. Even after the others had left the dining room, he and Trudy admired their gifts in the kitchen and helped Tippy put her doll to bed.

"Your dad is pretty swell," David said to Carrol as they strolled out to the porch. "He made us all feel that we have given him so much more than he did us."

"He does feel that way, David. Why, suppose you were all frozen up inside, and you found a family as wonderful as this one; and they helped you see where you'd been wrong. Wouldn't you be grateful?"

"Yes, I guess I would." David thought it over. "But I don't see where we're so wonderful."

"I know you don't." Carrol tucked her hand through his arm and patted it. "To you, you're just the Parrishes. That's what makes you all so nice."

CHAPTER SEVENTEEN

FAREWELL TO SUMMER

PENNY BENT over the big suitcase she was packing and tried to wipe a tearstain from a freshly laundered slip. She smoothed out the lace blindly and her head was bent over it so long that Trudy, standing beside her with a pile of silk and satin, leaned over to see what was wrong.

"Why, honey-chile," she crooned, dropping to her knees and cuddling Penny's quivering body to her. "You mustn't cry."

"But I can't help it, Trudy," Penny sobbed, her face pressed into Trudy's comforting shoulder. "You don't know how lonesome I'm going to be."

"Sure, I knows. It's always the one 'at gets lef' behind 'at's the lonesomest. But you mus' jus' think how nice it is fo' Miss Carrol to be goin' off with her papa an' Mr. David havin' his school. Your time's acommin', Miss Penny, honey."

"Do you think so, Trudy?"

"Sure. Now you run along an' let me pack up these things. I jus' thought you'd like to have something to do while Miss Carrol was at the doctors, but stayin' up here and cryin' ain't goin' to help you none. Miss Carrol'll be back in a minute and you'd better have your face washed so's you'll look happy. It ain't goin' to make her feel very good to see you lookin' so sad, nor your mamma neither."

"I know it. But Trudy, we didn't get to do half the things we'd planned. Carrol couldn't ride Ragamuffin again; and we just had to go down and say goodbye to him; and we didn't have our last ice cream soda at the Post Exchange, or—or—" Penny dissolved in tears again and Trudy sighed as she patted the bent head.

"I think you're bein' awful foolish," she said at last. "But I know trouble is mighty real when it's your trouble, an' there ain't much anyone can say to help yo'. But Miss Carrol an' Mr. David ain't gone yet, an' it seems to me as long as you're plannin' to shed a lotta tears you might as well save 'em up an' shed 'em all at once."

"I guess you're right, Trudy." Penny blinked and gulped as she used Trudy's clean apron for a handkerchief and even managed a smile as she got to her feet. "I feel better anyway."

"Course you do." Trudy looked at her ruined apron but said no more as she began to lay the piles of lingerie into the case. She could hear Penny sighing in the bathroom and presently the dragging footsteps went down the stairs.

There was no one in the hall when Penny came down,

but David's big kit bag stood in the vestibule and Bobby and Tippy were inspecting it thoroughly. "David's going away," Bobby volunteered as he spit on a soiled handkerchief and polished a buckle.

"And he says he won't come back till he's twenty years old." Tippy looked up at Penny solemnly. "Will he be an old man then, Penny?"

"Yes, with a long grey beard."

She went out to sit disconsolately in the swing. "It's today," she told herself. "And there's the rest of this summer and all winter, and I can't have any fun. And maybe we won't even go to see David next summer if Dad gets ordered to some terrible place." She bit her lips and pressed her fingers firmly against her eyes as she rocked the glider. "I know I'm being a ninny, but I just can't help it."

It was a relief when the car drove up and Carrol and her father got out. "I wish I'd gone with you," she said as she met them at the door. "Trudy took over the packing and I've been wandering around."

Carrol came in and put her arm around her and Mr. Houghton looked at her keenly. "Penny Parrish," he said, tipping her chin up, "you've been crying."

"No. I . . ." Penny tried to wiggle her chin free, knowing that the tears were coming again, but her captor laughed and pulled her to him. "You wrote me a letter once," he said, "about rescuing a princess in a tower. Now you're in a tower. You don't think I'm going to let you stay there, do you?"

"But I'm not in a tower." Penny's brown eyes looked miserably into his. "I'm here with Mother and Daddy."

"People are in towers whenever they are lonely and unhappy. We aren't going to have any more towers. Not ever." He smoothed her curls and put her arm around Carrol's waist. "The thing for you two to do," he said, "is to go over to the Post Exchange and order the biggest ice cream soda you ever ate. Make plans. If you don't trust me, trust that fairy you told me about."

He pushed them toward the door but hearing voices, stopped with his arms around them. Major and Mrs. Parrish came out with David and Mrs. Parrish said:

"We're sorry to be away so long but we were giving David the money he must deposit at the Point."

"And a lot of directions," David added, grinning. "And a package of post cards and a few dozen self-addressed envelopes."

"David! You don't have to tell everything," his mother scolded. "After all, I want to be sure I'm going to hear from you. Where were you three going?"

"The girls were thinking about a last ice cream soda, but that can wait." Mr. Houghton turned Penny and Carrol around and leaned against the screen. "Have you any leave coming this summer, Dave?" he asked.

"The usual month. Why?"

"My little place in Connecticut is pretty nice in summertime—and it's near West Point."

"I see your drift." Major Parrish smiled but shook his head at the same time. "I can't get away."

"We talked about it," Mrs. Parrish said, "when we thought we could drive David east. Dave asked for leave but they told him there would be training camps here and maneuvers. The general said he could go in September, but the children have to be in school then. Why don't we sit down?"

She went to the swing, her arm around David and the others followed her. They sat in silence until David said, "This is the most mournful looking outfit I ever saw. Somebody tell a joke."

"I will." Mr. Houghton spoke up promptly. "I may not get very far but I'll start. It's only this. Why don't you think about that leave in September, Dave? School doesn't matter much to Bobby, and Penny can easily make up a month. We have a number of things in New York that are an education in themselves; and I think it is much better to come and see David later than to have taken him to the Point and left him there."

"Oh, Daddy," Penny breathed. "Could we?"

"Why—I don't know." Major Parrish looked at his wife. "We hadn't thought about that. If we didn't take

David, there didn't seem much point in making the trip. What do you think, Marge?"

"Well," Mrs. Parrish carefully creased a pleat in her skirt before she met her husband's eyes. "I don't want to influence you, Dave," she said, "but I know I shouldn't mind so much letting David go if I thought I could see him soon."

Major Parrish clapped his hands together and grinned. "All right. It's a little sudden, but the Parrishes go to New York," he said.

"Oh, Daddy! Oh, Mummy! Oh, Mr. Houghton!" Penny danced about the porch, hugging first one and then another. She swooped on Carrol, then on David and finally waved her arms in the air. "Come on plane," she invited. "I don't mind now!"

David, leaning toward his mother, whispered: "I guess I'm an awful kid, but I was homesick already."

There was so much excitement, so much talking and planning, especially when Bobby and Tippy wandered in and found they were going somewhere, that Trudy came to the door. "Has something happened?" she asked.

"Yes!" Penny danced toward her. "We're going to New York! Is Trudy going too?" she asked her father.

"Oh, sure." Major Parrish nodded his head. "I guess we're all going but Woofy and Williams—and I wouldn't bet that Woofy doesn't get there."

"Glory be." Trudy hugged Penny, then looked up anxiously. "We ain't goin' in the airplane, is we?"

"No, Trudy." Mrs. Parrish sprang up from the swing.

"We're going in the car just as the Parrishes always do. Same seats and everything." She looked at her new watch and suggested, "Let's tell Williams to bring the bags down." She went behind her husband, put her arms around his neck and rested her chin on the top of his head. "Thank you, Dave," she said. "I feel lots happier, don't you?"

"Much."

Luggage came, bumping down the stairs and David went in to help. "The plane came in this morning," he called as he moved his own bag out of the way. "Dad and I went down to see her; she's a beauty."

"I saw it when it flew over." Mr. Houghton looked at Carrol and Penny whispering in the swing. "You didn't get your soda, did you?"

"No, but we don't mind." Carrol hugged Penny. "We'll get one in Schraffts when Penny comes to New York."

The bags were brought out and set in a row beside the screen. Penny and Carrol dashed upstairs to search for forgotten trifles and Carrol walked about the room touching everything lovingly. "I'm going to miss it so," she said, smoothing an organdy spread. "But Daddy says I can have my room done anyway I like and we'll have such fun choosing pillows and things when you come."

"When I come! Oh, Carrol!" Penny closed her eyes and clasped her hands over her heart so dramatically, that David coming down the hall stopped at the door.

"Penny, the actress," he teased. "I suppose, when you get in New York and see one play you'll think you have to go on the stage."

"I suppose I will." Penny held out her arms and swayed toward him. "Come in, my love, come in. Parting is such sweet sorrow."

"Not half as sweet as Shakespeare made it sound." David marched over to her and took her by both ears. "My little sun flower. Are you going to be a good girl while your brother is away?"

"The best I know how."

"Which isn't much." He doubled up his fist, tapped it lightly against her cheek and turned to Carrol. "About ready?"

"All ready." Carrol picked up her hat and coat, and the three went down the stairs.

Penny skipped out to the porch while David and Carrol went kitchenward for a last goodbye to Trudy. She was at the table, busy with a list, and her stubby pencil was flying over the paper.

"I can't make up my mind, Mr. David," she said as they came in, "how many suits I got to pack for Bobby."

"Well, you'll have plenty of time to think it over." David's eyes twinkled as he put his arms around her. "You aren't going until September."

"We ain't? Well then!" Trudy threw down her pencil and stood up. She put her hands on their shoulders and looked up at them, her heart full of love, her eyes brimming with emotion. "God bless you," she said. "Nobody ever had sweeter children."

"Trudy's a peach," David commented as he followed Carrol through the swinging door. "And she sure does like you."

"Does she?"

"Umhum. And I do, too." David grinned and added: "I guess I like you better than Trudy does."

"I can't believe this is us," Penny kept repeating as they got quietly into the car. "Look at us. No excitement, no fuss. Tippy and Bobby are clean and even David isn't late. Could it be that we're reforming?"

"It's because Mr. Houghton said he'd leave 'about' half past two. About is a very wonderful word." Her mother moved her feet to stride a small bag and lifted Tippy higher on her lap as she answered.

"Well, I've decided that the way to travel is by plane." Penny squeezed nearer to Carrol on the back seat and reached for Bobby. "You leave late and get there early."

The luggage compartment was closed, the car stretched its sides to hold the eight who were crowding into it, and Major Parrish gave the horn a cheerful toot. Williams saluted from the curb and Trudy's white apron flapped from the porch as they drove away. When they passed the flag pole Carrol managed one last glimpse at the Stars and Stripes so high above her.

David saw her looking and leaned out, too. "That's one thing we don't have to say goodbye to," he told her. "It will be with me at West Point and you can always see it in New York. I can hear taps at night, and though I may get homesick for this special flag, it's like the silver horse; I've got another one I can look at."

Carrol nodded as she noticed three waiting figures under a tree. "There are Mary and Bob and Jane at the corner," she exclaimed, pointing. "I think they're waiting for us."

Major Parrish stopped the car and hands reached

through the windows. "We told you goodbye this morning," Mary said, "but we wanted one last shake."

Major Parrish let them talk nonsense for a few moments, then he threw the car into gear and they got behind pretending to push. David tapped on the glass behind him and called:

"See you at the Point next year, Bob. Don't fail us."

The powerful plane, perched on the field like a great silver bird, was ready. Its cabin door stood open and a runway reached from it to the ground. Two pilots were talking with an officer, and a pretty girl in uniform was busy in a tiny kitchen compartment.

"Merciful heavens," Mrs. Parrish thought as she followed Bobby and Tippy inside and stood looking at the comfortable chairs, "David will never live this down." Penny and Carrol were exploring, and she watched them in a daze and jumped when David's arm pressed her shoulders.

"Pretty swell, isn't it, Mums? When I flew east in my private plane . . ." He waved his hand airily, then grinned. "I knew it was like this, this morning, but I wanted to watch your face when you saw it. Don't you think you will be a little in awe of me after this?"

"I'll never get over it." Mrs. Parrish shook her head solemnly, then reached up and stroked the blond hair that towered above her. "Oh, David, you seem so little to be going away."

David whooped. He hugged her to him and kissed her until she smiled. "Don't you worry, Mrs. Parrish," he told her, "I'm still your little boy. And if they aren't nice to me at school, and if the big boys are rough and noisy, I'll come home."

"Well, you'd better." She was herself again. "Time to get out," she called. "David, bring the children if you have to drag them. Come, Penny. Goodbye, Carrol, darling." She drew Carrol to her and whispered, "My other daughter," and was down the runway.

"All set?" Major Parrish came toward her. He kissed Carrol and wrung David's hand. "If you need anything, son, let me know. Take care of yourself."

"I will, Dad."

"Goodbye, Dave." Langdon Houghton's words were brief but his handclasp was firm. "Keep your chin up, Marjory. I'll keep an eye on your boy until you get there." His eyes squinted appraisingly. "Swell people." Then he bent down with David to Bobby and Tippy.

Near the plane, Carrol and Penny were clinging together. "It isn't so bad," Penny was saying, "because I'm coming. We'll both have such lots to do."

"Goodness, yes. And you'll ride Ragamuffin sometimes, and write me everything?"

"Oh, I'll write, and you'll write, too. And Carrol," Penny's eyes twinkled, "if you see Dick, and Michael, before I get there—tell them hello."

"I will. Nut."

They were in their normal laughing state when Carrol's father came to send her for her final farewells and to put his arm around Penny.

"The old fairy did all right, didn't she?" he said.

"Oh, she completely outdid herself. You know," Penny confided, "I've decided there must be two fairies;

a girl fairy and a boy fairy. No one fairy could possibly do so much."

"I believe you're right. And if you are, between them, we should do quite well."

He gave her a hug and drew her into the group. Last kisses, last promises were hurried. The gangway was moved aside, the heavy door was closed. Powerful motors began to roar and slowly the great ship moved away. Those on the ground looked up at the three they loved and their smiles trembled. Langdon Houghton waved from one window, and framed like a picture in another, David and Carrol smiled down together.

Gently the ship lifted, and like a bird soared off into the blue.